Facing Him

Susan Charter

Contents

Chapter 1- Risky — 1

Chapter 2- Nightmares — 9

Chapter 3- You Look Like Shit — 15

Chapter 4- Midnight Madness — 22

Chapter 5- The Backseat Was Invented For A Reason — 29

Chapter 6- You Have A Bond — 39

Chapter 7- Blackmailing The Blackmailer — 47

Chapter 8- Screw You — 53

Chapter 9- What Were You Thinking?! — 62

Chapter 10- The Truth — 72

Chapter 11- You Need Jesus — 79

Chapter 12- I Look Like Mr Tumnus from The Chronicles Of Narnia — 87

Chapter 13- Not In My Bed Please — 93

Chapter 14- Im Sorry, What? — 104

Chapter 15- I Had To Put A Ring On It Or She Wouldn't Let Me Smash   114

Character list   123

Chapter 16- I Love You   124

Chapter 17- How Heroic Of You   134

Chapter 18- Hey Mom   139

Chapter 19- This Day Went From 0-100 Real Fast   151

Chapter 20- You Promised   164

Chapter 21- This Is Not The Answer   178

Chapter 22- Gone   184

Chapter 23-Did You See Her   191

Chapter 24- Fight Until You Can't Fight Anymore   196

Chapter 25- Something Is Wrong   205

Chapter 26- That's Where You're Wrong   211

Chapter 27- Go To Hell   216

Chapter 28- What Have You Done   223

Chapter 29- I Can Save Her   235

Chapter 30- I'll Never Forget You   240

Chapter 31- Adrianna Daniels   247

Chapter 32- Kate Georgsson   254

Chapter 33- Ashley Davis and Morgan Sage   257

Chapter 34- Alison Carters   262

Chapter 35- Lydia Stone   269

Chapter 36- Perfect Life?   299

Epilogue   308

Chapter 1- Risky

Lydia's POV"Stef I'm nervous." I say to my older brother, he rolls his eyes. "Damn it Aide, how many times did I tell you we have to use our new names. It's Lorenzo now Lydia."

"Fine. I'm very nervous Enzo, I feel like something bad is going to happen and you know I'm never wrong." It feels like I have a rock in the pit of my stomach that's trying to push out. I'm scared.

"You can't be nervous, you just have to think positive-"

"How can I think positive when he's out there looking for us?" I snap angrily, he sighs and grabs my hand. "I promised myself that I would not let anything bad happen to you and I am going to keep that promise until the day I die. He's not going to find us this time, just keep your contacts in and keep your head held up high. We are going to go to school. We are going to make friends. And we are going to have a good life. From now on we have to forget about him and start focusing on our lives alright sis?"

I slowly nod. He's always found us, what says this time it's going to be any different?

"Okay good. Now get going, you're going to be late for your first day of senior year!" Before I could protest, he shoved my car keys in my hand and pushed me out the door. Stupid Stefano.

As I approached my new school, I couldn't help but admire the campus. It was big and very grassy and beautiful. Even the inside was beautiful, the walls were painted creatively, the hallways were decorated. This school is way better than any school I've been to by far.

I already knew the drill, it's the same thing over and over. Go to the office to get my schedule, I get a buddy and they show me around, blah blah blah. Unfortunately for me I got lost. Damn this school is huge.

I decided to ask this group of guys that was nearby. "Hey excuse me, do you know where the principals office is?" One of them that was wearing a SnapBack smirked. "Yeah, we know that place really well, we can show you-"

"Get lost douchebags. She's way out of your league." Some random girl interrupts leaving me a little curious. She was a lot taller than me, I would say maybe 5'9 but there was something about her that I wanted to get to know. She reminds me of my older sister.

"Rose?" I question, looking into her eyes with a smile. Once she shook her head I felt like an idiot. "I'm sorry I think you have me mistaken for someone else. I'm Piper, I hope my brother and his friends weren't bothering you. If they were I'll kick their asses don't worry." I didn't even look at her, I looked at the floor and wanted to cry. Truth is I haven't seen my sister in years, she said she would come back one day but she never did, and it's all my fathers fault.

"That's not necessary, I was just asking directions to the principals office-"

"Oh yeah, they know that place very well but I'll show you." She replies earning a grunt out of the boys. "Sorry boys, she's off limits."

The walk was silent until she decided to break it. "You're the new girl right?"

"Is it that obvious?" She chuckles and shakes her head. "No, I live across the street from you and I saw moving boxes. What's your name?"

"Lydia."

"That's such a cool name. Well, here we are. I can wait for you if you'd like." I shake my head and put a fake smile on my face. "I think I will be able to find my way, thank you for helping me though."

"No problem, and hey if you have any questions ask for Piper Santiago. See you around Lydia." She walked a way with a smile on her face leaving me to go get my schedule. I was greeted by the principal as I walked into the office.

"Hello Lydia, it's so nice to meet you. I am mrs Thomas, welcome to Castle Hill High. Let's take a look at your records from your previous school. Cheer captain, debate team, lacrosse, and excellent academics? You're the full package." I looked at her confused, she laughed. "That's a good thing. I hope you will join some of our spring sports teams this semester. Here is your schedule, your first class is in room 104 which is down the hall to the right. Here is your locker number and combination and if you have any questions feel free to come into my office." The truth is, in all of my old schools I joined something to make my high school experience seem more real. Unfortunately for me, my father found me because of those records.

She handed me everything and sent me on my way. You would think that since this is a really big school they would have told someone to show me around or at last given me a map but no, they didn't.

This school has a bunch of different twists and turns not to mention the fact that finding my locker was hard enough. I ended up being late to my first period class but that was nothing compared to what it was like at lunch.

The cafeteria was packed inside so I decided to go to the quad where others have lunch, at first I was eating while reading my book alone until I was approached by the guy in the SnapBack from earlier. "10 Things I Hate About You, excellent choice but have you seen the movie?"

"Yes I have. Didn't think a guy like you would though." I replied sarcastically, he smirks. "What can I say? I guess I'm just a hopeless romantic. So do you have a phone?"

"Maybe I do maybe I don't. What's it to you?" I flipped to the next page in my book, not even looking up at him. "Maybe I can call you sometime."

"Yeah sure my number is 555-N-O-T- gonna happen." I looked up at him only to see him with a smirk plastered on his face. What is this guys' problem?

"You're tough, I like that." He winks, I rolled my eyes. "Yo Brandon! Let's go!" One of his friends called, he flipped them off and looked back at me with an innocent smile.

"Duty calls, see you around Lydia." I forgot to mention he is in my math, gym and drama classes so now he knows my name. Wonderful.

As soon as he left I was approached by two girls, one of which was Piper. "Were you just talking to Brandon Santiago?" The girl that approached me asks, I shrug. Wait, Santiago? Why does that name sound familiar.

"I don't know if you would call it talking, it was more of him trying to hit on me and me turning him down." Piper smiles and starts clapping. "Good for you, I apologize for Brandon, he may be my brother but he is a douche, along with all his friends." I nod in agreement. That's where I remembered it from.

"What is their problem anyways? They're looking at me as if I am a piece of fresh meat." Piper's friend starts laughing.

"You're not wrong. You see the boys he is with?" Piper asks, I nod. "Yeah, what about them?"

"They call themselves the overachievers, but basically they are all just a bunch of dumb jocks that like to keep score on taking girls' virginity. I would know I was put on the list." Piper's friend says sadly. "That's horrible. Why would someone do that?"

"You see that brunette?" Piper asks, pointing to a guy wearing a leather jacket, I nod. "That's Mrs Thomas' stepson Nathan, although he takes his birth mothers last name which is Davis. He runs the school along with my brother and their goon squad." Piper adds on with an eye roll. She clearly doesn't like them.

"The one that is playing the guitar is Grayson, he is the only good one in the group meaning he doesn't undress girls with his eyes like the rest do." Piper's friend says with a smile.

"The one with the jawline sculpted by god is Vince, him and Nathan are the ones you really have to watch out for. And lastly the one in the SnapBack that you were just talking to is my brother Brandon. Oh and this is my friend Blaire, she's pretty cool and her fashion sense is on point."

"I'm Lydia-"

"I know, you're the talk of the school! I mean a new girl in a town where everyone has known each other forever is very rare. Well that and you're the new target of the overachievers. It's very nice to meet you, I think we will be great friends." Blaire replied excitedly, I smile but inside I am mentally killing myself.

Everyone knows who I am which means that by asking one question someone can easily find out about what happened back home. Nobody can find out what happened. Nobody can find out what my father did. Darkness follows me... I can't drag anyone into that.

"Hello? Earth to Lydia!" Piper waves her hand in my face as Blaire snaps her fingers at me, making me snap out of my train of thought. "I'm sorry, I spaced out what were you saying?" I question, Blaire smiles.

"I said so when are we going to go shopping for midnight madness?" Blaire asks, I look at her confused. "What's midnight madness?"

"It is the biggest Halloween party of the year, the whole school is invited. People get dressed up, some bring kegs, they get drunk, dance, overall they just party hard and have a great time and it is thrown by Vince but I can assure you that it is a blast. You coming?" Piper questions with a big smile on her face, I sigh. I'm not really in a party mood.

"I don't know, parties aren't really my thing-"

"Oh come on Lydia, whatever happens at that party stays at that party. We have the first week of November off! Everybody forgets anything that happens at that party trust me I would know." Piper comments with a sigh, something obviously happened to her but I can tell she doesn't want to talk about it and I respect that, we all have our secrets.

"Please Lydia? I mean I know we just met but it will be really fun!" Blaire pleads with a pout, a face that I knew that over time I would not be able to say no to. "I'll think about it-"

"It's in a couple of weeks! You have to go!" Piper chimes in, I sigh. "Maybe. I'll tell you what, I will go shopping with you guys and if I see a costume I like then I'll get it and I'll go."

"YES!" Blaire shouts cheerfully, earning attention from everyone in the quad and unfortunately from Grayson and his friends as well. "Yo!Piper! Is it going to be you that I'm kissing at midnight?" Vince asks with a wink, scooting next to me.

"Maybe, that depends. How many girls have you asked already?" She asks, looking at her red painted nails, making it seem like she's not interested. "You know my heart is only set on you." He replies with a cheeky grin, I roll my eyes.

"Yeah yeah only for me and that girl over there and Becky with the good hair am I right?" She replies snarkily, causing him to chuckle. "I love it when you talk back to me."

"Go away Vince. We will talk later." She replies with a tone of annoyance in her voice, he smirks. "So there will be a later!"

"OH MY GOD VINCE LEAVE!" Piper snaps with a chuckle, clearly annoyed, Blaire and I start laughing. "Alright, bye Pipes."

"I told you to stop calling me that!" She calls out as he walks away, rolling her eyes. "Piper he's so into you!" Blaire says with a squeal, Piper shakes her head. "He's into what color underwear I'm wearing, not me."

"That's true, guys are jerks." I reply under my breath, they turn and look at me with a smile. "Did you get your heart broken too? Spill girl spill!" Blaire squeals, I shake my head. Geez isn't this girl nosy.

"Something like that... I don't really like talking about it. Let's change the subject!"

"Okay well then I am making it our job to find you a new guy. Brandon seems into you why don't you go for him?" Blaire questions with a wink, I look over at the boys only to see that they are staring right at me. "Not my type, sorry girls, I don't date bad boys."

"I respect that. That's exactly why I don't like Vince." She replied with a smile, Blaire chuckled. "Okay fine then you will have to go for Gray he's a sweetheart, he just hangs out with the wrong crowd." Blaire replied excitedly, I shook my head.

"No I'm just not looking for a relationship right now." Right on time the bell rang, I took that as my cue to leave. "Well that's the bell, I have to get to class I'll see you guys later."

That was close. I can't have them knowing what happened back home, it's too big of a risk.

Chapter 2- Nightmares

(Gif of Lorenzo) Lorenzo's POVI'm deeply worried about my sister. We have been through hell but we never managed to make it back because we are still on the run. I'm afraid he's going to get us too but I can't show it for the sake of her.

Everyday it's always the same thing, I fake a smile and tell her to think positive but the truth is he always finds us. Where there's a will there's a way and he's not going to stop till we are both dead.

I was knocked out of my train of thought when Lydia came through the door with an aggravated expression on her face. "Hey sis, how was your day?"

"Meh. I made a couple friends but who knows how long that's going to last. You know what happens every time I get my hopes up." She replied with a grunt, plopping on our couch.

"How do you expect to make any new friends with that attitude? You can't think that way you have to-"

"Oh my god Stef if you say I have to stay positive one more time I'm going to kill myself! I lose brain cells every time you say that. I'm tired of staying positive! Staying positive hasn't done shit for me! I want to be normal! I want to have friends and a boyfriend! I want to go to prom! I want to fucking graduate! But at this rate who knows?! He could find us any time any day and do you know what that is doing to me?" I hate seeing her like this, it's scary.

"Lydia, you're sick, you need to calm down-"

"No Stef, I'm not sick! I'm crazy and that bastard made me that way! I hate him! I hate him I hate him I hate him!" She starts screaming and pulling at her hair while walking back and fourth.

Ever since that first day we ran, I knew something was up with her. Who could blame her after what we saw? What we saw what indescribable, and what he made us do was unspeakable.

After our father found us the second time, I was 20 so I was able to sign documents at the therapy center. Her Psychiatrist diagnosed her with bipolar disorder, anxiety, and depression. It got really bad, she even attempted suicide which was how he found us the third time. After that we made a pact. No doctors, no help, we handle this on our own.

I went over to her and started stroking her hair, something that always calmed her down as a kid. "It's okay not to be okay Aide. We have been through hell but we can't let him depict what's going to happen to us forever. I will not let anything happen to you I promise. You and me against the world, remember? You are going to be able to enjoy your high school experience this year. You are going to go to dances, make friends, go to prom, go to parties and who knows, maybe you'll find yourself a boyfriend along the way."

"Yeah right"

"I promise you this time things are going to be different. Live life to the fullest, I have a good feeling here. I think we are going to do good here, you just have to believe it too. For now let's just eat dinner and get some rest okay?" I made sure to make my voice as soft as possible because that's how it always calmed her down when things got bad.

"Okay. I'm just going to lay here for a little while, tell me when dinner is ready." She yawns, I chuckle as I get up and walk to the kitchen.

"Hey Stef?"

"Yeah?" I reply, stopping in my tracks, she smiles. "Thanks."

"For what?"

"For being the best brother I could ask for. I love you." She replies with a yawn, I smile. "Love you too sis." I then made my entrance into the kitchen and started cooking Adrianna's favorite meal. Chicken Parmesan.

After I woke Lydia up, we ate dinner, she took a shower, and we both got ready to go to sleep because we both have an early morning ahead of us. I have a job interview tomorrow for a very important law firm and she obviously has school. Everything was fine until I woke up at 3AM to the sound of her screaming bloody murder.

Lydia's POV"You don't have to do this!" Wesley shouts, dad chuckles. "You don't know what I have to do. You know too much. And people who know to much snitch, you know what snitches get? Stitches!" Dad screams, tears are streaming down my face as Wesley turns around. Before he could say anything to me, my father shot him' making his blood splash over me in the process.

"NOOO! WHAT DID YOU DO?! WHAT THE FUCK DID YOU DO?!" I screamed while running over to Wesley, dad laughs. "That boy is dead as a door nail. You think you can leave me and go without me knowing? You and your brother think you're so slick but you're not Adrianna!

Oh wait, I forgot you go by Morgan now. Or was it Alison? I can't really remember ."

"You're a bastard!"

"Yeah, but so is your brother. And you're nothing but his little bitch. What, are the two of you into incest now or something?" He comments with a sly grin, I glare at him. "You're sick!" I shout while grabbing his knife and holding it to my wrists.

"Sick? No. Psychotic? Maybe. So why don't you put the knife down before you hurt yourself-"

"YOU'RE MAKING ME DO THIS! You fucked up my brain! You messed with my head! I JUST WANT THIS TO BE OVER! I WANNA DIE!"

"Don't do this Adrianna-"

"Or what? You can't kill me if I'm already dead! I loved Wes and YOU KILLED HIM!"

"He knew too much! My sweet, sweet girl." He goes to stroke my hair, but I stabbed his hand in the process. "YOU LITTLE BITCH!"

"I'd rather be a bitch than be your daughter. You're a psychotic piece of shit! You killed them! You killed them all! I'm gonna make sure you pay for it." I scream, he laughs.

"And what are you gonna do? Shoot me?"

"YOU KILLED THEM! Now it's your turn to die!"

Lorenzo's POV I jumped out of bed and ran to her room the minute I heard her screaming. "YOU KILLED THEM! GET THE FUCK AWAY FROM ME YOU SON OF A BITCH YOU KILLED THEM!"

I ran as fast as I could to her room only to see that she was sleeping, she was having a horrible nightmare. Unfortunately for us, her nightmare was our reality.

"Aide wake up! You're having a nightmare you need to wake up!" I shout while shaking her, breaking room number one of dream analysis. Never wake someone whose having a nightmare.

"AHHH GET AWAY! IM GOING TO KILL YOU!" She starts kicking and fighting and sweating, I have to hold her down. She's going to hurt herself.

"Please sis, you got to wake up!"

"I JUST WANT THIS TO BE OVER! STAY AWAY! YOU KILLED THEM!!!" She screamed at the top of her lungs, tears stream down my face. "WAKE UP!" I scream, making her open her eyes.

It was like the life was being thrown back into her. She was short of breath, hyperventilating, and crying. "Stefano?"

"Yes Aide, it's me. You were having a nightmare. I'm worried, this is the third time this week." She shakes her head and gives me a bear hug. "It's okay. As long as everything is alright, I'm okay. Go back to sleep, you have an important interview tomorrow."

"I don't want to leave you-"

"It's okay Stef, or should I say Enzo. This interview could be a start to a new life for us. You were right earlier, we have to fight this time. Wesley died in vain and I want to avenge him. If he finds us, this time I'm gonna find him. I'm going to hunt him. And I'm going to kill him." At this point, her teeth were grinding together. Guess I know for sure what she was dreaming about.

Like I said before, our father is a psychotic bastard. He will stop at nothing to find us meaning he will kill whoever gets in his way whenever he wants. He's dangerous, and this time we are putting an end to this.

Chapter 3- You Look Like Shit

Lydia's POVGoing to school this morning was so hard. I was exhausted to say the least, ever since my nightmare I stayed up with a baseball bat sitting in front of our front door. I got no sleep.

"Damn Lydia what happened to you?" Blaire questions with a look of sympathy, I grunt and hold my head. "I feel how I look. Like shit."

"Oh no. What happened? Who's ass do I have to kick?" Piper questions angrily, clearly something is bothering her. "My stupid dreams. I had a bad dream that kept me up, no big deal."

"Damn, I really felt like kicking ass today." Piper grunts causing me to chuckle. "Why?"

"Grace is up my ass today." She replies while face palming herself, I give her a questioning look. "Who's Grace?"

"Let us embrace you into the wonderful world that is my evil sister. She's blonde, she's perky, and most of all she's a stone cold bitch." Blaire says with a chuckle, I look at her as if she had three heads. "She can't possibly be that bad-"

"Hey hobbit. Who's the fresh meat? The boys are going to eat her up! Honey I don't know why you would hang out with my ugly sister and her dumb friends instead of living the cool life with me. Here's my number if you change your mind. Kisses!" First she took my phone and put her number in it, then she blew a kiss and walked away.

"Yeah never mind she's a bitch." I reply dryly as we watch her walk away, the girls just laugh. "I told you. She started referring to me as hobbit because she feels as if I resemble smeagol from Lord of The Rings." Blaire says with anger clear on her face, I shake my head.

"That's horrible. What do your parents say about it?" I question, making the look on Blaire's face do a complete 180. She went from angry to sad.

"My parents are dead. They um died in a car crash when I was twelve so we live with our grandmother who is too senile to function at the moment." At that moment I felt like I could feel her pain, not in a sympathetic way, but in an I get you kind of way.

"I'm sorry for your loss. I know you probably don't even want to hear that and just forget about it but it is okay to remember. Remember the good."

"Damn. That was deep." Blaire says with a smile, I chuckle. "I just know what it's like to lose someone close to you."

"I'm sorry for your loss-"

"Guys can we please stop talking about death. It's depressing!" Just as Piper was going to continue her sentence, the bell rang and she was off and left us in the dust. "That may have sounded kind of insensitive but I promise she's not like that. Her family has been through a lot this past year, she just doesn't want everything to be revolving around darkness and sadness, you know?"

"Trust me, I understand that very clearly." I reply with a nervous laugh, Blaire smiles. Unfortunately her smile was cut short by Brandon and his boys whistling at us.

"Sup babe." Brandon comments with a smirk, I chuckle. "Hey jackass." His smirk only grew wider and he wrapped his arm around me.

"Ah sarcasm! I love it. Glad to call you my babe-"

"Let me stop you right there B. First of all, I'm not your girlfriend so don't be calling me babe. Second, hell yes I'm sarcastic as shit so you better watch your back cuz you don't know when I'm being serious or not. And third, the bell just rang so will you and your mediocre friends move out of my way so Blaire and I can get to class? Thanks." I pushed him out of the way and grabbed Blaire's hand and pulled her to class.

"Ooh girl he's totally into you!" Blaire chants excitedly, I shake my head. "No, he's totally into my body."

"Look, I know Brandon can be a jerk but he's been through a lot-"

"So have I, do you see me acting like a piece of shit? No. I understand that people go through different things but it turns out good for them in the end. Some of us aren't so lucky. Let's just forget that it happened and go to English."

Blaire's POVI know she's hurting, and I know that deep down something serious is going on but that does not mean that she gets to assume things about people.

I'm not protecting Brandon and his little club of douchebags, I'm just saying that we have all been friends forever and we all bond over our struggles. All of us went through something life changing and I can tell that Lydia did too.

Friday is Midnight Madness, and wether or not she's going, I'm going to attempt to get something out of her. I want her to be able to open up to us and if that means being completely honest about what happened to me then so be it.

It's time for the drunken honesty circle.

5 days later (Lydia's POV) This week was very dramatic to say the least. To sum it up, it was a chain of events.

First, my brothers stupid drunk ass got a girl pregnant so now she has to stay with us. I mean she's actually really nice so I don't mind but it's just weird considering what we are actually running away from. To bring a baby into our mess is horrible, but things happen and I won't mind playing babysitter. Let's just hope our father doesn't find us.

Then Vince and Piper got together which is awesome for them but not so awesome for me and Blaire because Brandon and Nathan won't leave us alone now. And the icing on top the cake, Grace started dating Grayson so now we are being forced to hang out with her. Oh and my car broke down so now I have to take the bus home till we can get it fixed.

Tonight is midnight madness and apparently its tradition to kiss at midnight so apparently their Halloween is our New Years. Weirdos.

"So Lydia, what are you wearing tonight?" Piper questions, I smile. I'm confident in my answer. "I'm going to be a dark fairy."

"Oh come on! It's halloween! Be something hot! I've got a few things in my closet-"

"No way. I'm not trying to get attention drawn towards me-"

"Lydia, my brother, the biggest flirt in town is going to kiss you-"

"You mean he's going to attempt to kiss me-"

"Stop playing hard to get! It'll only make him want you more. I know you think you hate him but he's actually not that bad. All you have to do is talk to him for a little bit, he's been through a lot and this whole player thing is an act, trust me." Blaire says reassuringly, I chuckle.

"I've been through a lot too, you don't see me hooking up with every guy in my eye sight. I'm not trying to put any attention towards myself because my past will come back to haunt me. Trust me when I say you don't want that." Oh shit. Did I just say what I think I said? Stupid! Stupid! Stupid!

Right on time the bell rang. Thank god.

"Um I'll see you guys at the party. Bye." Right as I was walking to catch the bus, Nathan caught up with me. "Hey Lydia! Do you want a ride?" I decided to say yes because I don't feel like dealing with people's bullshit on the bus today.

"Sure." The minute me got into the car, it was silent. That was until he decided to break the silence and turn the radio on. "Can I ask you something?" He questions, I sigh while looking out the window.

"That depends on what you're going to ask." I reply with a chuckle, he smiles. "Why do you hide behind this tough wall of hate and bitchiness?"

"I don't know, why do you and your friends fuck everything without a penis?" I reply sarcastically, he smirks. "Touché"

"Alright well since you asked me I have to ask you now. What really is midnight madness? I keep getting bits and pieces of information but I don't know exact details." He starts laughing. What the hell is he laughing at?

"Well let me fill you in. Midnight madness is basically an excuse for every-one to get drunk, for girls to dress slutty and for everyone party hard. People get high, have sex, dance, and sing. After all of the craziness, Me, Blaire, Piper and Gray help Vince clean up and we usually get so drunk that we start spilling secrets but that's a story for another time. Oh and the iconic midnight kiss. To be honest I have no idea how that even came to light, it just became a thing. Any more questions?"

"Actually yes. This one is completely random but are you into Blaire? Because if you are I think you two would make a cute couple. I've seen the way you guys look at each other, it's got love written all over it."

"Nah, it's not like that-"

"Oh come on! You guys would be so adorable!"

"Lydia I don't think you understand." He replies with a chuckle, I look at him confused. "What do you mean?"

"She doesn't like me because she doesn't like boys. She's into girls." That was enough to make us go silent. "Oh." I said awkwardly, he just started laughing hysterically.

"It's not funny Nate I didn't know!" I punched his shoulder which only made him smirk. "You're cute when you're angry." He says randomly, I smirk.

"Only when I'm angry? Sorry dude, I'm cute all the time!" I reply while doing a hair flip. Its a joke. Don't get triggered.

"Yeah, You are." I didn't know how to respond. I was being sarcastic but I'll take it. "That was supposed to be a joke." I reply awkwardly with a chuckle, his face starts turning red.

"Well I mean it, you are. I know that I have no right saying it because it violates bro code with Brandon but-"

"I don't like Brandon. And I never will, he's too conceded for my taste. I like the nice guys." It felt like we were having a moment until we stopped right at my house and my brother basically pulled me out of the car.

"Where the hell have you been?" He snaps, I chuckle. "Chill out Enzo, my friend drove me home-"

"Oh well that's nice. Get in the house. We need to go. Now." There was a sense of panic in his voice, I chuckle again. "Why Enz-"

"Just get it the house!" He shouted, I sigh and get out. "Thanks for the ride Nate, I'll see you at the party." Once Nathan drove away, my brother started looking around frantically. I knew that could only mean one thing.

Our fathers coming. -------------------------------Hey guys! I am so sorry I took forever to update, school has had me so busy but I am back now and I have ideas. I am going to try to update faster but I can't promise anything. I want to make sure everything makes sense for you guys and that this book is at it's full potential.

Anyways, relating back to the book, what did you think about this chapter? Thoughts on Nathan's little moment with Lydia? Is their father really back? What do you think is going to happen next? Comment down below! Also don't forget to vote. Thanks,

~Jen

Chapter 4- Midnight Madness

"What's going on?" I snap, he just looks around frantically for what I am assuming are his car keys. "I said what's going on?!" He still didn't respond.

"Answer me Stef! What the hell is happening?!" Once he finally found his keys, he grabbed my arm and started dragging me out the door. "We need to go."

"No. You said it yourself, he's not going to find us here-"

"He's on the verge of finding us again Aide! We need to get out of here. Or even cut our losses if you want to stay here. No friends. No Boyfriend's. No crushes. No contact in the social media world."

"But I'm just starting to make friends-"

"Do you want them to end up like Wes? You once let him in and look where that got him. You need to cut your losses and stop drawing attention to yourself. One little mix up, that's all it takes. We need to change our styles again. Dye your hair any color, wear a wig I don't care just do something.

And keep your contacts in. We cannot slip up, not when we have every-thing going for us."

He's right. No one can get involved again. Not after what happened with Wes. But I want to be normal, he doesn't have to know. Yes, I am petrified that my father is going to find us but I deserve to at least try to be normal. When this mess all started, my brother was already out of high school so he at least got a normal high school experience. I've been on the run since I was 12 and I've had to figure out this life thing by myself.

"Okay. I'll stay away, you're right." I lie. There's no way he's letting me go to this party, I know what I have to do. I'm going to sneak out, but in order to do that, I have to give him some of my sleeping pills to knock him out, bad, I know.

"Good. So what do you want for dinner? I was thinking Chinese food, is that okay with you?" He questions, I nod my head vigorously. "Chicken and broccoli with noodles and dumplings please."

Once the food came and we ate, it was time for the hard part. I managed to slip two of my sleeping pills into his beer before we eat, he should be out like a light pretty soon, all I have to do is wait.

First I had to dye my hair again and put in my green contacts because I figured if I am going to completely go against my brothers rules, I might as well follow one of them. Then did the dishes and once I heard him snoring, I ran upstairs and changed.

I decided to go as the dark fairy despite what Piper said because I think it looks good. My hair is now a ombré effect of dark roots onto hot pink and it's really long so it gives off the dark vibe along with my costume. My dress is black and long sleeved but the sleeves get bigger going down to my wrists, I'm in love with it. And for my makeup, I decided to use dark colors such as black for lipstick and grey around my eyes to add to my dark fairy look. For shoes I just put on my black combat boots.

My main priority was figuring out how to sneak out of my room without waking my brother or his pregnant girlfriend. Luckily for me, I have a vine wall outside of my window so I could climb down that. Hopefully I don't fall and die.

I made sure to leave my window unlocked so I could get back in later. Step by step going down was so hard, I thought I was doing okay until I pricked my hand on a thorn and fell. Also I was so focused on getting out, I didn't even realize that I didn't grab my brothers car keys so now I have to walk in the cold. Great. This night just keeps getting better and better.

Since Vince's house is a half hour away by car, walking was just so fun. Luckily for me, I was stopped in the middle of my trip because a car pulled up to me, my first instinct was to run but then I heard the voice inside the car and recognized the car. "Lydia?" Nathan questions, I smile and wave.

"Hey Nate."

"Oh my god I almost didn't even stop because I didn't recognize you. I love your hair. Are you walking?" He questions, I shake my head and put a smirk on. "No, isn't it obvious I'm riding my magical unicorn into the sunset!" I replied sarcastically which caused him to smirk.

"Still loving that sarcasm I see. Do you want a ride? I know Vince's house is far from here." To say I nodded would be an understatement. I basically jumped in the passenger seat of his car and held my hands to the heater.

"I'm surprised you're not with Brandon or Grayson-"

"That's only because Piper is driving Brandon and Blaire, and Gray was driving with Grace and I'm sorry but I just can't stand that girl." We both start chuckling at our mutual dislike of Grace. "Watch her show up in a costume that barely qualifies as clothes."

"Yeah. Ever since eighth grade, the clothes kept getting shorter and shorter. It's crazy. Last year she pretty much went all Regina George on us and wore a bunny lingerie costume. I like your costume though, it's so dark and mysterious. Are you wearing a wig?" He questions, I shake my head.

"Nope, I dyed it myself. I felt like a change and I plan on embracing this change tonight, I'm going to go to that party, have a good time and maybe get a little drunk." I reply with a giggle. I need this. I need fun in my life.

"What happened earlier? Your brother seemed upset-"

"Yeah he was, um it's all okay now. I don't really feel like talking about it. I like your costume as well, very dark and kinda hot... Sorry that was weird." He just started laughing at my random outburst.

Damn it Adrianna! Focus. No relationships.

"Thanks. I meant to tell you this earlier but Brandon is planning on getting you alone at midnight-"

"Over my dead body! That boy wants to use me as a toy just for my body and I don't plan on letting him so promise me one thing, no matter how drunk I get, make sure I do not go anywhere with him." I said with all seriousness. I don't feel like getting raped, even though that doesn't usually happen I'm thinking the worst. Sorry, my brain automatically goes dark.

"I promise. I won't let anything bad happen to you." I heard him mumble the words "this time" which only made me feel confused. "What?"

"Nothing. Since we have some time to kill, want to play 20 questions?" It was so weird, he pulled one of my moves and completely changed the subject. Nice Nate. There is definitely something that this boy is hiding.

"Yeah sure." We played the game the rest of the ride and it was so awkward. We both obviously had things that we wanted to hide and then we would ask each other questions that we didn't want to answer and that made it even more awkward than it already was.

Once we arrived at the party, I couldn't even admire the view of the house because Piper and Blaire pulled me inside, I didn't even get to thank Nathan for driving me.

"Wow you two look great!" I said enthusiastically while admiring their costumes. Blaire had on a black furry cat suit on that had a good with ears which was absolutely adorable and her makeup was on point. Piper went the slutty route but she still looked fabulous. She was a slutty football player but I have to say she looked great.

"You too! I love the whole dark vibe, and your hair looks amazing! Did you dye it?" Piper questions excitedly, I nod. "Yeah, I felt like a change. Do you guys like it?"

"Like it? No. I'm with Piper on this one, it looks amazing! Oh and I was going to ask if you wanted to ride with us but you ran off so fast. How did you get here?" Blaire questions, I chuckle and look over at Nathan only to catch him looking at me so of course he snapped his head back to whoever he was talking to.

"Well at first I was walking but then I was stopped by Nathan and he gave me a ride and am I going crazy or is he staring at me again?" This time it was Piper who looked at him, judging the look on her face when she turned back I'll take it as a yes.

"Forget my brother, you and Nate's babies would be beautiful!" Piper comments with a smirk, I chuckle and shrug. "Well we kind of had a moment when he drove me home this afternoon-"

"Wait he drove you home too? He doesn't even drive Brandon home! He must really like you." Blaire teases, I smile. "Aw look Blaire she's blushing!"

"I am not!"

"Aww it's so cute how she's being all defensive!" It was as if I wasn't even there, they were just fawning over how "cute" I was. "Guys I'm right here! We are just friends-"

"But you said it yourself you guys had a moment. That means something. Midnight is in two hours, is he going to be the one you kiss?" Piper questions thoroughly, I chuckle.

"I told you, I'm not kissing anyone-"

"Let's see if you'll be saying that once the alcohol is in your system." Blaire interiors with a smirk while handing me a beer, I chuckle. Challenge excepted.

Throughout the night we sang, danced, had genuine fun and maybe got a little tipsy. The last thing I remember was singing Bodak Yellow to Grace and the rest of the night was blurry. That was until I woke up the next morning.

I woke up with a splitting headache. Once I felt a draft, my eyes popped open and I freaked out at the sight.

I was in only a t-shirt, In a bed. With a guy.

I freaked out even more when I saw who the guy was.

It was Nathan. ************************************Woah Drama! What do you guys think happened at the party? Did anything juicy happen between Nathan and Lydia? What happened to Brandon? Comment your predictions and don't forget to vote! Thanks,

~Jen

Chapter 5- The Backseat Was Invented For A Reason

- -

L ydia's POVOkay, to say I freaked out would be an understatement. I screamed which caused him to fall out of the bed. Then I started grabbing my hair and chanting "no no no! What did I do?" Over and over again.

Then he freaked out.

"Lydia?! What the hell?"

"What do you mean what the hell?! Look at us! I'm in nothing but your T-Shirt and all I remember is playing beer pong, singing to Grace somehow and then waking up, the rest is a blur. Shit did we-"

"God no! You really don't remember what happened last night?"

"Well were we even safe?!" I shouted apprehensively, tears starting to form at my eyes. He chuckles and shakes his head which only made me cry more.

"We didn't have sex Lydia. You were so drunk that we couldn't even put you in the car, everyone stayed here last night. You woke up screaming in the middle of the night and once I woke you up, you started crying and asked me to stay with you." This time it was my turn to sign in relief. That was until Vince came into the room which caused me to scream again and hit the floor. Thank god he didn't see me.

"Wakey wakey Nate! It's breakfast time, everyone is already downstairs. How was your night?" Vince questions, Nate chuckles.

"Very interesting. You all got pretty drunk though, do you remember what happened" Nathan asks, Vince shakes his head.

"I don't know man, I got pretty hammered. But I do remember you flirting with Lydia last night, and by the looks of it she was pretty into you too." Vince replied with a wink.

Me into Nathan? No way!

"Alright well thanks man, I'm going to finish getting dressed."

"I hope you two get together Nate, your connection seemed special. Anyways, breakfast is downstairs if you want it. I'll see you downstairs. Bye Lydia!" Vince closed the door and I popped my head up. I automatically frowned, Nathan just started hysterically laughing.

"How did he know I was in here?!" I whisper shouted, Nathan shook his head. "Well you started screaming last night which woke everyone up and then you screamed just now. I'm not going to lie, we were all pretty worried about you. Are you okay now?" He asks with a look of sympathy on his face, I chuckle.

"Of course I'm okay. Why wouldn't I be? Can I have my clothes now?" I snap, Nathan handed me my clothes and was looking at me up and down.

"Stop looking at me perv!" I snapped while putting my dress back on, he chuckled. "I mean we've already seen each other in our underwear-"

"I'm still curious about that. How did I end up naked in your shirt?" He starts laughing which only made me glare at him. "It's not funny! I'm not doing the walk of shame again! The first time was embarrassing enough so at least tell me what happened before I-"

"Wait this happened to you before?" He questions, still chuckling, I grunt at the memory. "Kind of, but it's not like I didn't remember what happened. Now stop joking around and tell me!"

"Okay so basically you kept complaining that you were hot so you stripped down in front of me, Piper and Blaire and then plopped on the bed. Piper made me give her my shirt and she kicked me out so I am guessing that she put it on you. Now come on, breakfast is downstairs."

Once we got downstairs, Nathan turned on his phone only to have it blowing up with all different messages, voicemails, snapchats, and Instagram tags. It was crazy.

Everyone was silent while eating, that was until Vince decided to break the silence. "So, I see that I'm not the only one getting tagged in stuff from last night. It was a crazy party, shit always happens. But this picture of Lydia and Nate at midnight is pretty aesthetically pleasing."

Everyone looked at the picture, including me and my eyes went wide. In the picture I am caught in a make out session with Nathan while holding a bottle of tequila in my hand. What the hell did I do last night?!

"What the hell happened last night?" I question apprehensively, Blaire chuckles. "Well we all did and said some crazy things but the best had to be when you sang Bodak Yellow to Grace because she was trying to give you trouble. I think I have the video." She pulled out her phone and pressed play, the minute I saw her costume, a memory popped into my head.

"Hey hobbit. Hey slut. Hey demon. Nice costumes." Grace says sneakily, smirking at the names she gave me, Blaire and Piper. I chuckle and take an intimidating step towards her.

"Hey Grace. Your costume is pretty nice too, what are you again? I forgot. Was it a hooker or a prostitute? Oh no wait I forgot this year you decided to go as the dumb blond! Hm, it suits you."

"Oh SHIt! Go babe!" Brandon chants, making a circle of people surround us. Grace and I find ourselves caught up in a stare down. She tried to look intimidating so she took a step forward just as I did. I'm not backing down. "I'd watch what I say if I were you-"

"Or what? You have nothing on me." I reply with a growl, she smirks evilly. "I can ruin you."

"I'm already ruined. Sorry, but your bitchiness can't bother me. I know that you are just sad and insecure and that is why you pick on everyone else. I really don't know how Grayson puts up with you, if I were him I would just throw you down the garbage shoot and take out the trash."

The crowd erupts in a spur of 'Oooohs'

I just chuckle as her cheeks go red. "You're gonna regret that bitch-"

"Yes I am a bitch and I'm proud. I don't regret anything and I never will. Your reign here as queen is over, move over there's a new bitch in town." I walked away without a care in the world and went over to the karaoke section.

"Grace, this ones for you." I stood up and made sure people could see me, specifically so Grace could see me and I started singing. "Said lil bitch you can't fuck with me if you wanted to!"

Once the video was done playing, we were all in shock. "Damn Lydia, who knew you were such a savage!" Brandon comments with a chuckle, Piper just starts clapping excitedly. "Unlike the rest of us, you weren't taking crap from her and I applaud you for it." She replies, I smile.

"Thanks, even though I don't remember any of it, I sounded pretty savage. What else happened after that?"

This time it was Vince's turn to speak. "Well, this ones a pretty funny story actually. After you sang and told Grace off, Gray got into a fight with Brandon saying things like 'control your girlfriend' and all of that and then Nate stepped in which only made him and Brandon start fighting over who was going to kiss you at midnight. Then you disappeared so Piper and Nate went to find you."

"I'm not going to question why Nate is still shirtless but I will bring up the fact that you scared the shit out of us last night. We thought you were getting murdered with the way you were screaming. You were screaming that someone was coming to get you and that he killed them. What were you talking about?" Blaire asks, clearly worried.

Shit.

Alright, what's the best solution to this?

Lie! Lie! Lie!

"Something bad happened a couple of years ago and I've been having nightmares ever since." I looked down at my hands and started scratching them, something I always did when I got nervous.

"What happened that would make you scream like that?" Brandon questions bluntly, earning a slap from Piper and glares from everyone else in the process. "You don't have to-"

"No, it's okay. My nightmares are just repressed memories of what happened that night. I'll never forget that night. A fire broke out in our house which killed two of our family members. My brother Lorenzo and I thought our father made it out alive because he was missing, the cops found his body three days later in the woods behind our house. After years of conspiracy theories going around the town about us, we thought it would be best to move."

It wasn't a complete lie, my mother and older sister were caught in the fire, however that was not their cause of death. Our father is the reason they are dead. He made us do the unspeakable and we have been on the run ever since. He truly is the devil, and once he finds us there is no turning back from hell.

"Oh my god, that's horrible. I'm so sorry." Nathan replies remorsefully while grabbing my hand, I shake my head. "Don't be, it's not your fault."

"I'm not trying to sound like a bitch and change the subject but I think the real question everyone wants to know and is just not saying is what the fuck happened with the two of you? That picture is pretty promising." Piper asks with her signature teasing smirk, I roll my eyes and look at Nathan with my arms crossed. I'm glad someone changed the subject, I can not afford for any more of my secrets to be released.

"I don't know, you were the sober one Nate so you tell me." His face turned red which automatically made Blaire and Piper say "awe!"

"Oh come on man, she was drunk and all over you and you didn't even sleep with her?" Brandon grunts, Nate glares at him. "Not all of us are incompetent douchebags B." Nate replies snarkily, I chuckle.

"You're starting to sound like your girlfriend man." Vince teases while shaking his head, Nate and I automatically denied. "No we aren't-"

"Everyone thinks you are. It's all over social media. That kiss sealed the deal. Someone even sent it to your brother-"

"What?! Oh shit. Crap. Fuck. I-I have to go. Please, can someone drive me home now?" I started freaking out. I lied to my brother and lied to my friends if they start talking to each other and their stories don't add up I'll be dead meat. Everything is on social media. I just murdered myself.

"I'll drive." Nathan stands up, Vince winks. "Have fun! Remember the backseat was made for a reason!" Blaire teases, I roll my eyes. The ride was once again silent, only this time we were avoiding the two elephants in the room.

"So are we going to talk about what just happened back there?" Nathan questions awkwardly, breaking the silence. I chuckle. "What? The kiss, it was nothing-"

"No, I mean the fact that you freaked out when we talked about the pictures being leaked. Is there something going on that you're not saying? Do I need to call child protective-"

"No! It's nothing like that. Just please delete the pictures. Delete them all. I can't be traced." That sounded so sketchy. Way to go Adrianna!

"I can't delete what others posted. What's so dangerous about one little picture? Are you afraid that your brother is going to ground you?" He questions, I shake my head. "Yeah, something like that."

If only you knew...

"If you're afraid about your brother, I can fight. I'll protect you-"

"That won't be necessary. I'll be fine in my own-"

"No. I insist-"

"I can't be in a relationship with you. I shouldn't even be friends with any of you. You need to stay away from me, I can take care of myself and-"

"That's ridiculous! Why would I stay way from you?" Jesus Nate just cooperate! "Because you don't want someone like me in your life. Where I go, danger follows. I don't expect you to understand."

"Then make me-"

"I can't Nate! You don't get it! I can't be with you nor can I be friends with someone like you! Thanks for the ride but I no longer need your assistance. Do me a favor a delete those photos." That was it, I snapped. I got out of the car and the front door of my house swung open. I could see the disappointment on Stefano's face.

I'm sorry.

I was yanked into the house by my brother and thrown onto the coach. "Are you insane?! What the hell is wrong with you! Did my speech mean nothing to you?!" He shouts, a tear falls down my face, but then anger consumes me.

"I deserve to live life to the fullest Stef! You got to live the high school dream and what did I get?! School after school! Name after name! Hair color after color! It's endless-"

"Your mistakes may have just cost you your life! Say goodbye to your friends, make an excuse, I really don't give a shit. You crossed a major line Aide! You not only disobeyed me, but you drugged me and then got yourself so drunk that it's all over social media! We stayed out of the news for a reason! No pictures. No phones. No technology. Nothing that can trace back to us Aide!" He screams, I'll admit I saw a bit of our father in him and that made me petrified.

"I need freedom!"

"Freedom my ass! You know what Carlyle will do once he finds us. If we don't run, if we don't hide! It'll be the end for everyone! I understand you're a teenager now, I understand you want to have fun, but this is your life now Aide! Our father is a monster and we are on the run! You want to be normal?! We will never be normal after what we saw! We will never be normal after what he made us do! HE'S A MONSTER AND I DON'T WANT TO DIE AT THE HANDS OF THAT BASTARD! So keep your nose out of everyone's business and stay away, otherwise I'll make you." The tone in his voice was indescribable. He was stern, he was angry, but most of all, he was scary. And that's all I needed to hear in order to get my act together.

"I hate you! Sometimes I feel as if you are just like him. You're trapping me-"

"I'm protecting you-"

"From what?! You can't protect me from the world Stef! I could die any day at the hands of our father! Might as well live it to the fullest." I screamed at him and then the world stopped. He hit me. He's never hit me before.

"I HATE YOU!"

Nathan's POV I watched as she got snatched into her house basically by her hair. I knew something was going on, I just had to get to the bottom of it. And once I heard screaming, I called Piper, knowing she was still with Blaire.

"Hey lover boy! How did it go with the princess?" Piper teases, I roll my eyes and chuckle. "Ha ha very funny. What do you know about her?"

"What do you mean? She's our friend Nate." Blaire questions, clearly interested. "Yeah she's our friend but what do we really know? She transferred in the middle of October, that's all we really know. Don't you guys think it's weird that at the mention of her brother and social media she freaked? I saw the way her and her brother were arguing yesterday-"

"What are you trying to say Nate?" Piper questions with a tone of worry in her face. "I'm saying that something is going on it that house. And I'm going to get to the bottom of it."

Chapter 6- You Have A Bond

Piper's POVWhen Nate suggested something was up with Lydia, I thought he was crazy. But once the week we came back rolled around, I figured something was wrong as well.

First off, there is no way for us to contact her because she doesn't have social media or a phone. What 17 year old doesn't have a phone? Second, she was late to school which at first I thought was because the bus was late but then I got a close look at her.

She had a bruise on her face and a cut near her eye, I was so worried. But finally, what really made me believe Nate was what happened when I confronted her.

"Oh my god Lydia, are you okay?" I questioned worriedly, she continued to try to cover her wounds with makeup and put on a fake smile. "Of course I'm okay. Why would you suggest otherwise?"

"I saw the wounds on your face and was wondering-"

"Look, whatever Nathan said to you about me is a lie. My brother is not sketchy, nor is my family life. You can tell Nate to take his opinions and shove them up his ass." She sounded angry. I don't blame her though, after all if someone tried snooping into my family business I would be pretty ticked off too.

"I know what he said wasn't right but-"

"Are you actually going to try and defend him? Oh I get it, you guys have known each other your whole lives and all of a sudden someone new comes to town and everyone is quick to make assumptions. I get that this is a small town and that people talk but you all need to stay out of it." Without another word, she slammed her locker shut and walked off to class.

I didn't want to upset her and fight back but what she said wasn't even true. I have only known Nate since I was 13, he moved here in seventh grade. The rest of us have known each other our whole lives and yes we have shared things that I am sure Lydia will never be comfortable with but that's only because we are close.

We all have gone through something bad and that's one of the reasons that our bond is so strong. I can tell that Lydia went through something traumatizing but she doesn't want to talk about it yet and I get that. But sooner or later she's going to have to say something.

I'm agreeing with Nate on this one. Something's going on.

I ran to Nathan's locker and interrupted his conversation with Grayson. "Sorry Gray, can I bother Nate for a moment?"

"Yeah sure. Remember what we talked about Nate." Grayson walked off mysteriously, I chuckle and look at Nate. "What was that about?"

The look on his face proved that he was worried about something. What could it be?

"Lydia is in trouble." He replies with a gulp, I frown and cross my arms. "Well we had our theories but-"

"No. You don't understand. Gray told me that if Lydia doesn't back off Grace is going to out her secret to everyone. Grace has dirt or is gathering up dirt and it's our job to protect Lydia. I don't know what's going on with her but this could be crucial for her. We need to let her know." He says worriedly. Nate is not one to show his emotions, but judging the look on his face this must be bad.

"We can't. She's mad at us. She knows about the theories we made about her brother and now she refuses to talk. What are we going to do?" A pit in my stomach was growing as my anxiety for her increased. When Grace finds dirt, she goes deep into finding what makes you tick, and if we piss her off who knows what's going to happen with Grace.

"First we are going to go to Grace. And we are going to find out what she has on Lydia." He says with a smirk. I knew that smirk only meant one thing, he was creating a diabolical plan. We are going to take down Grace.

"What if she doesn't say?"

"I happen to know a lot about our target. I've done research myself, I know plenty. So if she gives us trouble, we blackmail the blackmailer." His smirk only grew wider, I shook my head.

"That's not a very good idea. I've known Grace all my life and if you try to blackmail her all that is going to do create is chaos. She may be a bitch, but exposing her will also expose Blaire and I will not do anything to harm my best friend."

"You're right. But don't you at least want to know what I have on her? It has nothing to do with Blaire." I grunt and nod. I'm nosy. Don't judge me. "She's sleeping with coach Lawrence. That's how she's passing her classes, she got him to alter grades for her."

I knew Grace was evil but breaking the law and sleeping with a teacher just so he will change her grades is absolutely despicable.

"How did you find this out?" I question, he chuckles. "I have my sources. You're forgetting that Brandon dated her and that she has loyal followers, or should I say stalkers that will spill anything in order to get close to her. All I had to do was tell them that I'll give her their numbers and bam, they were open books." He replies with a chuckle, I roll my eyes. I know my brother wouldn't give any information without a price.

"And what did you tell Brandon?"

"I told him that I would get him a date with Lydia." I automatically punched him in the arm. "You idiot! Why would you do that?!"

"I did it to protect her. If things ever went bad, I know Brandon would be able to protect her-"

"But you like her! She's clearly into you and not him! You're such an idiot Nate I swear." He crosses his arms and shakes his head. "Who said I like her?"

"Dude. You're really going to play that card with me? Let's start with the fact that you fought with Brandon about kissing her. Then you actually did kiss her. And let's not forget how you reacted when she started screaming that night." I smile at the memory from Friday night.

"GET AWAY FROM ME!!! AHHH! YOU KILLED HIM! HOW DARE YOU?! HELP!! SOMEONE HELP ME!" Lydia was screaming at the top of her lungs, we all ran to the room she was sleeping in. Nate was the first one in her room.

Blaire stopped Nate right as he was going to wake her. "Are you crazy?! You could kill someone by waking them up from a nightmare!"

"Well what do you want he to do? She's in pain! Something is wrong, I can tell." Nate snaps with a look of worry clear on his face. I sigh and put my hand on his shoulder.

"Nate, she's right. You just have to wait this out-"

"I can't-"

"Fine. Everyone, go back to bed. I'll make sure he waits till she wakes up." Without hesitation Brandon, Vince and Blaire ran back to their rooms while I sat next to Nate and waited for Lydias scream fest to stop.

It looked as if she was gasping for air when she woke up, she just started crying. "Lydia, are you okay? You were having a bad dream." I question, she couldn't even respond, she was too busy crying hysterically. Damn, that must have been one bad nightmare.

"Shh it's alright. I'm here Lydia. You're safe, it's okay." Nate says softly, making Lydia calm down a little. "P-Please don't leave me." She whimpers, he strokes her hair and reassures her that it will be okay.

"I'm not going anywhere Lydia. I'm right here, you're safe." I couldn't even say anything, bad memories started popping in my head which made me speechless.

"It's okay Pipes, I can handle this. Go back to sleep." Nate says reassuringly, I nod. I didn't actually leave till ten minutes later once Lydia finally calmed down. I wasn't about to let him do this on his own. As creepy as it sounds, I kind of just watched from the shadows.

"Are you okay now?" Nate questions, Lydia shakes her head. "No, but I will be soon. I just have to calm down."

"Does this happen often?" He asks again, she nods. "It happens at least three times a week. It's always the same thing over and over. Some are repressed memories and some are just fragments of my imagination. I'll be okay, no need to worry."

"Are you sure?" Nate questioned, she nodded. He got up, but she stopped him.

"Nate... can you lay with me?" Lydia questions nervously, Nate gives her a worried look. "Are you sure? I don't want to step any boundaries-"

"I'm the one asking you Nate. As much as I hate to admit it I'm scared okay? please?"

"Alright. But don't try anything missy." Nate jokes, Lydia chuckles and shakes her head. "Wouldn't dream of it lover boy."

"I reacted how any friend would react." He says defensively, I sigh. "Nate Nate Nate, you really are in denial aren't you? You really like her just admit it!"

"I can't."

"Why not?" I snap angrily, he sighs. I could see a look of sadness spread across his face. "Before I moved here, I was best friends with this girl. Her name was Adrianna. She would always confide in me and tell me what was going on at home... it got really bad. I guess I'm just so protective of Lydia because I don't want her to end up like Adrianna."

"What happened to her?" I question curiously, he sighs. "Her father said that there was a car crash and that her and her family had died. I always believed that he had something to do with it but I never had any proof. Lydia reminds me so much of Aide and I don't want to lose her."

"Oh my god. That's horrible, I'm so sorry. But you can't let one event change your entire life. Do you think I let my mother's death control my life? Yes, it was horrible and yes you had time to mourn but it's time to move on. They wouldn't want you to be sad or depressed, but they would want you to do the thing they couldn't do and live life to the fullest. Take the chance with Lydia, it's what's best for you."

"I can't. She's mad at me, I really messed up Pipes. Yes I am worried because I know something is going on but I think it's best to just leave it alone. I'm sorry, just forget that I-"

"No don't forget it. You want to protect her then we fight against the danger which is Grace. If we take down Grace, we take down all evidence against Lydia. Just apologize to her, she connects most with you." I say with a smirk, he chuckles.

"Really?"

"Yes dumbass. She doesn't want to share anything with me or Blaire but she'll share her nightmare with you. You've got a bond-"

"Wait a minute. What did you just say?" Crap. Now he knows I was eavesdropping. "I said that you're a dumbass."

"No, the other thing." He says with a chuckle, clearly full of amusement. "I said you have a bond."

"You were listening that night when me and her were taking weren't you?" Right on time the late bell rang. "Whoops sorry can't hear you, have to get to class. Take what I said into consideration bye!" I ran as fast as I could. I knew I was guilty, but I didn't want to admit that.

I know that they like each other. So I am determined to make it my goal to get those two together. Whatever it takes.-------------------------------------S urprise! Nathan knew Adrianna when they were kids! So much drama. What do you think is going to happen next? Do you think that Nathan will find out that Lydia is Adrianna? What's the deal with Grace? Are you

Team Nathan or Team Brandon? Comment down below and don't forget to vote!

~Jen

Chapter 7- Blackmailing The Blackmailer

Blaire's POVAt lunch, Lydia refused to sit with us because of Nate which is upsetting but understandable. I had convinced Vince to come with me and sit with her but we were stopped by Piper.

"Is Nate here yet?" She questions eagerly, I shake my head as she squeals. "Great. Okay so I sort of kinda have a plan and I really really need the both of your help." The smirk on her face said it all, she was scheming about love. Piper always liked playing matchmaker since day one, every time she smirked and squealed I knew it had something to do with it.

"Who are you trying to get together?" I question with a grunt, Vince looks at me with a chuckle. "How did you know that was what she was going to say?" He questions, I roll my eyes.

"Let me educate you on your girlfriend. Now you guys can deny you're a thing all you want but that's besides the point. We all know that Piper has been playing matchmaker pretty much since the fifth grade. Whenever she makes a match, she smirks, squeals and asks for help. So Pipes, who are you trying to match?" She cringed at the upbringing of her nickname while Vince and I just chuckled.

"I'm trying to get Nate and Lydia together. I know it seems like a long shot but-"

"No it's not. You're completely right, he really likes her. He kept telling me that at the party, I could see that he was watching over her cautiously and that he really cared for her. He's very overprotective of her which I admire about him. I'll help." Vince interrupts, Piper smiles and looks at me, I grunt and nod. "Fine! I'm in."

"Great! But first we have to get Grace out of the picture." Vince and I looked at her as if she had three heads. "Ugh must I explain everything? Grace has dirt on Lydia which is the reason she isn't talking to Nate at the moment but now Nate got dirt on Grace and we are trying to fix everything. Meanwhile I have my own little plan on the side which you guys are going to help me with."

She's crazy. But that's what we love about her.

"Okay. How are we going to do this without the two of them knowing?" I question, Vince nods in agreement as Piper smirks. "Well, my father is hosting the winter ball this year and I feel that if they see each other all hot and dressed up then they will want to rip each other's clothes off. With our help of course. Blaire and I will sweet talk Lydia about Nate and you Vince, will do the same with Nate."

"Alright deal. When is the winter ball?" Vince questions, Piper smiles. "In a couple weeks, December 1st. I believe we can do this. Now if you'll excuse us, we have a friend to sweet talk, I'll call you later." Piper says while basically yanking me out of my seat and pulling me over to Lydia.

"Are these seats taken?" I question nervously, interrupting Lydia from reading her book. She looks up at us and I almost melted. She had bruises all over her face and it was clear that she had been crying. "That depends. Are you coming as my friends or his?" She snaps, we flash her our smiles.

"Yours of course. Us girls have to stick together right?" Piper says with a wink, Lydia shrugs as we sit down. I could easily see that she wasn't in the mood to talk but Piper kept pushing.

"So how was your day?" Piper questions with a smile, Lydia chuckles. "Pretty shitty. I had a bunch of people ask me if I was okay and I told them all the same thing. I'm fine, I'm just clumsy."

"Are you sure there is nothing going on?" I question nervously, Lydia nods. "I'm okay Blaire don't worry. I tripped over my backpack and fell down the stairs, no need to worry. Whatever Nate thinks happened is a lie, my brother did not hurt me, nor is anything bad happening in my house."

"We believe you. I'm pretty sure if you told Nate he would believe you too. Would you ever consider forgiving him?" Piper questions with a smile, I chuckle. I know what she's trying to do, she's trying to get Lydia to admit she likes him.

"Probably. I just need to tell him that whatever he thought is a lie, and that I am okay. His problem is that he worries too much-"

"He's overprotective because he likes you. He was there for you that night because he likes you. He stayed in bed with you until you calmed down because he likes you. Do you get the common factor here?" I can't believe Piper just said that. I'm glad she did though because Lydia is smiling like an idiot.

"Nathan likes me? I doubt that, who would ever like me?" I could tell that Lydia wasn't fishing for compliments because her face was in serious mode. She's just self conscious, aren't we all?

"Are you kidding me? You can ask Vince or Gray, you're all that he talks about. That one day when he drove you home from school, he never drives any of us home. He did it because he likes you. And who wouldn't like you? You're smart, beautiful, sarcastic and witty, plus you have a body sculpted by god. You have all the qualities guys like, embrace it." I said with a smile which only made a small smile come across her face.

"Maybe I will. Eventually. I don't like him like that-"

"Liar." Piper wanted to test her, she could do this all day. Wrong move Piper. "Yeah, okay. Believe whatever you want, I have to leave early so I'll see you guys tomorrow." Lydia walked away with a victorious smirk on her face while Piper just glared at her as she walked away.

"What are you thinking Piper?"

"This means war." Vince's POV The thought of Lydia and Nate together makes me feel awesome. So in order to help Piper, I'm going to talk to Nate about Lydia. Here goes nothing.

"Hey Nate, how was your day?" He sat down with a determined look on his face, once he started tapping his fingers I knew something was up. "What's wrong?"

"I need your help with something." He looked nervous which only made me worry. "Sure, what is it?"

"Revenge."

He only made me laugh. That was until he started glaring at me, that's when I knew he was serious. "Wait you're serious? What happened?"

"It's Grace. She has so much dirt on Lydia, no amount of explaining can make you understand. She's threatening me Vince."

I looked at him with wide eyes. "Why would she be threatening you?" I question, he sighs. "I knew she had something on Lydia because Gray told me to tell her to back off. I told Piper and our plan was to blackmail the blackmailer but Grace is always one step ahead. She has stuff against me too Vince. It's bad."

"What could she possibly have on you?" I question worriedly, he chuckles. "I made a big mistake before school started. If that gets out, Gray, Lydia and Blaire will hate me."

"Well what the hell did you do?" I question anxiously, he buried his head in his hands. "The week my brother died, Grace and I went to a end of summer party. I got really drunk and she started coming on to me, I used to like her you know that, but I also knew that Gray was in love with her. I was vulnerable and drunk and I just wanted to forget everything, I wanted everything to stop. We had sex that night. I didn't know that she taped it until this afternoon, she's threatening to release it. I really fucked up and I don't know what to do."

"Dude you really fucked up. What is she making you do in exchange for silence?" I question anxiously, a tear falls down his face. This must be bad. "She's breaking up with Gray. She's making me go out with her in exchange for silence. I don't want to go out with her, I want Lydia. Lydia makes me feel something that I haven't felt in a long time while Grace makes me feel like I want to throw up all the time and not in the good way."

Before I could even respond, Nate was pulled out of his chair by a very angry Grayson. "Is it true?!" He shouts, gaining attention from everyone in the cafeteria. I look over at the girls table and see that Lydia was gone but Piper and Blaire were running over to us.

"What the hell is going on?" Blaire whispers, I shake my head. "ANSWER ME NATE! IS IT TRUE?!"

"I don't know what you're talking about." Nate grunts in pain, I shake my head. Right as I was about to help Nate, I was held back by Piper. "Don't play dumb with me Nate. Are you with Grace? Did she break up with me for you?!" Gray shouts angrily while giving Nate a kick in the ribs, earning a gasp from everyone.

"Yes...it's true." Nathan grunts, clearly in pain. I wanted to help him so badly but I know he got himself into this mess and now it's his job to get himself out.

"Son of a bitch! How could you?!" This time Gray started punching and beating Nathan in the face. It got so bad that both Brandon and I had to pull Gray off of Nate. I don't blame Gray, if I were in his position I would be mad too.

"What the hell is going on?!" Piper shouts angrily, I look up at her and shake my head.

"Your plan backfired."-------------------------------------Woah, drama! What else do you think Grace has up her sleeve? Does Piper have another plan? Will Nate get out of his mess? Comment what you think is going to happen and don't forget to vote! Thanks.

~Jen

Chapter 8- Screw You

Lydia's POVOnce I went home yesterday, I couldn't stop thinking about what Piper said. He likes me. Nathan really likes me.

I had to leave school early to take my brother's girlfriend Haley to get a sonogram to check on the baby. I had plenty of time to ask her for advice since Stefano had to work. But first let me explain the story of Stefano and Haley.

Haley knows everything about us. She knows about my father, she knows about what she did and she knows my father is out for our blood. Back when we were Morgan and Jacob Sage, my brother fell in love. He risked everything for love, he told her everything even with the risk that she would run away and hate him forever. Lucky for him, she didn't run. They got married a year later but then our father found us and we had to leave, she came with us. Then a couple weeks ago we found out that she is 3 months pregnant. That is one of the reasons my brother wants me to stay away from people, for the sake of that baby living a good life.

In the waiting office, I decided to ask Haley about the Nathan situation. "So how was school?" She questions, I smile.

"Actually, it was okay. I found out that this boy I'm friends with has a crush on me."

"Ooooh yay! Are you going to go out with him?" She asks while wiggiling her eyebrows teasingly, I shake my head. "I don't think so. I can't risk that."

"Well do you like him?" I shrug which only made her laugh. "Honestly, he makes me feel something. But after what happened to Wesley I am afraid to love again. Stefano is right, maybe if I stay away then I can keep them from danger."

"Aide, if there's one thing I learned from marrying your brother, its that love is unpredictable. There are going to be obstacles but you will get through them. Don't live your life in fear, embrace the now." She grabs my hand and smiles as the doctor calls her in.

I spent all night thinking about what she said and I decided that she is right. I have to embrace the now and forget about the past for a little while. I'm going to tell Nate how I feel.

I woke up early just so I could dress all nice. I even did my hair and makeup. This was going to be a day to remember, I could sense it.

I drove to school with a smile on my face, I was ready to tell him everything. This was my chance. I held my head up high even as I got glares and glances by a bunch of people. I didn't care who was staring at me, I was going to go up to Nate and tell him.

I skipped over to his locker with a smile. "Hey Nate." I said flirtatiously, he didn't flinch. "Hey." He said shortly, I looked at him as if he had just said something wrong which in my opinion he did. He never talks dryly with me, I'm the only one he really opens up to.

"What's up?"

"The sky." He closed his locker and was slammed against the locker by some girl. I didn't think anything of it until the girl started kissing him. Then I got a good look at the girl who was looking right at me only to realize that it was Grace.

Anger started building up in my body. I hate her. I was so angry that tears started forming in my eyes. I would not let her win, I will not let them see me cry. I just ran in the opposite direction. I sat in home room, slammed my books on the floor and buried my head in my arms. I'm tired of getting spit on. Can't I just have one thing that is good in my life?!

"Lydia, are you okay?" Brandon questions, I glare at him with tears rolling down my face. "Do I look okay to you?" I snap angrily, he sighs.

"No you don't, that's why I'm asking you. Look I may act like a douchebag but I have feelings too, you can talk to me. What's wrong?" He goes to grab my hand but I pull away and sniffle.

"As if I would ever tell you. All you want is a ticket into my pants-"

"That's not true-"

"Oh really? Ever since I got here you have been talking about having sex with me to all of your stupid friends. You all have your stupid book and call yourselves the overachievers because you take pride in taking people's virginity. I'm not a virgin so forget about that and I'm not some ticket that you can use whenever you want either. I'm a person, and people have feelings." I let all my anger out on him but I didn't feel one inch of guilt.

"This is about Nate isn't it?" He questions, I roll my eyes and wipe away my tears. "You know what, just forget about it."

"No. What he did was not cool. He led you on and pretended to be Grayson's friend just so he could get to Grace. He's in the wrong-"

"Don't talk to me about being in the wrong. You've done bad things too Brandon. So don't try and pull the crap on me."

"Are you actually defending him? He first spread rumors about you, then led you on, broke up Gray and Grace, and then started going out with Grace. And yes, I admit I have done some bad things but thats not really me, I'm just hiding behind the death of my mom okay? But I'm done being like that. I want to be good. And you're going to help me." He replies with a smile, I roll my eyes and glare at him.

"And why would I do that?" I snap, he chuckles. "Because, if Nate sees you hanging out with me more and more then maybe he will start to get jealous. I know that what ever is happening to him is all because of Grace, she's a master manipulator and she's not gonna stop until she gets what she wants and that was Nate. You'll help me be good and I'll help you get Nate back. Think about it." He got up out of his seat and walked to his first period class as the bell rang.

I decided to follow him to his locker, once he closed his locker and saw me standing there he jumped. "Alright Santiago, I'll give it a shot. Lesson one of being good, get to class on time."

"Jesus Lydia! You scared the crap out of me!" He shouts, I chuckle and smirk. "Good. At least I know I have your attention now. See you later."

"Wait, you can't just do that!" He calls out, clearly shocked, I laugh. "I just did." I shout back while walking to class. ---------"So what's the deal with you and Brandon?" Piper questions with a tone of worry in her voice, I shake my head. "Nothing. We are helping each other that's all. I'm teaching him how to be a good person and in return he's helping me make Nate jealous."

"Wow. You really are evil." She replies with a big smirk, I chuckle. "I'm not evil. I just know what I want."

"So I was right, you do like Nate!" She starts clapping excitedly, I roll my eyes again and shake my head. "I felt something when I was with him that I haven't felt in a while. I was planning on telling him today but then I found out that he is with Grace now. I know she has something on him because he doesn't like her either, we established that in his car when he drove me home from school that day." A smirk automatically rose to Piper's face, I couldn't help but laugh.

"So you're teaching my brother how to be a good person while your intentions were actually evil. I like it. You know what we need? A party! My older sister is having a party for her sorority and she invited me, wanna be my plus one?"

"I don't think I can handle any more parties after last Friday-"

"Oh come on, you don't have to drink. In fact you will have to be the designated driver for the night since Blaire, Vince, Brandon and I get drunk. Please? We don't have school tomorrow so it'll be perfect." She pleads, I shake my head. "My brother isn't going to let me anyways-"

"Didn't you say he was working tonight? Just text him and say that you have a project due Thursday that you need to do with me. I can drive you to my house after school and I can lend you clothes and we can get ready and everything. What do you say?" She gave me the puppy dog eyes, I chuckle. "Fine. Give me your phone."

"Don't you have one?" She questions, I shake my head. "Nope. I'm not allowed. So can I borrow yours?" Lucky for us it was our free period so we can do whatever we want, we decided to go sit on the bleachers outside in the field.

She slowly nodded and handed me her phone. I got up and walked a few feet away, I then dialed my brothers work. "Hello, Lorenzo Stone please."

The receptionist connected me to his office and he answered with a tone that I have never heard from him before. It was joy.

"This is Mr. Stone speaking."

"Hey Enzo, it's Lydia. I just wanted to tell you not to worry if you don't see me tomorrow morning, I'm going to be doing a project with Piper and Blaire and it is going to take awhile so Piper's dad said I can stay over."

"I told you to stay away from them." He snarls, I roll my eyes. "Stef, I told you it's fine. He hasn't found us yet, let me live my life and stop worrying-"

"I got a letter Aide. I'm just worried okay?" My facial expression went from happy to sad. "What do you mean you got a letter?"

"I'll tell you tomorrow. Go do your project, and be careful. I have to go, I love you sis." A tear slipped down my face. "Love you too." I hung up without another word and turned around with a look of pure fear on my face.

The last time we got a letter, Wes was murdered shortly after. I knew this meant one thing.

My father was back.

But this time it's different. I will not let him hurt anyone I love.

"Hey, what's wrong are you okay?" Piper questions worriedly, I nod and put on a fake smile. "Yeah, I'm fine. How much time do we have until we can leave?"

She checks her phone and smiles widely when she responds "five minutes." Thank god, I could not do any more of school drama today. I haven't talked to Brandon since this morning even though we have classes together, my first step for him is making sure he gets to class on time. But now I guess I have to see him at Piper's house.

The bell rang five minutes later and Piper and I couldn't have gotten out of school faster. We ran to our lockers, grabbed our bags and met up with Brandon at her car.

"I have to get a couple of things at my house so I'll take my car and meet you guys at yours." I said with a smile, Brandon looks at Piper and then smirks. "Let me be a nice guy and walk you back to your car." As I was walking with him, I turned back to see that Piper was making a heart with her hands, I couldn't help but laugh.

"You didn't have to do this you know-"

"I know. But I am trying to be good which means doing good deeds and this, my beautiful friend, is one of my many good deeds to come." He winks at me as we approach my car, I lean against it and smile at him. "Are you flirting with me?" I question with a chuckle, he shrugs.

"Maybe I am, maybe I'm not. I'm just a guy that is trying to be good and it just so happens that a beautiful and smart girl is the one that is helping me." He replies with a smirk, I smile and tip toe up to his ear in which I whispered "flattering will get you nowhere." This only made his face turn red, I couldn't help but laugh again.

"Such a tease Stone. I-"

"Well what do we have here? I thought you hated him Lydia." A voice that I recognized as Nathan's says with a tone of anger in his voice, I chuckle. "Could've said the same about you with Grace."

"Whatever. Can we talk? Please?" I sigh and look at Brandon who is shaking his head. I look at him with a worried look which he noticed. "Do you want me to stay?"

"No B, it's okay. I'll be fine." Brandon didn't even look at me, he was glaring at Nathan instead. I had to make him look at me. I put my hand on his cheek which made made his facial expression go from angry to calm. "Brandon, look at me. I'll be okay, I'll meet you at the house okay?" He slowly nods and walks back to Pipers car, leaving me and Nate alone.

"What do you want Nate?" I snap, clearly angry. He just gives me a sad look, sorry but it's not going to work on me this time. "Look, I messed up-"

"Clearly. Your point?" I want him to know that I am furious. You don't get to lead me on and then spit on me. "My point is I'm sorry. What I did was not fair but I was trying to protect you."

"Trying to protect me by hurting all of your friends and me in the process. Bullshit." I spat angrily, he sighs. "I know you don't think I was being protective but I promise you I am. Grace was threatening you and-"

"The only way was for you to go out with her. I know you use to like her Nate so you can cut the crap and admit it. You wanted to go out with her. It's obvious she has something on you but if you really liked me you would have told her to screw off."

"She has things on you too-"

"No shit Sherlock. I can handle Grace on my own. No matter what she has on me I can handle it myself. I don't need protection, I've been protecting myself for years. But my point is I actually liked you and you knew that-"

"I like you too Lydia." I couldn't help but start laughing. I was laughing out of anger. He thinks this crap is going to work on me? Yeah, not going to happen. "If you like me so much then you wouldn't have led me on only to go sleep with the enemy. You claim that you're protecting me but you're really just protecting your image. You don't care about what she has on me, you only care about what she has on yourself. Screw you Nate." I got in my car and started the engine.

"I know about your father." He says with his arms crossed, I chuckle and shake my head. "You know nothing." I ignored the rest of what he said and just drove off. There's no way I'm letting him get the best of me, he's not worth it. What he did was trash, I guess he showed his true colors. I should've listened to Blaire when she said I had to watch out for him. Stupid feelings. -----------------------------------Ugh Nate, always have to mess things up smh. What did you guys think? Are you team Nathan or team Brandon? What do you think is going to happen at the party? Comment below and don't forget to vote! Thanks

~Jen

Chapter 9- What Were You Thinking?!

Lydia's POV I drove back to my house while blasting Demi Lovato songs. I don't know what it is but her music always calms me down whenever I'm upset or angry.

Once I arrived at my house, I unlocked the front door, greeted Haley and ran upstairs to grab my stuff. I packed my hairbrush, toothbrush, pajamas and a pair of clothes for tomorrow. I also packed my meds because without them I would be a mess, and then I headed across the street to Pipers house.

Piper opened the door with a smile and pulled me up to her room. "The party is an hour away so we better start getting ready. I'm going to give you the full makeover. Hair, nails, makeup, and shoes. You ready?" Piper questions excitedly, I look up at Brandon with a nervous look. He shakes his head and chuckles. "She's a stylist, don't worry she's really good."

Before I could even protest, Piper had pulled out all her beauty supplies and started working her magic. It took a half hour to make me up. "Done!"

"Finally!" She starts laughing. "Oh Lydia, this was just for a simple party. Wait until the winter ball, that's when I'll work my real magic."

"Real magic? You mean all this work was only for simple makeup?" I question curiously, she nods. "Correct my friend. Now let's get going, our friends are waiting."

"I'll meet you downstairs, I have to pee." I waited for her to close the door until I took my medication. When it comes to my meds, I am on a constant schedule, one slip up and I'll be taking a trip to crazy town, and trust me when I say that you don't want to see that.

Once I took my medication, I stuffed them in my purse and headed downstairs to meet with Brandon and Piper. "Damn Lydia, you look hot!" Brandon comments, I chuckle.

"Oh Brandi, flattery will get you nowhere. You don't tell a girl they look hot, you tell them they are beautiful. Do I have to go over politeness as well?" He shrugs and chuckles. "Maybe you do."

"All right love birds, get in the van." Piper comments with a chuckle. Seriously Pipes? I'm not dating Brandon!

On the way to the party, we picked up Vince and Blaire and blasted music in the car. We had our own dance party in the van, I could already tell that this night was going to be fun. That was until I got to the party, that freaked me out.

It wasn't like a high school party, this was a frat and sorority party which is only ten times worse. You got guys in robes, girls in barely any clothing, people swimming in the pool, people drinking and doing drugs, and then there was the occasional people that looked like they had just hooked up. I could tell that this night was going to be wild and that scared me so I popped one of my anti- anxiety pills and headed inside.

We were automatically greeted by Piper's sister who was lovely. She wasn't like your cliché sorority girl, she was pretty and nice and very welcoming.

Brandon and I had agreed on being the designated drivers for the night, two of us in case one changed their mind and decided to get a drink.

First I was pulled onto the dance floor by Piper and Blaire but I got really dizzy after awhile so I decided that I was going to sit down for a while. Brandon plopped next to me with a smile on his face. "Enjoying the party?"

"Yeah, your sister is great, I really like her. Are you being good tonight?" I question like a mother trying to discipline her child, he chuckles and nods.

"Yup. I haven't had one drink, but I have had the urge to flirt with a few sorority ladies if you know what I mean." He winks which only made me gag. "Okay, let me teach you something. Good people do not have sex the minute they meet someone. They wait."

"But where's the fun in that?" He whines, I shake my head. Just as I was about to respond, I looked at the door only to see Nate making out with Grace. Ugh what the hell are they doing here?

"I need a drink." Brandon saw that I was upset but I stormed away from him and made my way through the house, to the kitchen only to come face to face with one of the party hosts himself.

"Hey, is everything alright?" the guy asks, noticing my anger, I shrug. "I don't know, it just seems like every guy at this party is just a jerk." I say while pouring myself a drink.

"Yeah, they are. I guess the real reason I throw these parties is because I have no friends." He replied with a chuckle, I smile. "That makes two of us." I hold out my cup, he presses his against mine. "Cheers." We both chugged our drinks, but unfortunately after one sip I ended up coughing. I felt the burn as the liquor went down my throat and it was not pleasant.

"Ugh what is this stuff?"

"Tequila and scotch mixed together. I know it's really strong but it helps mend emotional wounds, trust me I would know."

"I feel you dude. Life is hard, and with a hard life comes complications." I take another sip of my drink and I feel a wave of heaviness hit me. "Are you okay?" He questions, I shake my head as everything starts spinning. "What do I do?"

"Get me out of here." He took my out to the backyard and that's when the hallucinations started. I saw him. I saw my father.

"Typical Adrianna. You always were a whore weren't you?" My father said with a smirk on his face, I shake my head and start backing up. "What's wrong Aide? You look like you've seen a ghost."

"You can't be here right now. You're not real." I shake my head and start pulling at it. I then looked over and saw my ex boyfriend Wesley with blood all over him but he had a smile on his face. "Come with me Aide. It'll be fun." The room started spinning faster, I closed my eyes and opened them only to come face to face with my mother and sister.

"R-Run Aide! He's going to get y-you!" My sister's face starts melting, I scream at the top of my lungs. "Do you see what you've done Adrianna? You've caused a mess. They are dead because of you. And soon, you'll be joining them."

"NOOOO! GET AWAY! GET OUT GET OUT GET OUT! YOU'RE NOT REAL! YOU'RE ALL DEAD. GET AWAY! AHHHHHHH!"

Brandon's POVOver the loud music, I heard screaming. I turned around to see that Lydia wasn't where she was before and I went running. Piper saw me run so she came after me. The girl was screaming bloody murder, I pushed the jerk that she was punching.

"What the hell did you do to her?!" I slammed him against the back wall, he looked angry. "I didn't do anything! She just started freaking out."

"You're not real. You're not real! YOU'RE NOT REAL!! Get out GET out GET OUT!!!" Lydia falls on the ground and starts pulling out patches of her hair, I cradle her. "Lydia! Lydia snap out of it, it's okay. It's Brandon! I'm right here."

"You're dead! You're all dead! You're not real!" It came out as a feared whisper before her eyes rolled to the back of her head. "No no no. Lydia wake up. Lydia open your eyes. LYDIA!"

It was as if everything started going in slow motion. The world had stopped. "CALL 911!" I screamed at Piper, she whipped her phone out fast and called an ambulance. "They won't be here for an hour-"

"We don't have that much time! She's not breathing. I'll drive her myself, I'm going to need you to do compressions while I drive to the nearest hospital. It's only 15 minutes away." Piper knows how to do CPR, we took a class together after our mother died. I swooped Lydia up in my arms and ran inside, ignoring all the looks we were getting from people and we put her in the van.

The minute I got in the car, I floored it. Piper did compressions and I continuously checked on them. "How's she doing Pipes?"

"Not good. She's finally breathing but her pulse is very weak. We need to get there fast, how much longer?" She questions worriedly, I sigh in relief as I pull in the front. I didn't even bother parking, I took Lydia in my arms and ran inside.

"HELP! SOMEONE HELP!"

Nurses automatically started asking me questions. "What did she have?"

"I don't know! I think she drank beer or something. I wasn't watching her-"

"Is she taking any medications?"

"I don't know-"

"Does she have any allergies?"

"Not that I know of. Oh god, please just help her." They started saying a bunch of medical codes to each other which only made me freak out even more. I started crying, this is history repeating itself.

Please God, if you're real I promise you that I will completely change. No more parties, no more girls, I'll look after Lydia with everything I have. Please let her be okay.

"Everything is going to be-"

"Don't you dare say it's going to be okay because it's not. I was supposed to be watching her and she walked away and did god knows what. It's all my fault." Tears fall down my face, Piper shakes her head.

"Why are you putting so much pressure on yourself?" She questions worriedly, I sigh. "I couldn't help mom, I need to be here for Lydia."

"Brandon, what happened to mom was not your fault, it was the guy who hit her that was at fault. There was nothing you could have done. As for Lydia, well we can still help her. All we can do is pray." She grabbed my hand and I put my head on her shoulder.

It was hours before we heard anything. The nurse from earlier finally came to us and said she was awake. I ran to her room only to see her with an IV stuck in her arm and that she was being questioned by the doctor. Words couldn't describe how relieved I felt.

Lydia's POV I woke up with a headache and a feeling of confusion. That was until I was told where I was. "M'am, are you aware that you're in the hospital?" I shake my head.

"What happened?" My body ached all over, it hurt to move. "You had to get your stomach pumped. I have to ask you a few questions okay?" The doctor says, I slowly nod.

"Are you on any medications?" I nod, even that hurt. Damn. What the hell did I do?! "Yes. I am on multiple anti-depressants."

"Did you have anything to drink?" He questions, once again I nod. "Are you aware that you took a drug?"

"What?! No I didn't!" I started getting defensive, that was when I noticed Piper and Brandon standing there. "Miss Stone, in your report it says that you had a drug in your system, a mixture of that and the alcohol plus the medication you already took is what made you pass out."

"I bet it was Sam. That was the only person you were with. He drugged you!" Brandon starts getting angry, the doctor's eyes bug out. "Would you like me to fill out a police report?"

"No-"

"Yes Lydia. This is a crime-"

"I'm fine Brandon-"

"Look at you! You had to get your stomach pumped, you're not fine!" He shouts back, clearly angry. Nobody can know where I am. Not after what I saw.

"I'm okay. No need for a report. Can you give us a few minutes alone please?" I question the doctor, he nods and walks out leaving me, Brandon and Piper to talk.

"How can you say its okay-"

"Why did you bring me here? Please tell me you didn't call my brother. He can't know!" I freak out, Piper sighs. "We had to Lydia, we didn't have a choice-"

"Do you have any idea what you've done?!" I start freaking out again, Brandon grabs my hand. "It was what's best. He needed to sign your medical reports-"

"We don't have medical records! There can't be any report without any past records. Why couldn't I just have listened to him?! No technology, no communication, no doctors. That was the rule. I broke every single rule by even talking to you guys, do you know what he's going to do if he finds out I lied to him?" They give me a worried look, I start crying. Of course they don't know, I never told them anything.

"Is what Nate said about your brother true?" Piper questions nervously, I shake my head. "Not my brother, my father. If he finds us I'm as good as dead. You don't understand."

"I thought you said your father died?" Brandon questions with a tone of shock, I shake my head. "I lied to cover the truth. It's going to come out anyways since Grace knows. My father is a very dangerous man that has done unspeakable things. I told you guys he was dead to cover the truth that he hasn't found us yet. I'll tell you the full story just not here, I can't. Please, you can't tell anyone. If word gets around, my father will find us and hunt us down again."

Piper had a delayed reaction, but it was as if Brandon didn't care because he started unhooking me from the machines and IV's.

"What are you doing?" I question, he chuckles. "What does it look like? I'm getting you out of here. Weak or not I will not let anyone come after you.

They will have to go through me first. Piper can call your brother back and say that it was a prank-"

"Or he could come discharge you himself. Get dressed Lydia, we're going home." I looked up to see my brother standing in the door frame with a look of pure anger on his face, I knew not to defy him again. "Are you sure you'll be okay Lydia?" Piper questions, I nod and tell her that I'll see her Friday. I know my brother, he's going to make me rest.

"Stef-"

"I don't wanna hear it Aide. We will talk about this when we get home, until then don't say a word. I don't even want to look at you right now." So I didn't say anything. I didn't even sing to the music in the car, I just drank plenty of fluids to get my hydration level back up.

I could tell he was pissed, I don't blame him. Both times I disobeyed him and both times I got into trouble. But this time I lied through my teeth, I don't know how he's going to react this time. Last time he was violent, who knows what he will be like this time. Please let Haley be home. She'll be able to talk some sense into him. Please.

Once we arrived home, I looked over at Brandon and waved, he gave me a look of fear, I shake my head as a way of telling him that I will be okay. My brother just yanked me inside by the arm.

"Is Haley home?" I question, he glares at me. "It's five AM, you almost died and you're asking if Haley is home? What the hell were you thinking Aide?!" He shouts making me jump, I shake my head.

"It was only a sip of one drink-"

"One drunk that was laced with a drug. Never accept drinks from strangers! Are you dumb?! And with all the meds you're on you'd think you would've thought about the chances of that."

"I know! But I didn't and I'm sorry!" A tear falls down my face, he laughs. "Ha sorry. You're sorry? Sorry you disobeyed me, or sorry that you got caught." I gave him a guilty look, he chuckles again.

"That's what I thought. I don't want you hanging out with them-"

"Stefano that's not fair!"

"What's not fair Aide, is having you disobey me multiple times when I am just trying to protect you! You know what happened last time I got a letter from him. Do you want one of those innocent kids to die? Because I don't! Stay away from them. Your one little mistake could have cost us our lives. You wanna talk about fair, let's talk about fair. If you want to be with them you have to tell them everything. Every thing he made us do, everything he did, what he did to mom and Rose, all of it. He's a sick and twisted man so I'll give you an ultimatum. You can either be grounded and tell them, or you can be lonely and grounded. I understand you want to live your life but to what extent? Do you want him to find us?!" I quickly shake my head.

"Neither do I. So there are your choices, either way you're grounded. And you can think about what you did by reading the letter, maybe that will knock some sense into you. I'm going to bed." He threw the letter at me and without another word stomped upstairs leaving me to read the letter.

My dearest Stefano,Once again it is time for our annual game of hide and go seek. I guess it's my turn to seek again. You can't hide from me forever, I always have a way of finding you. And with you working at a big shot law firm and your sisters hot pink hair, it is very easy. We will see each other soon, it may not be now but it will be when the moon sets upon the stars and the winter is coldest. See you soon my son, I can't wait. ~Carlyle

I knew this meant one thing. My father is back, and he's badder than ever. That scares the shit out of me.

Chapter 10- The Truth

Lydia's POVI didn't speak to my brother basically until Thursday night when Piper and Brandon asked to see me do we could go over the notes in class. My brother decided to keep me home until I get my strength back and the doctor said to keep me home for at least a week so I'll be back on Monday.

I was nervous to see them after my breakdown at the party, but I was even more nervous to tell them the whole story.

"Lydia! Your friends are coming upstairs!" Stefano shouts, I had about five seconds to clean my room. I still felt weak from the other day so I just shoved everything under my covers and sat down as they opened the door. "Hey Lydia, how are you feeling?" Piper asks with a smile on her face, I smile back.

"Well, I still feel weak but I'm starting to gain my strength back slowly. How was school today?" I question, Piper's smile fades to a frown as she pulls Brandon in my room. He had a black eye and a busted lip. "What the hell happened?!" I ask worriedly, he chuckles and scratches the back of his head which knowing Brandon is an indication that he's nervous.

"My idiot brother started a fight with Nathan. Nate got him pretty good as you can see-"

"I did it for you. If he hadn't been at the party then you wouldn't have drank anything and you would be okay. It's his fault, I wanted to make sure he paid for it." I roll my eyes at Brandon's attempt at being nice.

"Thanks for sticking up for me, but I don't need you to do that. I can protect myself-"

"Like you protected yourself at the party?" I glare at him and shake my head. "That's not fair-"

"No, what's not fair is lying to everyone about why you're really here. What's not fair is that you accepted a drink from a random guy who laced his shit with drugs. What's not fair is that I thought I was going to lose you and that would crush me Lydia." I could see the pain in his eyes, I went up and gave him a big hug and them I kissed him on the cheek and smiled.

"You're not going to lose me. I'm right here, I'm sorry I scared you. You saved my life, now I'll owe you." At this point he was smiling like an idiot while Piper was standing there looking grossed out.

"Lydia, we won't leave you no matter what it is you have to tell us." Piper said with a smile, I sigh. "I'm not sure you'll say that once I actually tell you what happened that night." I gestured for them to sit down, this was it. I finally can get it off my chest. Let's just hope they don't think I am a psycho when I'm finished.

"Growing up, my mother raised us and my father worked to bring the money home. We were a loving family up until my father lost his job, that's when he started drinking. And with the drinking came violence...He would always hit us and lock us up if we disobeyed him. Sometimes he would throw us down the basement stairs and leave us in the dark without food or water for days. When I was 12, we found out that dad owed some bad men money, but he had just gotten fired so obviously he couldn't give it to him. Once my older sister Rose found out, she told me she was leaving but she would be back to get us. We never heard from her again, that was until that night."

I took a deep breath before continuing. "That night was a night I will never forget. My brother and I were outside in the backyard playing football when we heard a loud scream. Automatically I ran inside because my 12 year old mind wanted to know what happened. I ran inside and saw my father coming down from the attic with blood all over him. I asked him what was wrong but he replied with nothing. Then I asked where my mom was and he freaked, I went running for the attic but was thrown back on the floor by my father. My brother obviously came to my rescue but that was what made my father freak out even more. He wouldn't let us go, he took me by the back of my shirt and pulled me up the stairs. My brother was screaming at him to put me down until we finally reached the attic, my father threw me to the floor where I was face to face our mother's dead body bleeding out and our sister with a bullet wound to the head."

"Oh my god, that's horrible!" Piper comments, I nod and wipe away a tear. "He made us hide mom's body in the woods behind our house, we tried saying no but he would always threaten us by saying he was going to kill one of us. Then when we got back to the house, we saw a trail of blood and realized it was coming from Rose. She was somehow still alive. But not for much longer. He made me finish her off, he said if I didn't then he would gut my brother right then and there and I would be stuck with him for the rest of my life... I had no choice." Tears start streaming down my face as I start breaking down. They grab my hands which was an indication of them telling me to continue so I did.

"Dad set her body on fire as well as the house. He said if we faked our death then we could make it look like an accident. As he was making sure the fire spread, my brother and I ran faster than we've ever ran in our lives. We contacted our uncle Tim who helped us get away. We drove as far away as possible, we changed our names, we wore contacts, and we changed our hair colors. He eventually found us. We moved multiple times and he still managed to find us each time. When I was fifteen we thought we were okay, I made friends, got good grades, joined some teams and even fell in love. I told him everything, he was willing to protect me when all hell broke loose. The day our father found us was the day everything changed. Wesley wanted to stick up for me but my father killed him in the process, hence my screaming fit at midnight madness in the middle of the night. I've been having nightmares about it ever since."

"Another time he found us because of my medical records. I tried committing suicide after everything but unfortunately I came back to life. I was diagnosed wth depression, anxiety, and bipolar disorder. Then we moved again and here we are today. No phones, no medical help, no technology. That was supposed to be the plan, but then I started getting close to all of you and in a small town like this, word spreads fast."

"Wait you changed your name again?" Brandon questions, I nod. "Yes. My name is not Lydia Stone, my birth name is Adrianna Samuels." It was as if something clicked in Pipers head because she looked at me confused.

"Why are you telling us this?" She questions, I sigh. "My brother got a letter from our father. He found us again, I wanted you guys to know for two reasons. One, because I might have to leave again and I want to keep you guys out of danger, and two because Grace knows everything somehow and I'm pretty sure that is what she has on me."

Piper immediately grabbed her stuff and got up. "I have to go. I'm sorry." She ran out as fast as she could leaving me to start crying again, while Brandon comforted me. "This is why I didn't want to tell you guys. I'm so sorry!"

"No, there is no reason the be sorry." He starts rubbing my back as I cry in him arms. I knew this was a bad idea, I shouldn't have brought them into this. "I was afraid to tell you because I was afraid that what Piper just did would happen. I shouldn't have dragged you into this. I should've just stayed away-"

"Hey, I'm right here. I'm not going anywhere." He tries to reassure me, I shake my head. "Brandon he's dangerous, I don't want what happened to my ex to happen to you. Or even Piper, Blaire or Vince." Nice save Aide, nice save.

"Let's just say I know how to fight-"

"B, you know what I mean. He's got weapons and power and he's all sorts of ruthless. I don't want you being in the middle of that. I did it once and look how that turned out." He grabs my hands and makes me look at him, he sighed before saying "let me ask you something. What are you really afraid of?"

"I'm afraid he's going to kill me and everyone I care about. I'm afraid that he's going to hurt everyone I care about just to get to me. I'm afraid that he will kill my brothers baby once he finds out. I'm afraid of many things Brandon, the list goes on and on. I can't let anything happen to any of you, all of your lives are in my hands and-"

"It's okay-"

"No it's not okay! If he finds us then it's game over. He will get into my head and make me do very bad things which will end in chaos and my main goal is protecting my little niece or nephew and I don't know if I can't do that and it's really freaking me out and-"

"Lydia."

"And hopefully everything will be fine because I'm really starting to like you and all your friends and if he finds me he-"

"Lydia!"

"He will find a way to hurt me mentally and then we are all screwed. I'm so sorry this is all my fault."

Brandon's POVI knew that she was having a panic attack so I tried calming her down. But when that didn't work, I did the most cliché thing in the world.

I kissed her.

Lydia's POVHe kissed me.

He kissed me?!

What. The. Fuck.

Piper's POVThe minute she said her name was Adrianna Samuels I ran out. I knew that name sounded familiar and then it clicked in my head.

"Nate Nate Nate, you really are in denial aren't you? You really like her just admit it!"

"I can't."

"Why not?" I snap angrily, he sighs. I could see a look of sadness spread across his face. "Before I moved here, I was best friends with this girl. Her name was Adrianna. She would always confide in me and tell me what was going on at home... it got really bad. I guess I'm just so protective of Lydia because I don't want her to end up like Adrianna."

"What happened to her?" I question curiously, he sighs. "Her father said that there was a car crash and that her and her family had died. I always believed that he had something to do with it but I never had any proof. Lydia reminds me so much of Aide and I don't want to lose her."

I automatically took out my phone and called Nate, he answered with an angered expression. "What? I'm busy."

"We need to talk."

Chapter 11- You Need Jesus

Nathan's POVI was already in a bad mood because of Brandon this morning, then I got home and had to run a bunch of errands for my siblings so that put me in an even worse mood, and now Piper showed up at my doorstep claiming "we need to talk". What could we possibly talk about.

"So what did you want to talk about?" I question while sitting on my couch, she chuckles. "You're not going to believe me when I say this but your friend Adrianna is alive."

I looked at her and started laughing. "Very funny. I told you, she's dead-"

"No. She's alive, and I know this because Adrianna is Lydia. You said you thought she was like Adrianna, that's because she is Aide. She told me the real reason she's here, ask your girlfriend she'll even tell you. That's the leverage she had on Lydia."

"I have to talk to her. Give me your phone, I'll call-"

"She doesn't have a phone-"

"Then I'll go by her house-"

"Brandon's still there-"

"Then what the fuck am I supposed to do Piper?! All these years I thought she was dead and now I find out she's actually alive!" I said cheerfully, she sighed. "Look, I know this is big for you but I don't think it's good you tell her. She's dealing with a lot right now and you did her dirty. You not only led her on but then you pawned her off to Brandon in exchange for leverage and then started dating her enemy who is using you to threaten her, that's cruel. And while you've been living it up with Grace a lot of shit happened and Brandon was truly there for her. You need to start getting your shit together if you know what you want, because you've already hurt all your friends. Don't do it again."

There was a tone of anger in her voice that petrified me. "I know I made mistakes, but I am willing to fix them-"

"No Nate. I told you that she was alive to give you closure, not so you can go and ruin everything again. If you want to be in her life then just be friends with her, nothing else. Don't fuck with her head." She walked off without another word which I'll admit really scared me. When Piper is mad at you, you need to do something extraordinary in order to get her to forgive you.

What have I gotten myself into. ----------Piper's POVAfter a couple hours of leaving technology to go to my thinking spot, I texted Blaire and told her to come over because she is the only one who really can ever cheer me up.

"So what's the deal with Lydia and Brandon?" Blaire questions, I chuckle. "When I left she was crying in his arms, I haven't seen or heard from him in hours. They totally were getting it on."

"Piper! Don't think so low of Lydia, Brandon maybe but definitely not her. She's very closed in when it comes to her feelings and emotions, what makes you so sure she would let Brandon in?"

"Because he saved her life the other night at the party. She would've died if it weren't for him." Her eyes pretty much bugged out of her head, she never saw Brandon and I take Lydia out, I just texted her and Vince and told them to find a ride home because something came up.

"What?! What the hell happened?!" She asks frantically, I sigh. "My sisters sorority friend's boyfriend drugged her, Lydia was already on meds so it caused hallucinations and for her to pass out. Brandon carried her into the car while I did chest compressions because she stopped breathing at one point. She ended up having to get her stomach pumped. If he hadn't said fuck the ambulance, in driving her she would be dead. He saved her life."

"Oh my god. I had no idea, I thought one of you guys got sick or something." She says with a worried expression, I shake my head. "Don't blame yourself, there's no way you could have known. Please don't say anything to her, she made us promise we wouldn't tell anyone."

"Why?"

"Because something bigger than we ever imagined is going on. And it involves her screaming fit nightmares. Do you want to go check on them? It's been a couple of hours." I question, quickly dismissing the nightmare situation, she nods and smirks. "This should be interesting."

We walked across the street and once again rang her doorbell, a pregnant lady answered. I didn't know that another person lived with them. Interesting.

Maybe since her brother was able to let a girl in, she's letting us in. The whole situation is weird so I don't know. "Hello girls, Lydia and Brandon are upstairs so you can go right on up." She knew who we are so Lydia must have talked about us, besides she already had most likely seen me earlier but I didn't see her.

"If you don't mind me asking, I don't think I've heard Lydia talk about you. What is your name?" I question politely, she smiles. "I am Lorenzo's wife Haley, I wouldn't be surprised if she hasn't mentioned me though because I just stay in the house all day basically but she's kept me up with the drama." She replies with a giggle, Blaire smiles.

"Are you team Nathan or team Brandon?" Blaire questions, Haley smiles widely. "Oh team Brandon all the way, if you go upstairs you'll see why." That automatically made me and Blaire smirk at each other and run upstairs.

I opened the door quickly only to be in awe. "I expected something dirty, but this is just adorable!" I whispered to Blaire excitedly, she nods in agreement. They are both asleep, but Lydia is wrapped in Brandon's arms and he is cuddling her like she is the most fragile thing on the planet.

"I have to get a picture of this." Blaire comments while snapping a picture on her phone. Then of course with me being the matchmaker I am, I had to wake them up. "Wakey Wakey lovebirds!"

They woke up so calmly and just smiled at each other before looking at us and jumping apart, Blaire and I couldn't help but laugh. "What happened in the past few hours?" I question, Brandon scratches the back of his head nervously, Lydia gets up. "I'll be right back, I have to go to the bathroom."

We waited until she left the room to ask Brandon what happened again, he started smiling like an idiot. Ugh I ship them so much.

"Well...she kind of freaked out and I didn't know what do so I kissed her as a spur of the moment thing and then we kinda acted all weird but we ended up watching a movie and I guess we fell asleep."

"You kissed her?!" Blaire and I say excitedly in unison, he nods. "Don't make it a big deal-"

"Why? Because you like her?" I tease, he glares at me, I only just chuckle. "Come on B, we all know you like her. You haven't had any interest in being a better person until this year, just admit it. You're changing for her."

"I don't know what you're talking about. Dad wants us home for family night so I guess it's a good thing you woke me up anyways. I just have to say bye to Lydia first." Right on time, Lydia walked into the room with a smile.

Lydia's POV"Everything okay?" I question, Piper and Brandon nod. "Yeah, dad wants Brandon and I back home for dinner. I'll see you tomorrow, I'll be back with more of your homework and you can fill me in on what happened here." Piper says with a wink, I roll her eyes as we hug. Then it was Brandon's turn. First he grabbed my hands and I felt a bolt of electricity go through my body.

That was weird.

"Remember what we talked about okay?" I nod in understanding, he gives me a hug and then kisses me on the forehead which I did not expect, but it left me smiling like an idiot. What is wrong with me?

Once we heard the door close, Haley walked into my room with a smirk on her face. "Tell me the drama, you two looked so cute sleeping I didn't want to wake you up." Haley says teasingly, I chuckle as Blaire looks at me the same way.

"You guys are acting as if he asked me out-"

"Well, he did kiss you." Blaire comments, I start blushing. "So...he told you about that." She nods with a wide smile on her face.

"Yup. Come on Lydia! We wanna know what happened with you two! Please?" Blaire and Haley gave me the puppy eyes, and when that didn't work, Blaire got in her knees and started chanting "all hail Lydia! For she is the holy one!". It was hilarious.

"Okay jeez. But if my brother ever found out he would kill me so Haley I'm trusting you not to tell him." I look at her as she smiles and crosses her heart. "Scouts honor. And yes I was a Girl Scout don't even question it. Continue with your love story."

I roll my eyes and sit on my bed, blushing at the memory. "Well, Lorenzo gave me an ultimatum. I could either tell you guys the real reason I'm here and be grounded after that frat party, or I could be lonely and grounded. I chose to tell the truth which I'll explain to you later because it's a long story. Anyways, I told Piper and Brandon because they came by with my homework and by the end of it Piper ran off and I started hysterically crying. Brandon tried comforting me but then I started rambling and freaking out and he kissed me. That's all."

"I may be older but I'm not dumb. There's more after that, you're just cutting it out." I glared at Haley which only made Blaire smirk. "Come on Lydia, let's hear what happened." Blaire says teasingly, I rolled my eyes and started to feel hotness raising to my cheeks.

"Ugh fine! I may or may not have kissed him back...which may have lead to a little more, but then we stopped and decided to watch movies instead, and I guess we must have fallen asleep." I felt even more heat rise to my cheeks as I think of the memory.

"Oh my god you totally did it!" They say in unison, I shake my head fast. "No no no no no no! We just made out a lot you dirty minded fools." They automatically start laughing, I could help but laugh myself as well.

"Well I think you guys would be cute together. Forget Nate, he's a jerk. Brandon on the other hand is trying to change, specifically for you. He may seem like a flirt, but he genuinely likes you. He even burned the overachievers book-"

"That's dedication." Haley interrupts, I chuckle and shake my head. "It could just be a coincidence-"

"Just admit you like him already!" Blaire chants, I shake my head again as they boo me. "Ugh you are so in denial Lydia!" Haley whines, I roll my eyes and cross my arms.

"No I'm not. I just don't want to get hurt again, and I specifically don't want dad to find out because then Brandon said he would fight him and wouldn't let anything happen to me but I can't let him do that because then he will just end up like Wesley and-"

"I'm only going to tell you this once. Follow your heart, live in the now, and if it ever comes down between life and death you fight until you can't fight anymore. I know about the letter and I know you are worried, but you can't spend your life wondering what if. Besides, you guys have a connection, you'd be idiots if you don't follow your hearts." Haley interrupts with a comforting smile. This is why I love Haley, no matter how sad I am she always is there to pick me up and lift my spirit.

"Yeah, and besides our senior trip to Vegas is this Monday, you guys can connect in our group room." Blaire adds on with a smirk, I chuckle. Our school apparently is very lenient when it comes to trips or overnight things. Anyone can stay anywhere and they don't care, just as long as you do the activities they have planned out. The trip is for the whole week and everyone usually comes out a different person, I don't believe that for a second.

"Oooo yeah you guys can get it on-"

"HALEY!" My face turned so red, I couldn't help but nervously laugh. "What? Just be safe, we don't want you to be in my situation." She replies teasingly while holding her baby bump, I shake my head. Not that there is anything wrong with having a baby young, I just have responsibilities and I'm on the run from my father so a baby would not be good.

"You're so annoying! I may have made out with the boy but that does not mean I'm going to have sex with him! You need jesus." I reply innocently which only made Haley chuckle. Blaire was looking at us back and fourth as if we were a movie, she was so amused we probably could've given her popcorn.

"Ugh fine. What about oral-"

"NO!" At that point Blaire starting laughing at Haley's options while Haley just shrugged. "What? Sometimes they are having a bad day, so to lighten the mood you tie your hair up and-"

"LA LA LA! I can't hear your dirty minded opinions. Please leave!" I opened the door and lightly pushed her out. I will not have my niece or nephew hear such bad phrases.

"T-that was a-a-amazing!" Blaire squeaks in between laughs, I roll my eyes. "No, that was disturbing. Now sit down because I need you to know why I am here in case something happens to me."

"What are you talking about?" She looked at me as if I had 3 heads, I shake my head and tell her the story that I told Brandon and Piper which all led up to me being in this very spot. I knew this was going to be a long night. ----------------------------Hey guys! I'm sorry this chapter was really boring, but I promise the next few chapters will be filled with juicy drama. What do you think is going to happen on the trip? Now that Nathan knows that Adrianna is Lydia, do you think he's going to do anything? Thoughts on Brandon and Lydia? Comment below and don't forget to vote! Thanks,

~Jen

Chapter 12- I Look Like Mr Tumnus from The Chronicles Of Narnia

----

(Gif of Grayson)

Lydia's POVIt was the day of the trip, and after a whole weekend of begging my brother to let me go, he finally caved after talking to Haley. I agreed to his terms:1- No Drinking2-No sex3-No Drugs

Sounds pretty good to me. Especially after what happened last week, I do not need a repeat of that.

"Hey Lydia! Are you ready for a week of no parents and parties?" Piper questions excitedly, I chuckle. "Piper, it's not a vacation-"

"It practically is. The teachers don't watch what we do, especially the ones chaperoning us, we can go and do whatever we please." Gray interrupts with a smile, I chuckle and reply "Sweet."

"You know what's even more sweet? Gray gave up his seat so you could sit next to lover boy." Piper teases with a wink, I glare at her. "What? You guys can't avoid each other forever. You guys made out and had a moment, you can't ignore that."

"Piper, I'm not mad at the fact that you're trying to get us to talk. I'm mad at the fact that it's five in the morning, I look disgusting and you're making me sit next to a hot guy-"

"So you admit you find him attractive!" She teases, I roll my eyes and then glare at her. "I don't know what I'm saying! I'm suffering from sleep deprivation!" I shouted back as I got on the bus. Here goes nothing.

As I got on the bus, I couldn't ignore the stares that I was getting from everyone. Not that I blame them though, I have no makeup on, I'm in my pajamas, and I didn't even bother to do my hair. I just rolled out of bed, grabbed a muffin, and had Haley drive me to school. I probably look like Mr Tumnus from The Chronicles Of Narnia movie.

I sat next to Brandon with a pout as he looked at me with wide eyes. "Go on, say it. I look horrible, I know." He shakes his head and smiles. "That's not it at all. Different yes but horrible? Not one bit." I couldn't help but smile. I know he's sugar coating it but I'll take the compliment anyways.

"I think we need to talk about what happened Friday-"

"I agree. Look, I was out of line when I kissed you. You were vulnerable yet I did it anyways, good guys don't do things like that." He says sincerely, I sigh and shake my head. "No, I kissed you back-"

"But it was my fault, what I'm trying to say here is I'm sorry." He starts rambling on until I just grabbed his face and made him look at me. "Brandon! Listen to me! You did nothing wrong!"

"I like you Lydia, more then I have ever liked anyone and that scares me. I know it scares you too after what happened to your last boyfriend, so I'm not going to pressure you into anything. I don't know what we are but as long as I don't lose you I don't care." I couldn't help but smile again. I put my head on his shoulder, grabbed his hand and intertwined our fingers.

"We have the whole week to do whatever we want. Think of this as an escape from reality. We can be whoever we want to be and not have a care in the world." I reply honestly. He chuckles. "Okay, perfect life, go."

"Me, my friends, and my siblings would have our annual movie nights. We would have a big backyard and set up a projector screen while our mom would be baking cookies in the kitchen as our dad comes home and greets all of us with hugs and presents. I would be cuddled up with my boyfriend on our picnic blanket while my friends teased us, he would tell me he loves me which will only make my brother want to hurt him but Haley holds him back and let's me enjoy the moment. It would be perfect." I reply with a big smile as I actually close my eyes and imagine it.

"That sounds beautiful." I look up at him and smile. "What about you? What would your perfect life be like?" I question, he chuckles.

"This sounds really cheesy but my perfect life would be how things were before my mom died, just with you in it and without the whole overachievers thing. Everything wouldn't be complicated, instead it would be simple and romantic. We would all be happy. That's all I wish for."

"That is absolutely adorable. I love it." We locked eyes with each other and we smiled. I remember Haley telling me that's how her and Stefano really knew they were in love with each other. They locked eyes, smiled and kissed. I couldn't help but wonder if this was that moment. Could I possibly have a relationship with Brandon?

"Just go out already!" Vince, Blaire, Gray and Piper chant, we both laugh. I look back at Nathan only to see that he is looking at me with a sympathetic expression. All feelings I had for him are gone, I'm starting to feel things for Brandon that I didn't feel for Nate. Nate was a distraction when I was drunk, Brandon actually understands my problems and is there to comfort me. Maybe I could be friends with Nate but that's all.

"What do you say we forget the distractions for this week and work on us?" I question with a smile which only made him smile wider. "Are you sure? I don't wanna pressure you-"

"It's my idea dummy. Think of this as a trial relationship. So that when this whole deal with my father is over, maybe we can be a real thing." He didn't even answer, he just kissed my forehead and let me lay my head on his shoulder which I thought was adorable. I was still holding his hand when I fell asleep.

Brandon's POVPiper, Vince, Gray and Blaire were looking at us in awe, especially when she fell asleep on my shoulder. I don't blame her, it's 5am and we have a three and a half hour drive from here.

Once she was off in dreamland, Piper spoke. "So are you guys a thing now?"

"I'm fine with whatever it is we are. Are you okay with it?" I question her, in the past I have dated a few of her friends and it didn't end well so they stopped talking to both of us. I felt really bad, that was one of the reasons Piper hated me after our mom's death. She felt as if everyone she loved was gone because of me.

"Um of course! You guys are my freakin OTP. But if you break her heart I'll break your face. Brother or not, sisters will always be before misters. So don't mess this up." Vince and Gray started laughing which only caused Blaire to glare at them. "What are you guys laughing at? Vince you'll become Veronica if you hurt Piper and Gray, once you get a girl that is not a monster like Grace that actually wants to be friends with us, the same will go for you. Girls are crazy, don't mess with us." She replies with a smirk.

That shut them up. I couldn't help but put my hand over my balls because I can imagine what Blaire will do, and it's not pretty.

"Mhm Brandon..." Lydia mumbles with a chuckle in her sleep, Gray and Vince smirk. "Well, looks like lover girl is having a dream about you. Let's hope it's a good one." Piper teases with a wink, I roll my eyes. But I can't help but wonder what she actually is dreaming about.

Lydia only nuzzles her head into my neck even more which earned an "awwww!" from everyone. Everyone except Nate that is. He is such an asshole, he led her on and then dumped her like garbage just because of Grace. Lydia even knew Grace had shit on her and she was going to handle it but Nate decided to try to pawn her off to me as payment for dirt on Grace. It was a dick move and I wasn't taking it.

"Look man, I need you to go out with Lydia for me." Nate said with all seriousness, I looked at him like he had three heads. "Excuse me?"

"Grace has things on Lydia that are beyond explanation, and if those secrets get out it could ruin everything. You dated Grace in the past so you know some of her dark secrets, so spill the secrets and in exchange I'll get you a date with Lydia." To say my eyes bugged out would be an understatement. It was like he was trying to sell her to me. What the actual fuck?

"I don't want to be part of your little scheme-"

"Oh come on! I know you like her, she is a fine piece of womanhood. Just swoon her, I need her attention to be off of me for awhile. I need her to hate me." He says in all seriousness, anger starts fueling in my body as I shake my head.

"No Nate. I will not be part of your little scheme because Lydia is going to be the one that gets hurt in the process. You're just trying to pawn her off to me and that's a dick move. Lydia's a big girl that can handle her own problems, I really don't know what she sees in you. You want dirt on Grace I'll give it to you for free, but I will not be part of your screwed up scheme."

He had his chance and he ruined it. Now it's my turn. --Hey guys! Short chapter I'm sorry, but I promise the next few will be longer and more filled with drama. For those of you that didn't like Brandon in the beginning, what do you think now that you know the truth? What is Nathan doing? Will Grace release Lydia's secret? Team Nathan or team Brandon? Comment down below and don't forget to vote! Thanks,

~Jen

Chapter 13- Not In My Bed Please

Lydia's POVWhen I woke up I was confused and in what looked like a hotel room. It was dark. After my experience with darkness I kind of freaked out, especially when I saw Grayson on the floor and Piper sprawled across another bed. A memory of my past popped into my head which only made me freak out even more.

"WHAT THE HELL DID YOU JUST SAY?!" My father screams. What the heck is going on. I have to go see. "No." I was held back by my sister Rose, I punched her and ran outside to the staircase to see what was going on. I only saw my father yelling at my mom.

"You're a drunken loser Carlyle! Ever since you lost your job all you do is drink your days away! You promised you would get a job, YOU FUCKING PROMISED! But instead you go and make a deal with Cade? You're a loser-" She was cut off by having him slap her.

"DON'T YOU EVER TALK TO ME LIKE THAT AGAIN YOU BITCH!" He starts kicking her, that's when I ran downstairs screaming. "STOP! STOP IT! YOU ARE HURTING HER!"

I tried punching and hitting him but he only threw me into the wall in the process. "Look what you did Katherine! It's because of you that our children hate me!"

"We hate you because you're an insensitive bastard who betrayed us!" I spat angrily while holding my now injured leg, he laughs and takes an intimidating step towards me. "I am your father and I will not have you talk to me like that without consequences."

I only laughed in his face. "You're not my father, you're just DNA-"

"DON'T SAY THAT!" He shouts, throwing his beer bottle into the wall and holding the shards of what is left of it up to my face. "Or what? You're gonna kill me? We are all as good as dead if we stay here anyways so what are you waiting for?"

"Adrianna don't-"

"Why not mom? Look at what he's doing-"

"You don't know what you're talking about! You're only a little girl." My father replies with a chuckle. I glare at him. "I am old enough to know that you sold yourself to the devil-" He slapped me hard which only made my cheek start bleeding.

"Carlyle what the hell do you think you're doing?!" Mom screams, dad laughs. "I'm teaching her a lesson." Before I could even question it I was knocked out by my father.

I woke up in complete darkness. I tried screaming. But it was as if my screams had been masked by a bubble. My leg was in pain and my ankles were chained to the wall. "WHAT IS THIS?! WHAT DO YOU WANT FROM ME?!"

Tears started streaming down my face as I was left cold, alone and bleeding on our basement floor.

"It'll be okay. It'll all be okay."

"It'll be okay. It'll all be okay. It'll be okay. It'll all be okay-"

"Lydia! Snap out of it! We're right here it's okay!" I came face to face with Piper and Grayson who had concerned looks on their faces. Once I saw them I started shaking. "W-where are we? Are the others okay?" I asked frantically, they nod.

"They are in the other room, but I don't know how long for. Something's wrong Lydia." Gray says sadly which makes me look at him only to see that his eyes are bleeding.

"Y-your eyes! What's going on? What's happening?" I question frantically, they just shake their heads. The creepy thing about it was that they were doing it in unison, then Piper's eyes started bleeding as the door got kicked in. I came face to face with my father.

"Rise and shine bitches!" Panic automatically sinks in and I freak out. "AHHHHHHHHHHHHHHHHHH!!!"

"LYDIA! WAKE UP! YOU'RE DREAMING!" A voice I recognized as Brandon's screams, I open my eyes and see that we are on the bus so I held onto him for dear life and started crying.

"Are you okay? You were screaming and kicking, I was afraid to wake you up but I'm glad we did because you were starting to scratch yourself." Brandon says nervously, I don't answer, I just cling onto him.

"Where is everyone?" I question, trying to change the subject, Piper smiles. "They are inside. We told the teachers that we would wake you up because you were out cold. We have been trying for the past ten minutes, once we saw you screaming we knew we had to wake you up. It was like the night of midnight madness, did you have a nightmare again?" She asks, I nod fast.

"Do you want to talk about it?" Vince questions nicely, I shook my head. "I need to call my brother. Can I borrow one of your phones?" Piper was the first to give me her phone, I frantically called Stefano.

"Hello?" Haley questions with a tone of scratchiness in her voice, I probably woke her up. "Did I wake you? I'm so sorry-"

"No, it's okay. What's wrong?" How did she know? "I fell asleep on the bus and had another nightmare... this one was bad Haley."

"Did you start scratching again?" Even though she couldn't see me, I nodded anyways before replying "yes."

"Okay. Listen to me. Take a few deep breaths, after that take your medication. Think happy thoughts, you have your friends by your side, let them be your light. You just have to breathe. Don't panic. He's not there. Take deep deep breaths." I do as she says and take a deep breath, but when I close my eyes I can only see my father and Grayson's eyes bleeding. I only start coughing, she knows what this means.

"Okay Lydia. Put Brandon on the phone please." Haley says calmly, I know internally she's freaking out but she just doesn't want to show it. I do what she says and hand Brandon the phone.

Brandon's POV When Lydia handed me the phone I was beyond confused, but once her hands started shaking I understood. "Hello?"

"Hi Brandon, this is Haley. I asked Lydia to give you the phone because I know you are the only one who can truly calm her down. Tell me what is she doing now?" Haley demands, I look back at Lydia only to see that she's crying. "Her hands are shaking and she's crying hard."

"She's having a panic attack. You need to calm her down. Is anyone there with you?"

"Yes, I have Piper, Vince, Blaire and Gray-"

"You need to get them away from her. Make her focus only on you, it will help with the process. Do it now, if she starts hyperventilating and scratching herself, then we have a problem. You might have to kiss her again, it'll distract her. Once she's calmed down, make sure she takes her medication. Got it?"

"Y-yes."

"You can do this Brandon. You're good for her, don't second guess yourself. Call me when she's okay." I nod and hang up the phone, I look at Lydia to see that she's still shaking, then I look at the others who are giving me a worried expression. "What did he say?" Blaire questions referring to Lorenzo, I shake my head.

"It was Haley. She told me that you guys have to get off the bus-"

"Bullshit! I'm not leaving her-"

"Do you want her to hurt herself Piper?!" She shakes her head. "Then get off the bus. If we are not out in 20 minutes, call an ambulance. She's having a panic tack and this could get bad." She doesn't move, she just stares at Lydia with a blank expression on her face.

"PIPER! Let's go!" Vince pulls her off the bus, I sit next to Lydia and hold her hand. "Lydia talk to me, what's wrong?"

She starts shaking even more. "So much blood..."

"Blood? Who's bleeding Lydia?" She looks at me with a feared expression and starts crying harder. "Everyone."

"I'm not bleeding. It was just a dream Lydia, look at me. I don't have a scratch on me-"

"Their eyes... they were gone. It's all his fault. He's here." She starts scratching herself, I knew this was bad. I had to distract her somehow. What do I do?

What do I do?

I have an idea!

"Perfect life Lydia. Remember? Movie night, fireplace, presents, love, family, that is what's happening right now. Blaire and I have presents for you outside, and Piper, Vince and Gray set up the movie. We just have to get off the bus. Just open your eyes Lydia." She had her eyes closed, she refused to open them. I intertwined our fingers, she pulled away and kept scratching and crying.

"Its going to be okay Lydia, all you have to do is open your eyes and I'll protect you. I promise you that I will not let anything happen to you, you just have to open your eyes. Come on, let me show you that there is good in this world."

"I c-can't. He's here for me. He's here for all of us." She starts hyperventilating, I sigh. "I really wish it didn't have to come to this." I grabbed her chin and kissed her which automatically made her open her eyes. She looked at me with such a helpless look. "See? Nobody is here to hurt you. I won't let anything bad happen to you." I started stroking her cheek with my thumb and wiped away her tears as she slowly started to calm down.

"I wish it didn't have to come down to me kissing you, but I figured that would serve as a distraction and it worked. You're calming down, just look into my eyes and listen to my words okay?" She slowly nodded, I sighed in relief and smiled.

"I am going to make sure you get to your perfect life. It may not have your mother, father or sister in it, but it will have all of us. We can all get a house after graduation, one of those big houses with a nice backyard. On summer nights we can all sit by the fire, make s'mores, and even sing karaoke. And during the winter, we can all sit in the living room and watch Christmas movies as Haley bakes cookies. Does that sound good?" She nods again, finally catching her breath.

"We can do all of that. All you have to do is take a couple of deep breaths. We can get through this together, you're safe with me. In and out, you're doing great." She grabs my hand and intertwined our fingers, that's how I knew for sure that she was slowly coming back. She takes a few deep breaths and that's how she stopped crying. I didn't stop looking at her until she completely calmed down.

"It's all going to be okay Lydia." I lifted my arm so that she could put her head on my chest and I started stroking her hair which I knew for a fact would help in the process of making her stop. "Thank you Brandon." She mumbled, I kiss her head and smile.

"Any time. I'll always be here no matter what. Whatever you need, whenever you need it , I'll be here. I'm just a phone call away." She squeezes my hand as her breathing finally became normal.

"Can you stay with me tonight? I don't want to be alone." She questions, I chuckle. "Are you kidding me? After what just happened I'm never letting you out of my sight again."

"I'm sorry that I'm bothering you-"

"Stop it. You're not bothering me, if you were do you think I would be sitting her for the past ten minutes trying to calm you down? I told you Lydia, I'm in this for the long run because I like you." Ugh why did I say that?! I'm so stupid. Every time she's vulnerable, what the fuck is wrong with me.

She sighs. "I like you too B, I like you very much. It's just with everything going on with my dad, I can't be perfect, I can't give it my all because I'm constantly afraid that something horrible is going to happen."

"Nobody is perfect Lydia. Look at me, I was probably one of the most flawed people you have met, but somehow you saw something in me. You're teaching me how to be good-"

"You are good. You just hid that deep down because of what happened to your mom and I get that. When you asked me to bring that out again, I was willing to do it for free but then you had to go and mention Nate and I was in. He made me weak, but you make me strong and I highly admire that about you." Just the mention of his name made me cringe.

"Why did you like him? I'm not judging, I'm just curious." I question, she sighs and shrugs. "I thought he was one of the good ones. Piper warned me about him on my first day and I didn't listen. I thought he understood me,but then he started spreading rumors and you know what he did to Grayson. I thought he was good, but I was wrong. My problem is I trust to easily."

"That's why you were so reluctant in telling us about your past?" I question again, her face turns red. "Kind of. I don't know, it's complicated. When I feel betrayed I will block myself off. After what happened to my ex, I didn't plan on making friends or even liking anyone. I didn't want to get anyone involved, but you guys never gave up on me and for some reason I really respected that. So I purposely defied my brothers orders and might have potentially gotten us caught but for some reason I didn't even care. The night of the frat party was one of the greatest nights of my life up until what happened. I showed my weakness for Nate and that almost got me killed. After that my brother made me tell you guys, if I didn't then we wouldn't be here right now. Just promise me one thing... No matter how far away I try to push you, never leave."

"I'm here for the long run Lydia, nothing will change that. Not even if your father finds you, I will fight until I have no fight left in me. We should go, the others are waiting outside, I told them to call an ambulance if we aren't out in 20 minutes. But we do need to get you to the nurse because you're bleeding." She looks at her arms and a look of sadness spreads across her face.

Lydia's POVAs we got off of the bus, I couldn't help but look at my arms and be sad. I've been clean for so long, I haven't cut or scratched since Wesley was murdered, 3 years. 3 years and I haven't had such bad anxiety and panic attacks. What is this town doing to me.

"Are you okay? I was so worried!" Piper looked down at my arms and the look her eyes made me want to cry. When I saw she was okay I hugged her and clung onto her for dear life. "You're okay!" I mumbled excitedly while taking a deep breath.

"I'm okay. We are all okay Lydia, let's get you to the nurse." ----------------------I ended up getting yelled at by one of our supervising teachers for getting hurt but luckily I was okay. I only needed to bandage my wounds and not do anything hectic. I have been avoiding everyone after my breakdown back on the bus because I am afraid to face them.

What if they think I'm a monster? What if they think I'm a psycho just like my father? Oh god I hope not.

There was a knock on my door, it was Blaire. "Hey, can I come in?" She asks, I nod. She sits on the bed next to me but I don't flinch. Instead, I apologize. "I'm sorry about earlier-"

"You have nothing to be sorry about-"

"Yes I do. I worried all of you and I'm so sorry. When I have nightmares, most of the time they are repressed memories but the small percent that they are just dreams, I wake up not being able to tell what's real and what's not. I was petrified and I only made you guys feel the same, I'm sorry."

"Don't be sorry, nobody is mad or blaming you. Come with me, I have a little surprise for you. In fact, we all do. Get dressed, I think you're going to like this." She says with a smile. I'm not in the party mood but I can tell she's not taking no for an answer so I got dressed anyways only to have her put a blindfold on me.

"Um what are you doing-"

"Shh it's part of the surprise. You'll love it I promise." It felt like we had been walking for at least ten minutes before I was able to take the blindfold off but it was worth it because what I se made me smile.

In front of me was Brandon, Piper, Vince and Grayson, all with instruments in their hands. Once Gray started playing guitar I knew something was up.

Then Piper started playing drums, Vince playing bass, and then Blaire joined them with a tambourine. When Brandon started singing I almost cried, not because he was singing, but because of the song he was singing. It was Keep Holding On by Avril Lavigne.

When they were finished, I was smiling like an idiot and crying. "We are here for you no matter what. You told us the truth and all we need you to do is keep holding him because we whatever it take to make sure that you're safe." Brandon says with a genuine smile, I chuckle.

"Yeah, we are willing to do whatever it takes. Even if that means helping in the fight against your father. We are in this together now Lydia, nothing will change that." Vince adds on, I give them all a hug and smile bright.

"You guys have no idea how much this means to me, thank you-"

"Don't thank us, thank Brandon. It was his idea." Blaire says with a wink. Piper catches on to what Blaire was insinuating so she decided to add on. "Yeah. Thank him, but please not in my bed." We all started laughing, I didn't even want to fight her on it, I was enjoying this moment too much.

"Alright, enough with the dirty jokes! We have a karaoke machine rented out for the next two hours, let's have some fun!" Gray replies, we all smile and cheer.

We spent the next two hours singing and dancing our hearts out, after that we went back to our hotel room and talked till the sun came up, it was truly amazing. And after everything that happened today, I needed this. Now let's just hope that the rest of this trip is as fun as tonight.

Chapter 14- Im Sorry, What?

(A/N- gif of Grace)Brandon's POVThings this week have been very calm, luckily I was successful with my mission of making Lydia forget what is going on in her life for awhile. We actually were having fun, that was until Piper suggested that we all go out to a club.

"Oh come on guys, I think it'll be fun!" Piper pleads, Lydia shakes her head. "Not after last time." This time it was Grayson's turn to plead.

"Please? Everyone's going! It'll be fun, and after what happened with Grace I need fun. Pretty please?" Gray adds on, I shake my head. "She said no, you guys can go-"

"But we all are most likely going to get drunk so then can you be our designated driver B?" Piper questions, I look at Lydia before quickly shaking my head. "I won't leave her alone-"

"I'll go under one condition. Brandon has to be sober too because I am not drinking at all after the last party, especially because I just took my meds. So go get dressed, I'll make sure you guys don't get too drunk or do anything stupid." The minute Lydia give the okay, they all ran into their rooms and changed it was hilarious.

"I don't want you to be pressured into going-"

"I'm not, I'm going of my free will. Sometimes we have to face our fears to get passed the bigger obstacles right? Anyways, I have to stay alert, I haven't said anything but I have been having very bad nightmares about my father and they aren't repressed memories which scares the hell out of me. I'm just very afraid."

"Of what? I'm not going to let anything happen to you. I promised and I don't break promises anymore." I went to grab her hand but just like that she pulled away again. "I can't do this Brandon. I really thought I could but I can't. You're amazing and I love you for it, but the last time I had nightmares like this something really really bad happened so j have to be on my A game... I can't have any distractions. I hope you understand, I'm really sorry."

I know I shouldn't be angry because I expected that she would back out but I am angry. She let her walls down and now she's slowly putting them back up. As much as I hate to do this, I know what I have to do.

"Yeah fine. Whatever, I have to go, see you later." I could tell she was upset but I had to do this. I went to the one person who first helped tear down her walls.

I knocked on his door and he answered with a smile, that was until he saw me. "What do you want B?"

"I need your help Nate. It's about Lydia."

"What makes you think I-"

"I know why you're hooking up with Grace. You are doing it to protect her, and you are pushing Lydia away just so she wouldn't know the truth. I know because it is something I would do. I love her Nate, and I know you do too. You are my only hope."

"Fine. Come in, we'll talk."Lydia's POVI felt horrible. Brandon was the one thing that made me feel good and happy. But of course my father had to go and ruin it.

Last night I had a nightmare that was more like a memory, just instead of Wesley being killed by my father it was Brandon. Plus I got a call from Stefano and Haley saying that they received another letter from our father that said he will see us soon so to say I am on edge would be an understatement.

I need to cut Brandon out romantically and treat all of them the same. I do not want a repeat of what happened with Wesley. It will break me.

Piper was the first one to come back into the room and she saw that I was upset, when I told her nothing was wrong she wasn't buying it.

"Come on Lydia, tell me what's wrong? What did Brandon do? Do I have to chop his balls off?" She questions angrily, a tear falls down my face as I shake my head. "No. I'm the one who messed up."

"What happened? You can talk to me." She starts rubbing my back gently which made me only cry harder. "It's all my fault. If I hadn't come here then you all would be friends and everything would be perfect. You guys would've been better without me-"

"Don't you dare say that. If it weren't for you, I wouldn't have gotten together with Vince, the overachievers would still be a thing, Gray would still be dating Grace, and my brother would still be the worlds ultimate douchebag. You changed us for the good. Now tell me what's bothering you." She pleads, I shake my head and show her the letter that Stefano sent me over her phone and she just looked at me confused.

"He's coming back Piper. He found us again and I don't know when he's coming back but he's made it pretty clear that he will see us. I found this out today and I know if I told Brandon that he would freak and go into overprotective mode. So I pushed him away, and I know that sounds like a horrible move but I don't want him to end up dead which is exactly what would happen if my father found out. My father takes away everything that I love, so I figured if I pushed him away then everything could be okay."

"Did you just say you love him?" She questions with a huge smile, I sigh and chuckle. "I don't know, he makes me feel something that I haven't felt in awhile and that scares me. But I have to put my feelings aside for the sake of his life. I need to do what's right if I want to stay." I heard the door being opened so I quickly wiped away my tears, dried my eyes and put on a fake smile.

It was the rest of the group. "Lydia, get dressed, we are leaving soon!" Blaire says with a chuckle while pushing me into the bathroom, I shake my head. "I didn't bring any party clothes-"

"I got you girl! Boys we are gonna be a little bit, meet you outside." Piper pushed Vince and Gray out the door and looked at me with smirks on their faces. First they put me in a skin tight black dress that shows off my curves, and then they curled my hair and did my makeup. By the end I looked fierce, and fierce is exactly what I need right now.

Let's party. ----------------My party mood was soon cut short when I discovered that Nate and Grace were coming with us as well. So I'm just peachy.

So far I have seen Gray and Blair flirt with a few girls, Piper has been taking shots and basically threatening to have sex with Vince right on the dance floor which none of us wants to see. So at the moment I am with Piper and Brandon is with Vince.

"Come on Lydia! Let a girl have some fun! Please?" Piper pleads, I shake my head. "Piper, if Brandon and I don't do this then you and Vince will rip each other's clothes off on the dance floor-"

"And what's wrong with that? We're in love!" She slurs with a giggle, I shake my head with a chuckle. "Nobody needs to see that Pipes." We both start laughing.

"Oh a joke, I like jokes, can I join in?" Nate questions, making my smile turn into a frown. "Ooooh it's lover boy numero dos. Gotta go!" Before I could even stop Piper, she ran away and left me alone with Nate. Just wonderful.

"I heard about what happened on the bus, are you okay?" Nate questions, I chuckle and cross my arms. "Yeah, I actually am. Not that you actually care anyways."

"I do care-"

"That's bullshit and we both know it. I actually was starting to have feelings for you and that got thrown in my face. So what are you really doing here Nate?" I spat dryly, he sighs.

"It may not seem like I do but trust me Aide I know." Did he just call me Aide? "What did you just call me?" I snap. On the inside I'm worried, but I refuse to show it.

"I know who you are, and you know me as well." I grabbed his wrist and pulled him into a private room where no one could hear our conversation. Then I pinned him against the wall and started the interrogation.

"What do you know Nate. Spill." I say while glaring at him. All I could say is if looks could kill. "Piper told me about you only because of the story I told her. I told her that when I was 12 I fell for a girl named Adrianna Samuels, and that The reason I was so overprotective of you was because you reminded me of her. Then she told me your story and I was so happy you were alive-"

"Adrianna is dead. I'm Lydia Stone now. Who are you really?" I question eagerly, he chuckles. "You once knew me as Nathanial Flynn. However once you and my father died, I took my mother's last name and we moved here."

My eyes grew wide. I can't believe it. "If you were really Flynn, tell me something only the two of us would know."

"That's easy. When we were kids and your mom and dad would fight, you would run to my house and we would eat cookies in our tree house. We called it cookie land." I smiled so brightly and hugged him tight. "It really is you!"

"I knew you reminded me of Aide, but once I found out that you guys are actually the same person I wanted to talk to you. But after my mistakes with you, Piper thought it was best if I kept my mouth shut. I already know the story but that is because Grace only knows part of it, all she knows is that you changed your names multiple times and ran away from the fire that spread around your house. I don't know how she knows, but I thought maybe if I gave her what she wanted it would go away, but that only made it worse. I'm really sorry."

"If you would've told me that awhile ago I would've put up with the bitch and forgiven you already but no! You had to act like a jerk saying stuff like I have my reasons. What kind of bullshit excuse is that? Shaking my head Nate." I reply teasingly, we both laugh.

"Enough about me, tell me what's going on with you. I know you and Brandon had a little thing, but he came to me upset so what's going on?" He questions sincerely, I sigh and shake my head. "It's my dad. He's a monster."

"I always got creepy vibes from that guy, and at your funeral he didn't even shed a single tear, who does that?"

"Wait what funeral?" I ask worriedly, he chuckles. "Your father made it seem like you all died in the house fire yet he told me and my mom that you died in a car accident. He's a psycho, he even had a funeral for your family, closed casket so no one could tell that there were no actual bodies."

"Damn. I knew he was twisted, but that's a whole new level." He nods in agreement as we lock eyes. It was intense but I don't like him anymore, I care for Brandon. "Gosh I missed you."

"Yeah. Um we should probably get back to the dance floor before people think we are doing anything-"

"Eh let them think what they want! They're all drunk anyways." He replies with a chuckle, I shake my head. "Sorry to disappoint you Nate but I like Brandon. You and me are better off as friends."

"You can't tell me you don't feel anything for me-"

"Watch me." I grabbed his face and planted a kiss on him. "See? Nothing! Now let's get back to the party."

I left him to find Brandon only to see that he is drinking. Great, well looks like I'll be the only sober driver tonight.

Next I looked around for Piper only to see that both her and Vince are gone, probably thanks to Brandon. Blaire disappeared as well which only left Gray whom I finally found. But of course life just hates me today because as I was walking over to Gray, Grace decides to "accidentally" spill her drink down my bra. Wonderful.

"You bitch." I spat angrily, she laughed. "Sorry Lydia, my hand just slipped."

"Yeah just like my hand is gonna slip into your face!" I was held back by both Gray and Nate who were simultaneously laughing. "Awe, is that a threat?" She questions, I chuckle.

"Nope. It's a promise." I broke free of their hold and socked her right across the face. Her nose started bleeding, I just laughed as she screamed. "You're gonna regret that bitch."

"And you're gonna regret messing with her. We're done Grace." Nate replies with a smirk, she looks at him blankly before flipping her hair. "That's fine, I have Gray-"

"Nope. Sorry Grace but I don't date two timing sluts. You can't control us anymore." Grayson cuts her off, leaving her mouth to hang open. "I'm sorry, what?" She asks unbelievingly, I chuckle and take an intimidating step forward.

"You can't control any of us anymore. And that incriminating evidence you have against me is nothing, you want to spread it then fine. I'm sure that your father would love to hear about his precious little girl banging the football coach, especially with the senatorial election coming up, he'll lose for sure." I reply victoriously, she just stood there with a blank expression.

"Alright well, I've had enough of your bullshit for one night so I'll see you back at the hotel. Tootles!" I say mockingly while walking away. Gray and Nate follow while laughing. "That was awesome!" Gray replies excitedly, I chuckle and do a fake bow.

"Thank you, thank you! Now if you will excuse me for a moment, I need to talk to Brandon." A look of disappointment spread across Nathan's face but I just brushed it off and walked over to Brandon who was sitting at the bar with a very frisky brunette. Seeing her hands on him only made my blood boil. "Brandon, we need to talk-"

"Can't you see I'm having a moment with uh what's your name?" He asks the girl with a chuckle, she tells him it's Lauren. "I'm having a moment with Lauren. Now if you will be so kind as to go away that would be great!"

"What's wrong with you?" He just laughs. "Nothings wrong with me baby! You clearly don't want me but Lauren here does so move along-"

"You're acting like a jerk."

"Maybe I am a jerk. Did you ever think of that? Oh wait, I forgot you don't think before you hurt someone's feelings. Come on Lauren, let's go somewhere a little more comfortable." He took her by the hand and lead her into the private room upstairs. Wonderful. I know why he's being like this, and it's once again all my fault.

"You okay?" Gray asks, I chuckle. "I'm just peachy! Gray go find Blaire, make sure she's home by eleven. Nate and I are going to find Vince and Piper, hopefully they didn't get into too much trouble." Without another word, I walked out of the club with Nate and frantically searched the area for the two of them. When I couldn't find then I started freaking out.

"Give me your phone." Nate didn't even protest as I called Piper. No surprise it went to voicemail. Then I called Vince, once again I got voicemail. "No no no! This is bad, this is really really bad. I can't let them out of my sight-"

"Lydia you need to calm down, you're getting like how you got on Halloween. You need to take some deep breaths."

"I don't have any time for taking some stupid deep breaths! My friends are missing and my father is on the loose! Put two and two together. What if he has them? What if their hurt? Oh my god oh my god." I started pulling at my hair, he shook his head and firmly placed his hands on my face, making sure to cup my cheeks.

"Lydia. Look at me. They are okay. They are probably back at the hotel ripping each other's clothes off. Your father doesn't know where you are. Brandon is just being an asshole because that's his self defense mechanism. Everything is fine. Just breathe." I took a deep breath which made my breathing calm down a little. "Good girl. Breathe in and out. It's all going to be okay. Let's just go back to the hotel and wait for them to come back, I'll wait up all night okay?" I slowly nod as I control my breathing.

We walked back to the hotel which was only a few blocks from the club and sat down in my room.

Now we wait.

The next day... (Piper's POV) I woke up with a raging headache. Everything was blurry and loud. "Ugh how much did I have to drink last night Lydia?" I groan. No answer.

I say up nervously and looked around only to scream at the sight. Not only was I in a random room I didn't recognize, but I was in a wedding dress, and I had a ring on my finger.

What the fuck happened last night?!

Chapter 15- I Had To Put A Ring On It Or She Wouldn't Let Me Smash

L ydia's POVWe were up looking for them all night until Gray finally got a call from Piper, I automatically grabbed it from him and put it on speaker.

"Piper are you guys okay? We've been searching for you two all night, you worried the crap out of me!" I scold, she chuckles, but I can tell it's a nervous chuckle. "Yeah! We're fine! I just woke up somewhere I don't recognize in a wedding dress next to Vince with a wedding ring on my finger and everything. I'm not fine! What the fuck did I do last night?!"

"Well for starters, you two got really drunk. Then when I got back from to talking to Lydia, Brandon said he let you guys go while he got drunk as well." Nate replies with a tone of anger in his voice. "Wait, you and Nate are talking again? Damn, the one day I get blackout drunk all the crazy stuff happens."

"Yeah. Well wake up Vince and text us where you are, we will come and get everything sorted out. Save your battery, we will see you soon." Once Gray hung up the phone we all started laughing hysterically.

"Alright she texted me. She said they are at the wedding chapel of Las Vegas. I'm searching it up now and it's downtown, so we are going to have to catch a bus or call an uber." Gray says anxiously, Nate nods but I knew something was up. "What's wrong? I can tell you skipped over something."

"She said they told the guy what happened and he said that unless they pay they can't leave, otherwise they'll be arrested."

"Then we have to act fast. Let's do this."---------------It look about an hour for us to finally find this so called chapel, Brandon was MIA and Nate and I had to pretend that we were looking to get married just because they aren't allowed to give out their guests names and since the guy at the desk said that the guests staying there are invited to the wedding so we decided to fake being engaged.

"Okay fine, well I guess we were actually asking because our friends got married here and we wanted to share the joy with our recent engagement and all. You can invite everyone, when can we book an appointment? My honey bear and I wanna get hitched as soon as possible!" I fake slur, Nate catches on to my plan and winks.

"Yeah man! I had to put a ring on it otherwise she wouldn't let me smash. Virgins, am I right?" He replied while acting drunk as well. This time Grayson stepped forward, he was going to pretend to be the sober one that talks the drunks out of things. "Sir, I am the only sober one here but you have to understand how kids do dumb things when they are drunk. So what do you say we have a fake wedding but make it look real for them?" Gray added on with a chuckle, the guy wasn't having it.

"We don't do fake marriages-"

"Fake?! OUR LOVE IS REAL!" I pretend slur, the guy smiles. "That'll be $450."

"Deal. Do you take fifty dollar bills?" My eyes bugged out, I pulled Gray aside. "Gray, that's too much money. I can't ask you to do that, it's all the money you have for this trip-"

"Piper is like a sister to me. And since her brother is being a dickhead at the moment, I'll step up. You guys can get a divorce very easily, I won't tell Brandon that you guys are married as long as we can get Piper and Vince the hell out of here. The school bus leaves in 4 hours, we have to act fast."

"Sir, how fast can my sugar bear and I get married?" I question going back into drunk mode, the guy smiles. "We happen to have an opening in an hour, dresses, room, rings, and tuxes are included in the price so you can go pick them out now if you'd like. I'll come knock on the bridal sweet door when it's time, here is your room key. Have fun!"

The three of us ran as fast as we could upstairs and called Piper and told her and Vince to come to the sweet.

I finally found the perfect dress for me. It was beautiful:

I don't even want to marry Nate, but if it'll save Piper then I'm willing to do whatever it takes. I would've been able to avoid getting hitched by paying for their stay and stuff but it would've been $900 and Gray only had what he gave us and I used my money throughout the whole trip. Stupid Vince and Piper left their wallets and bags at the hotel so they couldn't even pay! We wouldn't be in this mess in the first place had they brought their shit.

I stepped out of the bathroom feeling uneasy. I was about to marry a guy that I had just spent the last two weeks hating but also the guy that I apparently have known my whole life. Stefano can not find out about this.

"Wow... You look... Gorgeous." I was knocked out of my train of thought by Nathan, I couldn't help but smile. "Thanks, and you look handsome. But did you have to say 'I had to put a ring on it cuz she wouldn't let me smash' and then call me a virgin? I'm not even a virgin! Come on." I tease, he chuckles.

"Hey it was better than sugar and honey bear." We both start laughing hysterically, that was until Gray opened to door to reveal Piper and Vince. Once she saw me in the wedding dress she was so confused, she was even more confused when she saw Nate in the tux.

"What the hell did you get yourselves into?" She asks anxiously, I chuckle and shake my head. "Well if it weren't for the two of you forgetting your wallets we wouldn't have to get married right now."

"Why him? Why couldn't you marry Gray?"

"Hey I don't have time to be tied down! Besides, I'm the one paying for the whole thing. If you two idiots hadn't gotten blackout drunk and gotten married then non of us would have to do this. So tell them the plan Lydia." Gray responds while glaring at me, I sigh.

"Okay well first we have to go on with the ceremony and get married blah blah blah. Then we act like a happy couple and go back up to our room but really we will head for the back exit, run a couple blocks to get the bus then get on it, get back to the hotel, change our clothes, pack our stuff, grab a granola bar or something to eat, run to catch the school bus before it leaves, sneak past Brandon and all without getting arrested."

"You're crazy." Vince says with a laugh, Piper smirks. "Sometimes crazy is what can get a person out of something. Hopefully for us we can get out no problem, the question is are you guys really ready to get hitched for real? There's no turning back."

"I'd do anything to save you guys, you're like a second family to me. So I'm putting my hand in and I'm saying let's do this!"-------------------After an hour, the guy from the chapel desk knocked on the door and we went downstairs to begin the ceremony. It was so awkward but I couldn't help but get flashbacks of when Nate and I were little and we used to pretend to get married.

I didn't really pay attention during the ceremony, all I know is that it was over within an hour. We kissed, everyone clapped and then we ran the hell out of there.

"We got a problem. If we go out the back then we will set off the alarms and they will know everything-"

"Then we will run for our lives." I reply with a chuckle, Nate smirks. "You're crazy. You are so lucky I like that about you. Let's do this!"

We casually walked out the back door hoping that the alarms wouldn't go off. However they did and that was the moment my life flashed before my eyes, and believe me when I tell you it was pretty shitty.

When we saw the security guards we knew we had to make a break for the bus. So I took off my heels and started sprinting towards the bus stop. Lucky for us it was just about to take off. The guards were banging on the bus door as the driver took off and that's how I knew we were semi out of the clear.

"That was so close! What would've happened if they had caught us?" Gray questions, I laugh. "Well then we probably would be on our way to jail right now. Lucky for you guys I know how to make a fast getaway."

"And how exactly do you know that?" Vince questions worriedly, I smirk and fold my hands together. "Well let's just say my dad made me steal a lot of alcohol as a child. My mother hated it but I knew it was the only way to keep her safe from him."

"Your father really was Satan wasn't he?" Grayson questions with a chuckle, I nod. "Basically. He's the anti Christ."

"Thank god you got away." Nate says while holding my hand, I shake my head and sigh. "But I didn't. My brother and I have been running from him for years and now he claims he's found us again but that could be a lie. All he knows is where my brother works and my brother works out of town so I think we are okay for now. But that's the reason I broke things off with Brandon... I'm afraid to chase my demons because chasing them might lead to a repeat of the past and I can't do that. I can't lose him, or any of you guys, I love all of you like family. And if I lost one of you I would consume myself with guilt and probably let him kill me. I know it sounds dramatic but you can't tell him, please."

"You're the sister I never had Lydia, I'll do anything for you. You have my word, I won't say anything." Gray replies, I smile and thank him.

"We all have to make a pact. This never happened. We all have to work out ways to get divorces-"

"Wait, we never signed a marriage paper because we made a run for it, so technically we are not actually married. As for you two, only God knows. You two were so drunk you were probably going at it all night."

"That's the one thing I do remember." Vince says to Piper with a wink. "Eww!" Me, Gray and Nate say in unison while they just laugh.

The rest of the bus ride was pretty silent, we got a few congratulations from people on the bus and it was super funny. Once we got off the bus, we had to run back to the hotel because we leave in a half hour.

We had to make sure nobody saw us so we took the back staircase, ran up to our rooms and luckily Brandon wasn't there because he would just have a fit. Then we had to quickly change pack our stuff, grab an apple or something and run back downstairs in time to make it before the buses leave.

"Where the hell have you guys been?" Blaire questions worriedly, I chuckle and reply "it's a long story"

"We've got time. Now explain yourselves!" She wouldn't stop bugging us about it so eventually we told her, to say she freaked out would be an understatement. "You guys got married?!"

"Shhh! Keep your voice down! Someone might hear." Piper says while covering her mouth, Blaire acted like a five year old and licked Piper's hand just so she could talk again.

"Fine I'll whisper. How could you get married to Nate?! If anything we all thought that it would be Brandon-"

"And it should've been. Look I've been a jerk to him, I know that but I'm only doing it to protect him, and I know he would do the same for me. But once I told him that I think we should stay friends he kind of flipped out and then at the party he let Vince be with Piper and he went upstairs with some frisky brunette to do god knows what and I'm pretty sure he hates me now. Plus we had no choice, it was either get married and see Piper and Vince again or leave them to rot in jail because they couldn't pay their bill. I'm sorry I didn't tell you sooner, I was just-"

"Don't worry about it, I completely understand. Besides, there is no way Brandon hates you. You changed him Lydia, he's a different person because of you."

"Are you sure about that? Because his tongue down Elena's throat right now is telling me otherwise. I don't blame him, I crushed his spirit and I'm sorry for that. I just couldn't let him know the real truth because that would be repeating history." I sigh while looking at Brandon. Blaire just gives me a blank stare which is really code for "go on"

"I left out a couple of details about my father because I was afraid that things would be different... but I'm ready now. Back when I was dating Wesley, my ex, my father started threatening us. First he said if I didn't distance myself from my friends that they would end up dead, of course I was a stupid 15 year old and I didn't listen. I regret not listening because it was the worst mistake I ever made. First it was my best friends Nina and Joshua, he kidnapped the three of us and killed them in front of me. He scooped out their eyeballs and made me watch them die. That is why I was freaking out on the bus, I had a dream that it was Piper and Gray instead."

"Oh my god that's horrible!"

"That's not all. My father texted Wesley from my phone saying that I needed help and he came to the rescue. Unfortunately for him, I wasn't the one who needed to be rescued. He tried fighting my father but my father only shot him in the process. There was no service so I couldn't even call 911 to save him, and I didn't even know where we were so I couldn't take him to a hospital or anything and my father refused to help him because I didn't obey his rules. So there I was, watching him bleed out as he told me he loved me. I haven't been able to say I love someone the way I said it to Wesley. But then Brandon came along and I started having those feelings again. Once we received that second letter from my father I knew I had to distance myself from him romantically. He hates me now, but I'd rather have him hate me and be alive then love me and be dead."

"Oh my god, I can't believe it. You two belong together, and maybe one day when this is all over you can be together, but for now I understand because he would do the same thing for you. Your father is a horrible man and I think that when the time comes and he finds you, you will have to be able to protect yourself and I can help you with that. After brother was killed a couple years ago my mom made me and my other siblings start taking self defense classes, and she even opened her own kind of dojo underground and it was awesome. I've been going ever since, if you want I can teach you some self defense moves." Blaire says with a sympathetic look, I nod and smile.

"That would be great. For now I suggest we sit back, relax and enjoy this bus ride."

"I agree with Lydia. This whole trip my father has been up my ass about the stupid winter ball or whatever the hell its called. Of course he decides to take charge this year but I'm actually the one who is doing everything. I called for the decorations, the catering, the DJ, the hall, the invitations and the website with details while he sat on his ass and bugged me about it. Enjoying this bus ride home with no service is exactly what I need." Piper kicked up her feet and sighed in relief while Blaire and I chuckled.

"Why is he so stressed out, when is this ball thing?" I question, she grunts. "That's right I forgot to tell you that day that Gray fought Nate because you left early. Anyways, my father's on my ass about it because it's next week-"

"Holy crap, next week is December 1st?" Blaire questions, Piper nods with a sad expression on her face. "We have been so busy with drama, family stuff, and this trip that we lost track of time. But the dance is next week and I don't wanna think about it because I am going to be super stressed out that day so for now I'm gonna sit back here, relax and not give a shit about anything except you guys."

If only it was that simple. Just when we thought this ride home was going to be relaxing and peaceful, the bus stopped working and we were stuck in the middle of nowhere.

But it wasn't actually nowhere. It was my home town, and I knew it wasn't a mistake we were here. We are here for a reason, but the question is, why?

Character list

Vanessa Hudgens as Adrianna (Lydia)

Dave Franco as Stefano

Holland Roden as Piper

Daren Kagasoff as Brandon

Sophia Bush as Blaire

Alex Pettyfer as Vince

Colton Haynes as Nathan

Matt Lanter as Grayson

Margot Robbie as Grace

Jeffrey Dean Morgan as Carlyle

Chapter 16- I Love You

- -

Brandon's POVIt wasn't a crash. It was more of a boom noise. We thought it was an explosion, well technically it was because the engine blew out but that's beyond the point.

We were stuck in a sketchy town with no cellphone reception, and Nate decided to be the hero and step up because he actually knew where we were. "Everyone, stay calm. I happen to know where this is, and if I'm right then there is a hotel about a mile down that always has vacancy. My step-uncle owns the place, we can get in for free until the bus gets fixed. It's probably going to take a couple of days before the engine can be fixed so we need to walk fast. It's getting dark out, and when it's dark here bad things happen." Nate says worriedly, Lydia nods in agreement.

"He's right. We need to get moving and fast-"

"Oh and how would you know that Lydia?" Grace teases with a smirk, I give her a questioning look. "Just trust me okay? We need to get to that hotel where we will be safe for the night. What do you say mrs Daniels?" Lydia asks our supervising teacher, she nods.

"I say get your stuff and let's get the hell out of here. Nate and Lydia, lead the way!" We all got out of the bus, grabbed our stuff and started walking.

I had so many questions of my own, and this time I was going to get answers. I refuse to be pushed aside by Lydia again. I know she knows what's going on, and I'm going to do everything I can to stop it.

The walk was silent, as it grew darker weird things started happening. First it was Elena who casually sprained her ankle. Then one by one everyone started feeling funky. Lydia and Nate were being so secretive, I had to ask them.

"Can one of you explain to me what the hell is going on?" I whisper shout at them, Lydia shakes her head. "It's none of your concern Brandon-"

"Bullshit! We are dropping like flies! Elena with her ankle, Greg with his leg, Blaire with her headache, even mrs Daniels is acting as if she's high on something and you two know what's going on so fill me in. If there is a solution, I want to help. So please, fill me in."

"It's this town okay?! This is my hometown Brandon. This is where my mother and sister died! This is where all hell broke loose. This town... it changes people, and not for the better. This town forms monsters, and I am one of them. It's not a coincidence that we are here, we are here for a reason, and we are going to find out what that reason is." I looked at her like she was crazy, and then jealously overcame me when I realized she wasn't talking about me and her, she was talking about her and him.

"Why him? I thought you hated him! Why didn't you tell me this before?" I shout, causing everyone to look at us, she glares at me. "Shh keep your voice down Brandon-"

"No. I want to know the truth!"

"The truth is you were too busy being a jerk to even realize what was going on! Just because I told you that I couldn't be in a relationship with you, you went back to your playerish ways! I told you to keep an eye on Piper and Vince and you couldn't even do that because you were being childish

Brandon. You think I would tell you something like this? How could I tell you something so big when you genuinely don't give a shit?" She snaps back, I sigh and try to grab her hand which she only pulled away.

"I know I've been an idiot and an asshole these past few days but I genuinely want to help. Whatever this is, we can get through it-"

"No we can't. Don't you get it? There is no us and there is no me and Nate either! Nate and I were friends way back when we both lived here and now all of a sudden five years later we are back by weird circumstances. I know it's not just me who thinks it's fishy, it's almost as if history is repeating itself and I'm going to get to the bottom of it. You want to help? You can help us make sure everyone gets to the hotel in one piece while I find out why this is happening." I've never seen that look in her eyes, it kind of scared to to be honest. It was a mixture of anger and pain, but mostly it was fear.

What is going on in that head of yours Lydia?

Lydia's POVThis is bad. This is really bad, we have to get to that hotel fast. Things already started happening, and I'm afraid if we don't get there fast then more people are going to be hallucinating.

As it got dark we finally reached the hotel and I realized that I remember this place. This is where Nate and I met as little kids, I remember that day so well because my mother told my sister to take me and Stefano here so she could "talk" to our dad. Looking back on it now, when she came to pick us up she had a black eye so obviously they were fighting and she just didn't want us in the house while it happened.

I know Brandon is pissed at me because I won't tell him what I actually believe is going on but it's for the better. The less he knows the better, I don't want to drag him into this.

Nate managed to get us all rooms but that is when everyone really started tripping out. You had people fighting with walls, you had the casual couple making out, you had the nerdy girl in the corner rocking herself back and fourth, and then there was the 7 of us. We were just acting normal.

"What the hell is wrong with everyone? It's like the fumes from the bus made them high or something!" Vince apprehensively says, I sigh.

"I told you guys, it's this town. It does things to people, but as far as the hallucinations go, this has my father written all over it." To say I was nervous would be an understatement, I was petrified.

"What do you mean? Are you saying he was following us?" Piper questions, I slowly nod as Piper's phone goes off, she answers nervously and then hands the phone to me.

"Hello?"

"Hello Adrianna, what a pleasure it is to hear your voice again!" I shivered at the sound of his voice. "I wish I could say the same Carlyle. What do you want?"

"Oh how I wish we could go back to the times when you called me dad. Those were great weren't they?"

"Maybc for you. It was hell for me. Now answer the question, what do you want?" I snap, he chuckles. "Well look at you, thinking you're in charge. Cute. Meet me at the house and nobody dies. If you bring any of your little friends I will make sure that they all end up like Wesley, just with longer and more painful deaths. Got it?"

"Fine! Just don't hurt them. I'll be there soon." I hung up the phone and looked at them with a sad expression. "What's wrong Lydia? What did he say?" Nate questions, a tear falls down my face as I shake my head.

"I'm sorry I dragged you guys into this. It's all my fault, I have to go if anything happens I want you guys to know that you have been the greatest friends I could ever ask for-"

"Wait what?! What do you mean if anything happens?" Brandon asks, stepping forward and giving me a sad look. "You're going to meet him aren't you?" Blaire was the first to understand, I nodded.

"We love you, you know that. Just be careful okay? And come back to us in one piece." Vince says with a smile, Brandon looks at them like they are crazy. "You're all going to just stand here and let her go?! Are you crazy!" He shouted, they all gave him a look of sympathy as I walked away.

Brandon's POVThey are all insane! She told them the story of her father and now they are going to just sit there and watch her leave to meet him. There is no doubt he has a trick up his sleeve.

I'm not letting her go. Not this time.

Lydia's POV"Lydia wait!" It was Brandon, he was running after me, I shook my head. "You have to go back Brandon-"

"No. Not without you." He shakes his head and grabs my hands, I sigh. "I have to do this Brandon, you don't understand-"

"Then make me understand! He's dangerous Lydia and he could kill you! If something happened to you I don't know what I would do. You saw light in me when nobody else did and you brought it back out in me. I know you say you don't want to be anything and that's okay but I can't stand seeing you walk into a trap. It's suicide!" I cupped his face with my hand, hoping that this will make him understand.

"I couldn't live with myself if something bad happened to any of them, especially you. You make me feel something that I haven't felt in a very long time. But you have to understand that my father is dangerous, and he will kill whoever gets in between him and my brother and I. I'm going to be as careful as I can, don't worry he's not going to hurt me. He wants me and my brother alive for now, you can't follow me or he will kill you. So please, if not for yourself then do this for me. Stay here and make sure that nobody leaves, go into everyone's room and lock all windows and doors to make sure no one can get out. Nobody is going to die on my watch today."

"You really are a hero Lydia Stone." He replies with a big smile, unfortunately a tear also fell down his face which I wiped away with my thumb. "Don't be sad. I am going to be okay. I promise. I'll be back before you know it." I decided that now was the time to show him how I feel without actually saying it, I kissed him so passionately it felt like the world around us had stopped. Time stood still and it was just the two of us.

Sadly I had to pull away because I had to leave. "I'll be back soon. Stay safe okay?" I reply while giving him a hug and smiling. He always smells so good, I don't know what cologne he uses but it is very comforting. And if this is the last thing I ever get to smell then at least it'll be something good.

As I was walking to the staircase, - because elevators are the route of all evil- he said something that gave me hope. I knew I had to come back for him.

"Hey Lydia?" I turned back with a smile. "Yeah?"

"I love you."

"I love you too Brandon." I wish I could've stayed, but I needed to do this. This ends today.

My house was only a couple of blocks away, so I ran as if my life depended on it. I made sure to check the perimeter, when I saw my father wasn't there I was confused. But I decided that I was going to visit my family's grave and keep my guard up just in case.

I decided to take a seat next to the grave of my mother and start talking. "Hey mom, it's Adrianna. I know it's been awhile since we've talked but that is only because Stefano and I are carrying out your wish. We got out as soon as he started the fire, Stefano knew it was something that you would tell us to do so we ran. It's been five years and he's found us yet again. He's created chaos and I don't know what I'm going to do to stop it. I'm sorry I failed you."

All of a sudden I heard a slow clap and laughing, I looked up to see the devil himself. "A family reunion, how precious! I knew I would find you back here."

"What do you want Carlyle?" I snap, he smirks. "Please stop with the formalities, call me dad Adrianna-"

"It's Lydia now and I will never call you my father."

"That's not what you said when I killed that boyfriend of yours." Anger fueled through my body at the mention of Wesley. "You didn't ask my question. What do you want?"

"Well, part of me wants to kill you but the other part of me wants you and Stefano to come back so we could be a family again-"

"You know, I really would it's just you are a narcissistic psychopath and I don't want to sleep with one eye open every night because of the constant reminder of what you made me do-"

"Oh you loved it! I saw the look in your eyes when you drove the knife through your sisters heart. Why do you think I chose you and not Stefano? I chose you because you're special Adrianna. You had the same look in your eye that I did when I first killed someone. Come back home, I can teach you my ways."

"Never. Tell me what you did to my class." I demand, he chuckles and pulls out a knife. "Oh that was nothing! First I just had to cut the oil tank so that the bus would stop, then I made sure to put a little something extra in your classes breakfast. Eggs and a bit of drugs, whoops! The plan was to make you hallucinate so that you'd come back with me but you weren't even there for breakfast so here we are."

"If you brought me here just to threaten me into coming back, it's not going to work. I will never work with you. You're a monster!" I shout angrily, he slashes my arm with the knife.

"Don't you dare talk to me like that-"

"And why not Carlyle? You're not my father anymore. My father was a kind and generous man until he got into the drug and alcohol business. You are not my father, you're nothing but DNA and I hate you for it!" He slashed me again, I winced in pain. "Go ahead dad, what are you going to do? Kill me, Your precious little girl? You've already killed my spirit, I died the day you murdered my mother so go ahead. Kill me. I know you won't do it because you're a coward!"

"SHUT UP!" This time he punched me right in the eye, that was gonna leave a mark. I could feel the blood dripping from me but I was not going to give up. "No. You need to know what kind of a monster you really are! Remember that day you gave me a concussion because you pushed me down the stairs? Or the time we refused to come home so you decided to melt my friends eyes with acid? Or the time you murdered my boyfriend? Or even when you killed your own wife and daughter!"

"I HAD NO CHOICE! She was digging into my business and she saw too much! It had to be done. But I didn't even touch your sister, you killed her-"

"YOU MADE ME! I LOVED THEM AND YOU MADE ME KILL HER AND I HATE YOU FOR IT! I FUCKING HATE YOU! You're a monster, you're a thief and most importantly you're a psychotic murderer."

"Fine, I'll give you an ultimatum. Either you come back with me after graduation and help me pay my debts or we will just have to have the past repeat themselves. Brandon is it?"

"Don't you touch him! I'll kill you-"

"I'd watch what you say to me Adrianna, all it takes is one little slip and that'll be two of your Boyfriend's whose blood I have on my hands. Now you are going to join me when you graduate, or your friends will all undergo slow painful deaths. Oh and you have to follow my rules as well. Number one, you can't tell anyone except for your brother, try to convince him to help as well. Number two, if you disobey me I will kill you. And number three, you need a cellphone so we can keep in touch. Understand?" He says with a smug smirk, I rolled my eyes because I was trying to hold back tears and when he saw that he started laughing.

"Good. We are on the same page. Oh and just as a reminder, I am going to give you a little present." He took the knife and plunged it into my leg, I screamed in pain. "Think of this as a little reminder. If you disobey me your consequence will be a lot worse. You better get going Adrianna, we don't want you to bleed out before they can take you to the hospital." He said smugly. I was so angry that I was holding back tears. I will not let him see me cry.

I got up which was absolute hell, I was in indescribable pain. My leg was bleeding so badly I was leaving a trail of blood as I walked back to the hotel. If I die, my blood will be on Carlyle's hands.

When I finally got to the hotel, I collapsed. All I remember is hearing a bunch of people yelling and screaming as I went down. Specifically, I heard Brandon's voice before I knocked out.
---Woah! Lydia's father really is a dirtbag. What do you think is going to happen next? How do you feel about Brandon and Lydia's moment? How do you think everyone is going to react to Lydia's injury? Comment down below and don't for get to vote! Thanks,

-Jen

Chapter 17- How Heroic Of You

Brandon's POVEverything was going perfect until she came back injured. I told everyone that we said I love you and kissed and we were all happy. Up until now.

"HELP! SOMEBODY PLEASE HELP ME!" I screamed for dear life as I walked through the hospital with Lydia in my arms. There were no cars that could come for two hours and I knew that she didn't have enough time, so I swooped her up in my arms and ran for my life to the hospital. Lucky for me I used to take track and football, so the mile run with her in my arms was easy.

Someone finally caught my attention and put her on a gurney. I followed them all the way to the surgical room where they wouldn't let me pass. "Sir, you have to stay out here-"

"Bullshit! She's my girlfriend, I need to be there for her!" I snap back at the nurse while shaking my head as Nate and Piper hold me back.

"You can't go in there Brandon. They are going to do their best to save her-"

"Oh and of course you are going to play mister perfect again! She needs support-"

"No Brandon! She needs surgery! Her father hit an artery in her leg. Not everything is about you so sit down and shut the fuck up!" I was in shock. I have seen Blaire in many different emotions and fazes in her life, but I've never seen Blaire angry before.

I did as she said and kept quiet but on the inside I was tearing myself apart. It's all my fault. If I would've gone after her and followed her then maybe I could've protected her and she would not be here right now.

The nurses refused to tell us what condition she was in but I knew that Blaire knows. She wants to become a doctor so she studies all the anatomy and blood stuff, I want to ask her but instead I keep silent.

"We shouldn't have let her go alone." Gray comments while shaking his head, they all nod in agreement. "I know." Nate replies, anger starts to fill through me.

"Then why did you? You spend all this time saying what if but none of you actually did! You guys let her leave-"

"You didn't do anything either. All you did was say how much you love her-"

"That's not true. I begged her not to go but she was persistent that she had to or someone would die. So yes I told her I loved her, because if those are the last words from me she ever heard then at least she knew how I felt."

"Oh how heroic of you!" Nate mocks, I glare at him. I wanted to punch him so badly but I have to hold on to that piece of Good that Lydia brought out in me. "And what exactly did you do Nate? Oh that's right, you let her go get stabbed and maybe killed!"

His stupid ass decided to use me as a human punching bag. It was so hard to resist punching him but I had to do it for the sake of Lydia. "Nate stop it." Blaire says worriedly, he kept punching, I started feeling light headed. "NATE STOP! YOU'RE GONNA KILL HIM!" Okay maybe she was being over dramatic but I was feeling really lightheaded by now.

Gray and Vince had to pull him off me and even so he was kicking and screaming. Security escorted him out. Piper and Vince went after him in order to make sure he didn't do anything stupid while Blaire and Gray helped me get cleaned up.

"Why did you let him do that to you? The old Brandon I knew would've fought back." Gray questions while shaking his head, I sigh. "The old player Brandon is gone. I'm starting to change, Lydia took a big part in that. I'm a better person because of her which is why I didn't fight back. She's in surgery right now possibly fighting for her life, and since I didn't follow her, the least I could do is respect what she taught me."

"You really love her don't you?" Blaire says with a wide smile, I wince in pain as we put an ice pack on my eye and nod. "She brings out the best in me. Ever since my mom died I went down a spiral path and she brought me back. The plan was supposed to be if she can help me be good again, I'll help her make Nate jealous and get him back. However, while he was busy being an ignorant asshole we connected and I guess we fell for each other. Saying I love you is hard for the both of us, but I don't regret saying it."

"Awe that's so adorable! You two are definitely my OTP. Her and Nate may have been childhood best friends but they would be too problematic as a couple. You two solve each others problems and that's what makes you so great. I've never seen you care so much about a girl, it really is amazing." I could tell she was being sincere and that made me happy. Unfortunately my happiness was cut short when I heard that beeping sound coming from the surgery room. I panicked.

"Her bp is dropping, we're losing her! Start doing compressions." I heard the doctor shout to the nurses, we ran to the window so we could see what was happening. I regretted it because it only brought up bad memories.

"She's gonna be okay Brandon-"

"You don't know that! You said it yourself he hit a major artery in her leg. Maybe if I was able to take her in a car then she wouldn't be dying right now!"

"You can't blame yourself-"

"Yes I can. If I would've followed her anyways and ignored her then I could've protected her. It's my fault." I wanted to cry, but I couldn't cry in front of them. "Brandon, we couldn't predict what would've happened. He could've killed you-"

"But at least I would've protected her!"

"Brandon, if you died she would not be able to live with herself. Yes you would've protected her, but she would've died anyways. She's going to be okay, they just got her pulse back to normal. She's most likely going to need a blood transfusion because she lost so much blood, you're gonna want to be here when she wakes up." Blaire says sympathetically, I shake my head. "The only thing we can do is wait and pray, she's going to be alright." Gray adds on, I nod.

There was one place I had to go to and that was the church inside the hospital. I kneeled down and started praying. "I don't really know how to start these things but um hey, it's Brandon. I know we haven't talked in awhile but that is because I lost a little of my faith when my mother died. Believe me when I say it broke me, but you probably knew that already.

When I first met Lydia I was a jerk and a player, but she changed me for the better. She made me see the good in things and I will forever be in debt to her, but ever since I came into her life she started having more problems and I'm so sorry. Please, if you really are up there, save her. I promise I won't cause any problems, I will avoid her if I have to just please let her live."

The doors swung open and I looked to see Piper. "Brandon, we can go see her soon. They were able to get her leg all stitched up and it turns out that Blaire was the perfect match for the transfusion, they are both recuperating now. Let's go see her!" Before I could do anything, Piper grabbed my arm and pulled me all the way to Lydia's room.

She was still asleep which was okay since she just had surgery, but she looked so adorable I didn't even want to move her.

"Go!" Blaire, Piper and Gray pushed me inside and closed the door. I tip toed over to her bed and grabbed her hand. "I know you're sleeping, but I want you to know that I'm here. I brought you to the hospital because I was horrified. I blamed myself for what happened to you and it's because of that pain I felt when I saw you hurt that I have to let you go. I love you so much that it hurts, and if anything would've happened to you today I don't know what I would've done. I'm so sorry." A tear fell down my face as I went to kiss her forehead. I wiped my tears away and walked out, all of them looked at me with sympathetic expressions.

They are all going to say that I'm being over dramatic but I have to do this. It's for her own good. ---Brandon Brandon Brandon, smh. What did you guys think of this chapter? Is Brandon being over dramatic? Or is he just being way too overprotective? What is Nathan's deal? Are you team Brandon or team Nathan? Comment down below and don't forget to vote! Thanks

-Jen

Chapter 18- Hey Mom

1 Week Later (Piper's POV)Lydia didn't get cleared for a few days, and by then the buses were fixed and we were all ready to go. Lorenzo came and took her home, I hope she's okay. She hasn't been to school in for couple of days and I'm getting worried.

"Hey Pipes, how are you?" Blaire asks with a sympathetic look, I put on a fake smile. "I'm fine. How are you?" Truth is I'm not fine, I don't think Brandon is either. Today is a very hard day for us, it's the one year anniversary of our mother's death.

"That fake smile isn't fooling anyone, really, how are you?" Right as I was about to answer, Lydia came walking in looking like she didn't have a care in the world. She looked brand new, makeup, new style, hair done, everything.

"Something is up with her." Blaire gives me a questioning look. Obviously something's wrong with her, she got stabbed by her psycho father a week ago and now here she is, walking in as if nothing happened.

"What do you mean?" I looked at her as if she had three heads. Is she crazy or just dumb? "Look at her! She just got stabbed a week ago and now she looks like she wasn't even hurt at all. Plus her and Brandon haven't spoken since. You don't just say you love each other and then not speak for a week. Plus Brandon is kissing any girl in sight today, I hate seeing him like this."

"Like what?" I turned around to see Lydia with a smile on her face. What's got her so happy? "Nothing, don't worry about it. What's up? How's the leg? You look great!" She does a little twirl but I can see it in her face that she's in pain.

"Thanks. It feels as if someone's running me over with a bus but the pain meds really work. Anyways, guess who finally got a phone!" She says excitedly causing me and Blaire to give each other questioning looks. When she told us her story, she said one of the number one rules were no phones. I'm so confused.

"I thought you couldn't have a phone?" she shakes her head and sighs. "I wasn't supposed to, but Lorenzo and I had a very long talk about what happened last week and he thought it would be best if I got one so that I could stay in touch with him at all times. He even dropped me off at school, annoying but understandable given the circumstances. Anyways, how are you guys?"

"Not so good but I'm okay. Today is the one year anniversary of our mother's death so it's a sad day. The worst part of it being that Brandon blames himself for it and that's the whole reason he became a player and everything. You should talk to him, he listens to you." I don't want to use grief to my advantage but there's got to be something that will get these two to talk.

"Oh. I'm so sorry, that must have been awful for you guys. If you need anything, I'm here for you." She puts her hand on my shoulder, I shake my head and shrug it off. "No, it's okay. I've been putting it off for months, you don't have to worry about me. It's Brandon you have to worry about, he's tearing himself up and I'm really worried. Will you please talk to him?"

"I'll do anything for you Piper, I got your back." Right as she said those words, the bell rang and she darted off. I think she's forgetting I have homeroom with her.

"I gotta go, I'll see you at lunch-"

"Piper wait. Are you actually ok? I'm worried about you." Blaire stops me, I nod and put on another smile. "I'm fine Blaire. The one we should be worried about is Brandon, you know he blames himself. I don't know what he will do, I have to get to homeroom I'll see you later." And with that said I walked off and made my way to class.

Lydia's POVI wasn't planning on talking to Brandon after having what my father said play in my head over and over for the past week. I don't exactly know what happened, but I know how he feels and that's why I'm going to talk to him.

I sat in my usual seat which was next to him in homeroom and greeted him. Of course he barely said anything to me, I wanted to break the silence.

"Are you okay?" He turned his head so slowly that I thought he could've been possessed, it was really scary. "Yes. Why does everyone keep asking me that?" The tone in his voice was anger and hatred. I know it wasn't hatred for me, but hatred for himself.

"Because I know what today is, and I know it's hard-"

"It's not hard. I'm completely fine." I could see that he was tearing up so I tried to grab his hand but he pulled away from me. "Brandon, you know you can talk to me about whatever-"

"I said I'm fine Lydia. Just leave me alone." And with that he stormed out of class which left me speechless. There is obviously some sort of pain going on in his head, and I know it's not anger at me or even grief for that matter.

No, something is wrong with him and I'm going to get to the bottom of it.

In all my other classes, he acted the same just instead he didn't talk or look at me at all. Gym was the class I had with Vince, I knew I could get something out of him.

Once we started walking around the track, I caught up with Vince which was absolute hell for me. The pain was unbearable, but I had to do this. "Hey Vince, what's up?"

"Nothing much, how about you?" He replied with a chuckle, I sigh. Here it goes. "Nothing interesting. I know what today is, and I know that's why everyone is acting depressed. You should take Piper out tonight to get her mind off things, I'm trying to work on Brandon-"

"Good luck with that. He blames himself for what happened, today must be hell for him." I could tell that there was a tone of pain in his voice and that only made me curious. "What exactly happened?"

"Oh no, you're not getting it out of me. You have to talk to Brandon." He went to walk away but I stepped in his way. "Don't you think I tried that? The guy hasn't talked to me since I had surgery-"

"Look Lydia, I believe the reason he's not talking to you is because it's too painful to talk about it. Bringing you to the hospital probably brought back bad memories for him." What bad memories could he be talking about? It's obviously about Brandon's mother's death, but what happened?

"I just need to-"

"Nope."

"You don't even know what I was going to say!" I protest, he rolls his eyes. "You were going to ask on a scale of one to ten how bad is what happened?"

"Damn you're good." He laughs, I looked over at the bleachers only to see Brandon getting high and drinking with the stoners. He's skipping class again, this isn't good. This is not a way to cope. "Go talk to him. Even though he doesn't want to admit it, he needs you. While we all bonded over the death of a family member, you're the only one who can really get through to him. He really loves you Lydia, he'll come around eventually, just go talk to him."

Here goes nothing.

I made my way over to Brandon and his new stoner friends. "What the hell do you think you're doing?" He started laughing, his stoner friends walked away from us as he replied "I'm having fun. Try it!" He blew the smoke in my face, I waved it away and grabbed the joint out of his hand and stomped it to the ground. He only got angry at me but I didn't care.

"Hey that was expensive-"

"I don't really give a shit Brandon. What are you doing huh? You're wasting your life, that's what you're doing! And for what? Because you're sad?"

"You don't know what it's like-"

"MY MOTHER WAS MURDERED BY MY FATHER! And you say I don't know what it's like? Bullshit. I know what it's like to blame yourself, I know what it's like to feel numb and I know what it feels like to lose a mother."

"I don't know what to think anymore! I'm tired of everyone questioning me today! I'm tired of all this drama and most importantly, I'm tired of you. I'm out of here!" Tears were forming in my eyes but I refused to let them fall. I just followed him to the parking lot and sat in his car.

"Get out." He growls, I shake my head as anger flows through me. Stay calm Lydia. Stay calm."No. You don't get to do that. You don't get to say you love me and then take it back when you're sad, that's not how things work! Talk to me B. I've confided in you for all my issues, now it's your turn. Come on, this isn't you-"

"You don't know who I am-"

"Yes I do. You used to be this ball of sunshine and then your mother's death turned you into a player, I knew that. But you were able to come back to your good self and I know you are still that person. Brandon just talk to me." His face starts to turn red, indicating that he is about to cry.

"It was all my fault." He buries his head in his hands and starts to cry, I rub his back. "No, whatever happened was not your fault. I know how you feel right now. You blame yourself and you feel numb. You feel as if you can't breathe and like someone is literally shattering your heart into pieces. It's good to let it out, it's okay to cry."

"No it's not. It was my fault, I'm the reason she's dead. Everyone blamed me, my father blamed me, Piper blamed me, even my grandmother blamed me, I even fucking blame me because it was my fault."

"Tell me what happened, you can talk to me." I grabbed his hand and intertwined our fingers, I saw a small smile appear on his face, but that smile was soon turned into a frown when he remembered what happened.

"We were on vacation at a ski resort and I went to a party with this girl I met at the resort. I got really drunk and I had sex for the first time with that girl and my mom caught us. She started yelling at me and I yelled back and said things I shouldn't have and she hit me. So I ran downstairs and got in the car, I wanted to blow off steam but she got in the car with me. I never planned on it, but I knew she hated when I drove fast so I was driving real fast. We were arguing and I turned to face her for one second and then I heard a truck honking. It was coming at us so fast, it was out of control. Mom grabbed the wheel and the car swerved away from the direction of the truck but the car spun around on the slippery road and hit us. We went off the cliff and into the frozen lake and I got knocked out. When I woke up in the hospital, they told me what happened and that she didn't make it. I killed my mother and last thing I said to her was that I hated her... I never even got to apologize."

He starts hysterically crying, I hug him as an attempt to get him to feel better, obviously it didn't work. "It wasn't your fault Brandon. The roads were icy and the guy driving the truck was in the wrong lane. That wasn't your fault. And while it was unfortunate that things went down the way they did, everyone fights with their parents. She grabbed the wheel because she wanted to protect you. She knew you didn't mean it, believe me."

"I never got to say I'm sorry! It's all my fault...she probably hates me. And now I'll never see her again." I made him look at me before I cupped his face with my hands and wiped away his tears. "Listen to me. If there's one thing I've learned about mother's, it's that they will always forgive you no matter what. There is nothing more special then a bond between a mother and her child. Where is she buried?"

"Evergreen. Why?" He gives me a questioning look, I smile and grab his hand again. "Because I want to meet the woman who birthed such a wonderful human being that had a huge impact on my life."

For once, I actually saw his lips twitch, turning into a little smile. It made me so happy. "But first, we have to make a little pit stop so let's switch spots because you can't cry and drive, and I know how you feel about your car but-"

"You can drive it. If there's one person I trust, it's you." I was surprised he let me drive his car, he treats his car like his child. He doesn't even let Piper touch it, I feel special.

We switched seats and I drove to the nearest flower shop and picked up pink roses, I knew they were her favorite flower because Piper said they were her favorite as well. The drive to the cemetery was quiet, but once we were approaching his mother's grave I was holding his hand.

The tombstone said "Here lies Kathleen Danielle Santiago, loving daughter, mother, and wife." I could tell he was nervous, his hands were shaking, but I only smiled at him and whispered "You can do this." He just gave me a look of fear so I reassured him by sitting down next to her grave.

"We are going to be here awhile. It's okay to sit down, this way it'll feel as if the two of you are face to face. Don't be nervous, it's okay." He placed the flowers on the grave and sat next to me.

"H-hi mom. I brought your favorite flowers, I hope you like them... but most of all I h-hope that you're not mad at me. I have made so many mistakes in my life and saying what I said to you before the crash was one of them. I don't hate you, I never hated you mom. I love you with all my heart and I'm so so sorry. This past year I have carried so much guilt with me and that made me do so many things that I am not proud of. But I guess the truth is that I did those bad things because I blamed myself. I always thought maybe if I hadn't gone to that stupid party or even met that girl, you would still be alive. Now I understand that god has a plan for everyone, and you are in a better place." A tear falls down his face, I place my hand on top of his as a way to tell him it's okay.

"These past few months have been an emotional rollercoaster. But I think you would be proud of me when I tell you that there is one person that was able to bring me out of my spiral downwards, and that is this girl right here. Mom, this is Lydia. She has made such a huge impact on our lives. She brought me back to my old self, and she even got Piper to start smiling and laughing instead of thinking bitterly like she used to. I love her mom, and I hope that you are able to watch over us growing old together. I want you to know that I really miss you, and I guess when my time comes which hopefully isn't for a long time, that we will find each other some day." He kissed his fingers and then touched the grave, I smiled. I'm so proud of him, I knew what I had to do next.

As he got up, I stopped him and told him that I wanted to talk to her for a little bit, he looked so happy. I told him to wait in the car so that it could be just us girls and he nodded, understanding what I was about to do. I made sure he was far away before I started talking to her.

"Hi mrs Santiago, I'm Lydia. I wanted to talk to you because I wanted to let you know what an amazing son and daughter you have. Piper is always sarcastic but that is what I love about her, her humor is hilarious and she never fails to make me laugh when I'm feeling down. She's like a sister to me and I love her for that. Both her and Brandon are always there for me with all my family drama, and believe me when I tell you there's a lot of drama in my life. Piper was so welcoming on my first day but Brandon is a whole mother story. On my first day, him and his friends were still part of the overachievers group which you probably know about. But down the road something sparked between us and I fell for him."

I took a deep breath before continuing. "He may have started out like a jerk, however over time he asked me to help him be good again and I did. Last week on our senior trip was the first time we said I love you and it was so special. I really do love your son, he's truly an amazing person and I think you would be really proud of him...but it's because I love him so much that I have to try to keep him out of my family drama no matter how hard he tried to get in. I guess I'm telling you this because I can't talk about this with my own mother. She's dead as well but I blame myself for her death. I know I shouldn't but I do because I'm the reason they were arguing that night." A tear falls down my face at the memory.

"I was 12 at the time and my dad had hurt me the night before and locked me in the basement. I had no food or water and I was bleeding, luckily my older sister snuck down to help me otherwise I could've bled out. She was studying to be a doctor, so she sewed up my wound and brought me back upstairs. The next day was when all the bad stuff happened... I don't want this to change your views of me but I need to let this out. The full truth." I took another deep breath before continuing.

"The day my mother and sister died is a day I'll never forget. I believe that my mother knew something bad was going to happen, if she didn't then she wouldn't have written us a letter. My brother Stefano and I went to the store that morning to get supplies for us, the plan was we were going to leave in the middle of the night but my father found out and decided to stop us and it was too late. I was still too young to understand why she made us go outside and throw around a football but now I get it. She knew my father was dangerous, and she knew that if we stayed we would get killed too. My sister Rose refused to come with us no matter how much we begged her and now I realize why. We weren't actually throwing a football, we were packing everything in the truck. Rose didn't come because she knew what was going to happen. In my mother's letter she said Rose knew and Rose was willing to do whatever to protect her little brother and sister." Tears start falling down my face, it was like Niagara Falls up in here. But I had to do this.

"We heard screaming and glass breaking and that's when we ran inside. I knew something was wrong when i saw Rose crying, I remember constantly asking for my mother but my father just kept shouting and me and pointing his gun at us. I figured out she was dead when I was standing under the attic door and blood started dropping down my face. When I went to open the door, my father pulled the trigger, but Rose jumped in front of me and got shot. She wasn't as lucky as my mother, my mother's death was quick and simple. Rose's was long and excruciatingly painful.

My father kept shouting at me saying 'you did this!' Over and over again until he grabbed out his knife. I tried running to the attic again, this time I actually managed to get up there, but my dad pulled Stefano and Rose up with him. I ran over to my mother and tried to help her but whenever I touched her, he would stab Rose. He made me end it for her, that was only after he stabbed her about ten times and she was still alive. She was strong, but my father made me choose. It was either her or Stefano, Rose told me that it was okay and that she was ready. I closed my eyes and pulled the trigger. It was so hard for me, I wanted to turn the gun on myself and just end it right there but I knew I needed to be strong. When my father set the house on fire, Stefano and I ran for our lives. Our uncle helped us get away..."

"But now he found us again and he threatened me. He doesn't know that my brother is having a baby and I would like to keep it that way, however he does know about Brandon and that was why I haven't talked to him this past week. Truth is my father hurt me last week and threatened to hurt him so I figured that if I stayed away then he would be safe but knowing my father, nobody is actually safe... I guess I'm telling you this because I want you to know that I promise I'll do whatever it takes to protect him and Piper and to keep them safe. I'll get back in contact with my uncle if I have to, I'll do anything to get my dad out of my life. And I want you to know that you have great children, and if anything were to happen to them I would make sure my father pays for it."

I got up and made sure that there was no grass stuck on me. I smiled and said my goodbyes. "I'm so glad I talked to you. It was so nice meeting you and I really hope we can talk again. Next time I'll make sure Piper comes with Brandon and they can both talk to you. And when this whole thing with my dad is over, I'll make sure that you're the first one to know. Thanks for listening."

As I walked away I couldn't help but actually feel good. All this time I have been hiding from my past but now I am actually facing it, and talking about it to Brandon's mom really made things clearer for me.

I know what I have to do now. And that's keeping everyone safe.

Chapter 19- This Day Went From 0-100 Real Fast

Lydia's POVOnce I dropped Brandon off at his house, I was greeted at my front door by Piper and Blaire. "Hey honey! Welcome home, now let's go." They pulled me upstairs before I could even protest.

"What's going on?" I ask with a chuckle, they plop on my bed and look at me like lost puppies. "What do you mean? It's 8 o'clock! You two left at 11 this morning! Spill!"

"Where's Lorenzo and Haley?" I question while intentionally changing the subject, Blaire rolls her eyes. "They left about a half our ago, they told us to tell you they went out for dinner. Stop changing the subject! What happened between you and Brandon!" I smile widely at the memory, they look at each other with smirks in their faces.

"Ooooh she's blushing! This must be good." Piper teases, I roll my eyes and sit down on the chair next to my bed and start telling the story.

"Well it wasn't easy at first. We started arguing and then he ran to his car so I got in and followed him and I got him to attempt to stop blaming himself. He told me what happened with your mother so I drove his car and took him to go see her at the cemetery and we talked to her and it was really nice, I think it brought the two of us closer together. After the cemetery, we went up to a spot that he said was special to him and we just cuddled in his car and watched the sun set. It was really romantic, and I'm glad I was able to get him to forget for awhile." The look on their faces was a mixture of shock and awe.

"He let you drive his car? He doesn't even let me touch it!" Piper whines, Blaire and I laugh. "He said he trusts me with it-"

"He must really love you Lydia. Piper is right, he hasn't let anyone go near or touch it. He only just started driving it to school a couple weeks ago... but I guess the real question you should be asking yourself is who do you like more? Brandon or Nathan."

"What? That's crazy!"

"Bullshit Lydia. I saw the way you two were looking at each other in the hotel room that day-"

"That doesn't mean I like him-"

"But it means you do feel something for him. You can't string the two of them along, you're going to need to choose eventually. Besides, the winter ball is Friday and you are obligated to go because you're my friend and I put this stupid thing together. So who are you going with?" Piper asks eagerly. There was a threatening look in her eye that really scared me, but it also got me thinking because she might be on to something.

"Okay fine I admit that I did feel something for Nate, but that's only because I found out who he really is. Besides, I love Brandon with all my heart. And I thought we weren't taking dates to this thing-"

"Don't change the subject Lydia. You need to figure this out before Grace figures it out for you. She's planning something, I have no idea what she's planning but I know it's going to be big. So if this has anything to do with it you need to get your feelings in tact before someone gets hurt." Blaire got up with an angry expression on her face and stormed out.

"What's her problem?" I snap, Piper shrugs. "Honestly, I don't know. She's been acting really weird lately. What ever it is, she isn't talking about it, and you know her, she's an open book. But the question is what exactly is going on with her?"

"When did this start?" I ask curiously. The face she made was as if a light-bulb went off in her head because she looked like a deer in headlights. "It started when you told her that we all got married. It started when you told her that you and Nate were taking again."

My eyes grow wide as it clicks in my head as well. "You don't think she-"

"It's possible." Piper nods, I shake my head. "But I thought she was-"

"Me too. That's why this is all weird for me."

"We need to talk to her." She shakes her head. "Why not?"

"Because if that's what's going on with her, we need to give her time. After what happened to her a couple years ago, she convinced herself that she was a lesbian. And after constantly telling herself that, she started to believe it. But if that's not actually the case and she does like Nate or Brandon, we need to give her some time to figure things out."

"You're right. I'm sorry." I say with a sigh, she chuckles. She had a certain look in her eye that made me just automatically know that she was planning something, and if I'm right it has to do with this whole love triangle thing.

"Just between us though, who are you leaning more towards?" She asks with her signature smile, I chuckle and cross my arms. "I think you already know the answer to that."

"Oh come on! You're not gonna leave me hanging are you?" She whines while stomping her foot, making the motion of a five year old that doesn't get what they want. "Piper it's not rocket science. Who has been there for me all along instead of running away from their problems?"

"I'm still lost. Both of them have run away from their problems and pushed you away. But look, Vince and I were talking and since his older brother is a lawyer, he said since you and Nate didn't actually sign the marriage papers you're not actually married. So if Grace tries to say anything about it to Brandon, she will have no actual proof. I'm telling you that because I think you're leaning more towards Brandon. You're thinking Brandon right?"

"I mean yeah I guess. He made me feel what it's like to be loved again, he brought that out in me. When I got here I had no intension of talking to anyone yet he was still there. Even when I liked Nate, he was willing to help me get him back. He's an amazing guy."

"But?"

"But Nate was my childhood crush and you're right, that day at the hotel there was a spark and I did feel something. I'm not sure if I really like him that way or if it's my defensive walls being put back up after my altercation with my father but I did feel something for him. And I know it sounds bad but Blaire is right, I do have to choose and I promise that I'll choose by the ball. I have two days, tell her I'll make my decision by then." She looked down at her phone and then back up at me with a sad face. There was a look in her eyes that worried me, it wasn't anger or uneasiness, it was fear.

"What's wrong? Why do you look afraid?" I question, she shakes her head and a tear falls down her face. "Because there's something you're not telling me... and I think I know what it is." She slowly shows me her phone and I gasp when I see the video of me at the cemetery telling her mother the full story.

"Piper-"

"Why didn't you tell me? We got this message earlier from an unknown number. The same number that called me when your father called. It was him. Why did you lie to me? Why did you lie to everyone?" She looked betrayed and I felt awful about it.

"I didn't tell you because I didn't want to worry you-"

"Bullshit! Tell the truth Lydia."

"I'm protecting everyone okay?! When my father hurt me he said that if I didn't do what he told me then someone was going to die. He threatened all of you and that's the real reason I wasn't talking to any of you this past week. But today I broke my promise to myself because I knew how badly the two of you were going to feel and now I might have just killed myself. He's going to come after me and I don't know when or where and it's killing me! I didn't tell you guys anything because I refuse to let history repeat itself. Last time this happened everyone ended up dead and I refuse to let anyone die. We are dealing with so many problems here because we are in high school! Nobody should be dragged into this at seventeen! I'm sorry."

"Yeah, me too. For once I thought I could trust someone and all they did was lie to me." A tear fell down her face as she grabbed her stuff and stormed out of my house.

Well that did not go as planned at all. My father wants to play games? Then game on.

----------The Next Day----------School was pretty awkward, neither Blaire or Piper talked to me. What was even weirder was not even Brandon was talking to me and that made me upset.

"Hey, what's wrong?" Nate asks as I grab my books from my locker, I shake my head and put on a wide fake smile. "Nothing, I'm just peachy!"

"Come on we both know that's a lie. Talk to me." I shook my head as sadness flowed through my body. "Everyone hates me. Blaire hates me, Piper hates me, hell I even think Brandon hates me and I don't understand why because we just had a wonderful day yesterday besides the part when we were fighting, but it was really nice and then I came home and everyone started getting angry with me."

"That's ridiculous! Why do you think they hate you?" He asks with a chuckle, I shake my head. "Because Piper found out something I was hiding from her, I'm pretty sure Brandon found out about Vegas, and Blaire has this ridiculous theory that I am in love with you and Brandon."

"Yeah um that's totally ridiculous... but you know, if it's not that's okay too because you know that I feel the same way about you-"

"Nate, I can't have feelings for you. I am in love with Brandon and all of this teenage high school drama is not for me. I have my own family drama to deal with and none of this is helping. Everyone needs to understand that I am not about the teen drama life. If don't do bullies, I don't do love triangles, and I don't do confrontation, yet everyone seems to think I do!" He grabs my hands and tells me to take a few deep breaths.

"You need to calm down. This is high school, and you're forgetting that we live in a town where everyone knows everything. I know you don't like it so do something about it. Convince Blaire you're not in love with me, tell Piper you're sorry, tell Brandon why we did what we did in Vegas, and mend things with Grace. You need to get out of here and get your mind off things, why don't I take you dress shopping?"

"I have to catch up on my work-"

"Come on, one day isn't going to kill you. I know you, you water till the day of to get a dress for the sixth grade dance so let me take you shopping for the ball. Come on! It'll take your mind off everything, and it'll be like old times. We can even invite Gray and Vince and even your sister in law if you'd like." Maybe he's right. I just need to get away from all this nonsense that is high school drama.

I don't even know where all this came from! One minute we were all fine and the next everyone is mad at each other. All I can say is all this drama went from 0-100 real fast.

But I guess he's right. I need some distraction, and no, not the romantic kind. "Fine. Go get Gray and Vince, I'll text Haley." A few minutes later, Nate was back with Vince and Gray and we were walking out to the parking lot. I passed Piper and Blaire who only glared at me, I just rolled my eyes and walked away.

"I texted Haley, she said she'll meet us at the mall." Nate nodded and we continued our walk, once we got in Nate's car we sat in silence. That was until Vince decided to break it with an uncomfortable question.

"So, what's up with you and Piper? I saw that glare her and Blaire were giving you." I must have given him the bitchiest smirk because he looked confused. "You tell me. She's your wife." He looked as if he forgot that they got married, I couldn't help but chuckle.

"Then what's going on with you and Blaire?" Gray questions, I shrug. "To be honest, I don't know. I think she either likes Gray or Brandon because she had this ridiculous theory that I like Brandon and Nate and she got angry because there is a love triangle." I made sure to put air quotes on love triangle so that they don't suspect anything. Vince and Gray look at me as if they are debating wether or not they believe me.

"Well..." Vince replies. Just by the pitch change in my voice, I could tell that he believed Blaire. "Well what?"

"I think what Vince is trying to say is that you have been hanging out with Nate a lot and one could assume that there is something going on. She's been acting unusually weird lately, maybe it's a best friend thing I don't know. And as far as the Blaire thing goes, it's a possibility. She told me she was bi at that party so it's a possibility she likes one of them. Anyways, enough about drama. Today is about going shopping for your dress."

"Can't we just skip dress shopping and go see a movie or something? I don't think I even want to go to this dance because Piper and Blaire don't want me there-"

"Nonsense. I'm calling Piper and telling her to meet us there. Whatever this problem is, you guys are going to resolve it." Vince demands, before I could even protest he calls her. "Hey Pipes, want to come to the mall?... Great! See you there."

"She said yes. You two are going to mend whatever drama this is today. With all the stuff you have going on right now, you don't need any high school drama." Finally someone gets it!

"I tried solving things with her this morning but Blaire pulled her away and then in English, Brandon said something weird. I don't know, I hate drama. Hopefully she will actually listen to my explanation."

When we got to the mall, I tried on multiple dresses and then I finally found one that I really loved but I refused to show them until the ball tomorrow. They did whine about it but I bribed them with food and they happily skipped over.

As we were eating, Piper came over and I waved at her with a smile, she ran away and I decided to follow her.

I opened the bathroom door and called out for her, I only heard the sound of her puking. "Piper? Is that you?"

"Go away."

"No. I'm one of your best friends Piper and I can see that something is wrong. I know you're mad at me but please, I need you to talk to me. Whatever it is, I'm sure I'll understand." She came out of the bathroom stall crying. She didn't look at me as she popped a breath mint and washed her hands, she looked at me when she was done and the look in her eyes was pure pain.

"I've been a bitch to you and I'm sorry. When I saw the video of you talking to my mother and telling her the truth, I lost it because I couldn't even come to terms with the truth myself." I looked at her confused. "What are you talking about?"

She sighs before continuing. "A couple of days ago, I noticed that I was late. I didn't think anything of it at the time because that usually happens to me, but this time it felt different. My stomach was in knots and I started getting nauseous and I threw up. Then I threw up again and again all weekend so I took a trip to the drug store and took an early pregnancy test-"

"You're not pregnant are you?" I ask apprehensively, tears fall down her face as she nods. "The test was positive!" She winces, I sigh and give her a hug as she cries into my shoulder.

"It's all going to be okay-"

"How could you say that? I'm bringing a baby into this world with your father in our lives. This baby was conceived because of a drunken mistake and now it is going to come in this world of hatred and murder. I don't even know if I want to have it, I'm a senior in high school! I'm not ready for a baby."

"It's your decision, but at least talk it over with Vince first. I suggest after the ball so that you guys could enjoy a night together. If you do decide to keep it, then I promise you that no harm will come to your family and I'll do whatever it takes to protect your family, even if that means leaving and going with my father to make sure no harm comes to any of you." She nods and smiles.

"I would want you to be in the baby's life if I decide to keep it. Which is why I am willing to do whatever it takes to get rid of this evil, but for now, you're right. Today and tomorrow are all about having fun, so let's get out there and have some fun. Maybe not in the food court though." We both start laughing. Once we could control our breathing, I decided to tell her that I've made my decision.

"So, I was going to tell you earlier but you were kinda busy ignoring me. But I want you to know that I made my decision on what you, Blaire and I talked about yesterday." She made a face that said she was hiding something. "What is it?"

"Well... Blaire might have told Grace about you two getting married and Grace might have said something to Brandon and-"

"WHAT?! I specifically didn't want to tell him because if he were to find out about that he would never speak to me again! Everything's ruined!" Tears start falling down my face. Ugh I'm so stupid!

"I know and I'm so sorry-"

"It's not your fault, it's Blaire's. And if she thinks I'm ever going to forgive her she's dead wrong." Anger started fueling through my body. How could she do this to me?!

"I know it sounds bad but-"

"No Piper it doesn't sound bad, it is bad! I have to go, thank you for telling me." With that I walked away, I texted Haley telling her to get the car and that I wanted to go home and I met her in the parking lot. I slammed the car door shut.

"Are you okay? You look upset-"

"I'm fine. I just want to go home." I looked out the window and at the blue sky which I hoped would calm me down. It didn't. No matter how many times I took a deep breath and tried to calm down, all I could think about was how angry I am.

Everything I have ever done was to protect all of them, and now that the two of them are angry at me, I know that they will be willing to do whatever it takes to spite me.

I tried everything to protect them, I've done everything to make sure that they are safe and that my father doesn't harm them and for what? So that I could have all of my secrets spilled by a girl who might be after my boyfriend? It's bullshit.

I opened up to her and she spilled everything. Who knows what else she could've told Grace! She could've told her about my dad, she could've told her everything. I can't even tell Stefano because he'll kill me.

Great. And now I have to pretend as if everything is okay and go to this stupid dance because I promised Gray, Nate and Vince that I would go.

I'm hating this dance already.

Haley tried asking me about it multiple times when we got home but I wouldn't budge. Then when Stefano got home from work, he tried but I still wouldn't talk because I couldn't even if I wanted to.

Stefano's POV I know something is up with her, she just refuses to tell me which must mean that it is big. I wasn't only going in there to talk to her because Haley wanted me too, I was going in there to talk to her about our father.

I got another letter from him. This is like the fifth time he's mentioned about the moon meeting the stars when the winter is coldest and I have no idea what that means. All I do know is that tomorrow is December first and that means winter is closing in on us and I have to figure out what this means.

Anyways, since she refuses to talk to me, I've decided to bring in someone that I know she will talk to no matter what. Hopefully he will answer.

"Hello?" YES! I'm so glad he answered. "Nate! I need you to come over as soon as you can, something is wrong with Lydia and she refuses to talk to me about it and I know you can get it out of her." He chuckles.

"Actually I'm already here. She kind of left the mall in a rush and left her stuff so I figured that I would return it." There was a knock on the door, I looked through the peep hole and saw him so I opened it.

"I'm glad you're here. She's upstairs in her room, she hasn't come out in hours, not even to eat and you know how she feels about her food. Go up and talk to her, she'll talk to you I know it. But no funny business, my room is right next door and if I hear even the slightest bit of that I'll castrate you." He chuckled and gave me a smile and went upstairs, hopefully he can get to her.

Lydia's POV I heard a knock on the door but I didn't budge. "Go away, I told you I'm fine Stef!" The door opened anyways and I just threw the blanket over my head and grunted.

"It's not Stefano, it's Nate. You left your stuff with us at the mall so I figured after dropping everyone off I would swing by and drop your stuff off."

"Thanks. Can you put them in my closet before you leave?" I felt the bottom of my bed push down, indicating that he sat down. Great now I actually have to talk to him. Maybe he'll understand how crucial this situation is.

"I knew something was up when Piper said you left. What's wrong?" I sat up and decided to tell him. I used to tell him everything as a kid and he always knew what to say, hopefully things haven't changed too much.

Unfortunately for me, this was his response.

"Be my date to the ball." Seriously? This guy can't take a hint! "What?" I just started chuckling, he laughed as well.

"Show Brandon what he's missing out on. Don't think of it as a date date, think of it as a way to get your jerk of a boyfriend back. I'm not even giving you an option, I'm picking you up at 8." And with that he got up and left.

What the actual fuck? Well this was a pretty shitty day .————————————————————-Woah, this chapter went from 0-100 real fast. What did you think? Who do you think Blaire really likes? Are you team Nathan or team Brandon? When is Carlyle coming back? Thoughts on what Piper should do about the baby? Comment below and don't forget to vote!

Also, please forgive my typos, I'm sick and I wanted to get this uploaded because it's been about a week since I uploaded. And things might be a little different format wise in the end of this chapter versus the beginning because while I was writing I got the new update on my phone and a lot of stuff changed so if you noticed, bare with me I'm working on it. The next chapter is going to be really long and even more dramatic then this one, hope you like surprises because a big one is coming your way!

-Jen

Chapter 20- You Promised

- -

Lydia's POV"WHAT DO YOU WANT FROM ME?! I GAVE YOU EVERYTHING! JUST LEAVE ME ALONE!" I scream, he chuckles as he walks closer towards me.

"Don't you get it? You can't escape me! There are no loopholes. Just join me." I shook my head, he laughed and grabbed Haley and started stabbing her. "STOP!"

"JOIN ME ADRIANNA!" Haley shakes her head as blood starts coming out of her mouth. "L-Lydia... D-Don't do it."

"She needs the hospital-"

"She goes to the hospital when you help me kill the last member of our little family, your nephew." I shake my head as tears fall down my face. I felt a pain in my chest that was hard to explain, I couldn't breathe, I couldn't talk, I just stood there and shook my head.

"You once made me choose between two people I love and I refuse to do it again! You're a killer! Let her go!" He looks between me and Haley and he smirks.

"You're right sweetheart. I am a killer." He slit Haley's stomach, snapped her neck and threw the body to the side like it was nothing. I must have screamed louder than Lydia did in Teen Wolf when Alison died because I felt my soul leave my body.

"YOU KILLED THEM! YOU KILLED THEM ALL! I'M GONNA HUNT YOU DOWN AND I AM GOING TO KILL YOU! DO YOU HEAR ME YOU SICK FUCK?! I'M GOING TO KILL YOU!!!!" I started screaming at the top of my lungs until suddenly I passed out.

"LYDIA WAKE UP!" Stefano screamed while shaking me, I opened my eyes and gasped for air. It felt like the life was being sucked out of me. I couldn't breathe. I can't breathe.

"H-Haley! Where's Haley?!" I asked, still hyperventilating. He grabbed my hand in attempts to slow down my heartbeat, but unfortunately it didn't work.

"I'm okay Lydia! I'm right here! I just went to get your medication. It's okay, it's all okay." She grabs my hand, I shake my head and try to catch my breath.

"N-n-no. He k-killed you! I-I saw it-"

"You were having another nightmare Aide. This one is the worst I've ever seen. You just need to breathe, otherwise you will have a panic attack. You're okay, Haley's okay-"

"What about the baby?" I ask apprehensively, Haley smiles and puts her hand on her stomach. "The baby is okay Lydia. Nothing is wrong, everything is fine. You were just having a night terror. Nobody is here except for us, but I'm pretty sure the whole neighborhood heard you screaming. You sounded as if someone was getting murdered." She said with a chuckle, I look at her as a tear falls down my face.

"You were. Promise me that you're not going out tonight, I just want to make sure everything is okay because you never know with Carlyle. Besides, he doesn't know about you or the baby yet and I want to keep it that way." I guess by the look on my face and the way that I was grabbing her hand, she understood my worry for her.

"Okay. I promise." She sat next to me on the bed and started stroking my hair. She's going to be a great mom, I know it. "Nothing bad is going to happen tonight Aide. You're gonna go with your friends and have fun. Nothing bad will happen, I promise." Stefano says reassuringly, I sigh.

"It just felt so real. I was so scared."

"I know. But it's okay now, he's not hurting you, we are right here and we aren't going anywhere, I promise you. Go back to sleep, we will be right here, we're not going anywhere." I nodded and closed my eyes. It took awhile before I could actually fall asleep but I guess I did after awhile because when I woke up, the sun was out and Grayson was staring at me.

"AH!" I screamed and fell out of bed because I was startled, you would be too if you woke up to one of your best friends starting at you. It's scary. He just laughed at me.

"Sorry! I just wanted to take you out on a spa day since Piper and Blaire couldn't. You'll get your hair, nails and makeup done, and I'll take you out for breakfast, my treat. So get up, we've got a lot of work to do in such little time. You slept till 12 and the dance is at 6, we have little time to get all done so come on get up, let's go!" He pulled the blankets off of me and pulled me out of bed, I just grunted.

"I don't wanna get up!" He chuckled and shook his head. "Too bad. Now get in the shower, we leave in fifteen minutes." He skipped out the door and went downstairs as I locked the bathroom door and got in the shower. I love my friendship with Gray, it's so adventurous.

After I got out of the shower, I got dressed, towel dried my hair, brushed my teeth and headed downstairs. "I'll see you guys later." I gave Stefano and Haley big hugs and then headed into Grayson's car. This day is going to be fun. ————————————-"Alright, so spill the tea. Why did you really leave yesterday?" Gray questions while shoveling a fork full of pancakes, I chuckle and shake my head. "I talked to Piper, but she's not the problem, it's Blaire. I told Piper that I made my decision on this whole Brandon and Nathan situation and she told me that Blaire went ahead and told Grace everything and she went and told Brandon about everything and that's most likely the reason he's not talking to me so I was pissed." His mouth was hanging open, I found it so funny.

"Say something!" I said with a chuckle, he shook his head in disbelief. "Why would she do that? Unless... oh my god! Do you think she likes Brandon?"

"It's a possibility but all I have to say is this chick better back off my mans before I have to fight her- "

"So you chose Brandon!" He starts flailing his arms in the air out of excitement, the old couple in front of us starts looking at him with an angry look, he laughs. "What? My friend is in love which I'm guessing you two were so don't judge." That was enough to get them to turn around, I couldn't help but laugh at the situation.

"I wanted to choose Brandon, but if he's going to be an asshole because of something Grace told him without him asking me face to face then maybe he's not worth it. Meanwhile, Nate was there for me and he made things all weird last night-"

"Wait wait wait, rewind. Last night? What do you mean?" He questions enthusiastically, I smile. "Last night, he brought over my stuff and we talked about it and he said he would take me to the dance to make Brandon jealous and before I even could speak he said he will pick me up at 8. So I think he wants it to be a date but I don't know and I don't know what to do because Brandon is being childish."

"So now you don't know?" I shrug and sigh, the look in his eyes said it's all, he was annoyed. "Maybe I'll just give them both up. My father already knows about Brandon, if he knew that Nate was my childhood best friend, I don't know what he would do. I love them both, but maybe it's best for everyone if I just stopped."

"What are you trying to say?" He questions with a worried expression on his face, I shake my head. "I had a horrible dream last night and I'm afraid something really bad is going to happen. So I guess I'm saying that in order to protect the ones I love, I'm going to go away for awhile. At least until things with my dad cool down-"

"What?! Lydia that's crazy! You can't run from your problems, you need to face them. You are going to get the happy ending you deserve, and I am going to make sure of it. I don't care how long it takes. If you leave you might as well take me with you because my dad is a P.I and I'll find you and bring you back whether you like it or not." I can see he cares. But I don't think he sees what could happen if I stay.

"People have died because of me Gray, If something like that were to happen to any of you, I couldn't forgive myself." He grand my hand and shakes his head. "Nobody is going to die except for your father, and we will make sure of that. Don't think about that, at least not today. Today is all about fun so come on, let's go get your hair and makeup done."

"You're a great friend, you know that?" I say with a smile, he smiles back and does a little bow. "I try my best. Now let's go, I booked your appointment for two o'clock."

The day went by surprisingly quick, I guess time flies when you're having fun. Next time I'm sad I'm going to go to Gray, forget Brandon or Nate, Gray can actually make me laugh and doesn't try to flirt with me in the process. I can gladly say that he's the coolest guy ever and that he is my best guy friend.

Before we knew it, it was eight and Nathan was downstairs like he promised. Gray decided that he was going to be my date as well to make sure Nate doesn't try anything which I thought was hilarious.

Haley of course had to have a photoshoot and took about a million pictures of the three of us but we didn't mind, it was pretty fun. I even took a picture with Stefano and then we got in Nates car and drove to the dance.

Once we arrived, I was in awe. The decorations were beautiful, the music was actually good and basically the whole town was there. When I caught Piper's eye, she looked me up and down before squealing. "OOOH GIRL YOU LOOK SO GOOD!"

"Me? Look at you! You look amazing! And you did a great job planning this thing like I'm speechless this is so cool." She smiles and did a hair flip which made me chuckle. She looked at Nate and then back at me and smirked. "So is this a date-"

"It's a triple single date." Gray interrupts defensively, Piper starts laughing. "Alright, cool. I'll tell Brandon and Vince that you guys are here, I want you guys to perform a song tonight." I looked at her with my eyes wide.

"What? I've never sang in front of anyone before-"

"Channel your energy into the song. You can sing any song you like! Gray agreed to play guitar, Vince plays drums and I got Brandon to agree to play keyboard. Please?" She put her hands together and gave me those puppy dog eyes that she knows I can't resist. I roll my eyes. "Fine! When?"

"In about five minutes. Go backstage and get yourselves situated!" Before I could even protest, she pushed me through the crowd of people and into the dressing room backstage where I came face to face with Brandon and saw Vince.

"Piper forced you guys into this too?" I question, Vince chuckles and nods while Brandon shakes his head. "I agreed because I have to talk to you and you've been avoiding me-"

"I think you have that backwards. You're the one who has been avoiding me. I just gave you your space because I thought you were mad." He smiles and shakes his head. "Why would I be mad?"

"I thought Grace might have told you something about me." I reply while looking at the floor nervously, he shakes his head. "What would she have said?"

Tell him. Tell him now.

"I have to tell you something-"

"Hey lovebirds, hate to break this up but we are on. You are going to sing the perfect song for Blaire and Grace. It's one of the new Taylor Swift songs, it's called This Is Why We Can't Have Nice Things." Vince says with a smirk, I smile wide as we walk on stage.

"Hello everybody, Piper said we could perform a song so we decided to sing this one. If you've ever had a fake friend, this ones for you." I looked at Blaire as the music started, I was smirking the whole time.

[There should be a GIF or video here. Update the app now to see it.]

When we were done playing and got off stage, a lot of people clapped but Piper's dad didn't look so happy. I don't understand why though because we kept the music clean, there were no bad words in it. It's a good song, why is he so grouchy?

"Your dad does not look happy." I say to Brandon, he shrugs. "He's never happy. That's just his face."

"Guys we did great! We should form a band!" Gray says enthusiastically, I shake my head and chuckle. "Maybe when this whole thing with my father is over-"

"LYDIA!" Piper shouts as she runs over to me, I look at her with an annoyed look. "I was talking Piper, what is it?"

"I need to talk to you, it's urgent." Before I could even protest, she was already pulling me through the crowd of people and into the bathroom. She made sure nobody was in there before she locked the door and started panicking.

"What's wrong Piper? Talk to me." I could see that she was about to freak out, but if I don't know what it is over I can't help her. "It's Nathan. He got into a fight with Grace and she said she was going to release everything! We need to stop her-"

"Let her. She's going to tell everyone anyways." She shook her head and grabbed my shoulders. "Listen to me Lydia! She is going to release everything and she has evidence. You need to talk to Nate, I'll talk to Blaire, hopefully she can get Grace to stop this madness."

Now I was mad, no, I was pissed.

Anger was fueling so fast through my body I could feel it in my veins. There is no way that I will have my secret blown. I need to cover my tracks.

I ran out of the bathroom to find Nathan, once I found him I firmly grabbed his arm and said "we need to talk." He knew what I was talking about because he started apologizing, I wouldn't have it.

"I'm sorry! She was talking bad about you and-"

"I told you in the beginning of the year that I could handle this problem myself. That's what got us into this mess in the first place, you were trying to protect me but you might have just killed me in the process. If my father finds out about this or this goes viral, we are all as good as dead and it'll be your fault!"

"I did it because I love you!" I was so angry that I slapped him across the face and stormed away to find Grayson. He saw how angry and worried I looked so he gave me a sympathetic look. "Lydia, what's wrong?"

"Everything! You need to get Brandon out of here before-"

"Excuse me everyone, I would like to make an announcement. In this town, we all know each other, but we all have our secrets. However, there is one secret that is especially different from all of ours and that is the secret of our newest family, the Stones. I'm only sharing this because we all have a right to know who and why this family is here. The Stone family are a bunch of liars. Their last name isn't even Stone! It's Daniels. I did my research and I found information about a little house fire that killed Lydia's mother and sister, but nothing about the rest of the family except for the fathers." She started pulling up pictures of me in the past.

"This is Adrianna Samuels."

"This is Kate Georgsson"

"This is Ashley Davis."

"This is Alison Carters"

"This is Morgan Sage."

"And this is Lydia Stone. All of these people are like her alter ego. If she's lying about her name, what else could she be lying about? You all deserve to know. First off, she's a drunk slut who sleeps with anyone who's willing. Second, she acts all tough but I can see that she's basically pissing her pants right now. Oh! I forgot the best one! Brandon I really hope you're listening for this one. In Vegas, she got married to Nathan at some cheap wedding chapel-"

"That's enough Grace! Look everybody, I know your shocked but there is a reason behind all of this. To sum it up really short, I am in the witness protection program. My mother and sister were murdered and we were sent into protection. We were told to change our names and identities for the sake of not being found. So there's the big secret! Grace probably just killed me so thanks a lot Grace!" I ran off stage with tears in my eyes. I had to find Brandon.

Stefano's POVI spent the day re-reading all of these letters that our father sent us, hoping that something would click in my head and it did.

I frantically searched for my car keys and kissed Haley goodbye. "Where are you going?" She asks apprehensively, I shook my head.

"I have to warn Lydia."

I hope I'm not too late.

Lydia's POVOnce I found Brandon, I saw he was fueled with anger. "B, I know your mad-"

"Mad? Ha funny. Mad would be an understatement Lydia, I'm furious! How could you? I t told you things that I could never tell anyone else, I trusted you, I opened up to you, I fucking changed for you! And for what?! For you to spit it all in my face?!" I shake my head as tears fall down my face.

"No! It's not like that! I'm in love with you-"

"Don't you dare say that word. You don't have a right to say that word. You don't love me and you never did! If you loved me then you would've have gotten married to one of my best friends behind my back!"

"But you don't understand"

"Oh I understand clearly Lydia. What, was this all some joke? Let's try to get him to trust me, maybe I can get him to fall for me! Right? I loved you more than I have ever loved anyone before, I let you into my home and I protected you multiple times all for nothing."

I shake my head as tears continue to stream down my face. "Brandon-"

"Don't text me. Don't call me. Don't even talk to me. I don't EVER want to see your face again! I hope your father finds you and takes you back to the hell hole you came from." With that said, he stormed off into the crowd of people that were watching our fight, I broke down. I was so upset and so angry that I screamed and punched a hole into the wall.

I was going to keep going but my phone started ringing. It was Stefano.

"What?" I snapped while answering. "Lydia listen carefully. You have to get out of there." The panic in his voice scared me, my heart started to race.

"Stefano, what's wrong? Why do you sound worried?"

"I'm coming up the block now, just listen. Get out now. The moon shit that he's been saying in his letters, I figured it out. That means today. He's here Lydia, you need to leave that party now!"

"Oh my god. I'm on my way out, I'll see you in the car." Piper found me right as I hung up the phone and she saw the look on my face. It was pure fear. "Lydia? Lydia talk to me, what's wrong?"

"Everything. I-I have to go." She grabbed my arm and chuckled. "What? That's ridiculous-"

"Piper. I need you to let me go before I punch you. I need to leave now or everyone in here is going to die."

"What are you talking about?" She asks apprehensively, I shake my head and try not to hyperventilate. "He's here. My brother just called me, he said that the moon meets the stars crap that my father has been saying in his letters means today. I need to get out of here right now."

"I'll go with you-"

"No, stay in here where it's safe. Get Grayson, Vince, Blaire, Nate and Brandon and lock yourselves in the bathroom. I'll call you when it's safe to come out but please, no matter what you hear, do not open that door. Promise me." She nods fast. There was a look of shock on her face, I feel so bad for springing this on her. "Okay. I'll do it. Stay safe." She gives me a bear hug, I return it.

We parted ways and I started walking out, I was about to call Stefano but I heard the sound of a speeding car and I panicked. I froze when I saw my father driving with a gun pointed at me.I dropped my phone, closed my eyes and waited for the pain.

"LYDIA!" I opened my eyes when the shots stopped firing and the car was nowhere to be found but I didn't feel any pain. I opened my eyes to see Stefano on the ground screaming in pain.

"NO! HELP! SOMEBODY PLEASE HELP!" I couldn't even use my phone because it broke when I dropped it. Please someone help.

A bunch of people from the party came out, I was staring at Stefano's eyes. His face started turning pale, his lips started turning blue. "You have to stay with me. You can't die! You promised nothing bad would happen!"

"M-mom told me t-t-to do whatever I h-had to do in order to p-protect-t you." He said with a smile. That was before he started coughing up blood. "She didn't tell you to take a bullet for me. Come on Stef, you have to stay with me. If you're not going to stay for me then stay for Haley and the baby. They need you! I need you! Please." His eyes started closing and his breathing got heavier.

"No! Stef! Stefano wake up! You can't die. You promised nothing bad would happen! You said everything would be okay! This is not okay! I need you! Please don't leave me!"

He grabbed my hand and smiled. "W-we will m-meet again. P-promise m-m-me y-you'll find h-him and k-kill him." I nodded fast and squeezed his hand.

"I promise. I promise you I will do whatever it takes for as long as it takes. But you're going to be okay, the ambulance is on its way! Everything will be fine." He shakes his head. "T-tell Haley I L-L-Love h-her."

He coughed one last time and he stopped breathing. I screamed so loud that I'm pretty sure the whole town could hear me. No amount of crying is going to bring him back. I want revenge. I want blood.

Pipers POV"Piper what the hell are we doing in here?" Brandon questions angrily, I sigh. "I'm afraid I have some bad news. Lydia told me to lock us all in here because her father found them-."

"We have to go after her." Brandon interrupted, I shake my head. He really must care for her. Minutes ago he was screaming at her and now he's overprotective of her. "We can't. Lorenzo is picking her up now, she went outside-". I was interrupted by the sound of gunshots and screams for help.

Brandon ran for the door, unlocked it and started running outside, we followed him. As bad as it sounds, I sighed in relief when it wasn't her lying on the ground.

"Lydia, what happened?" Gray asks, she looks up at us with tears streaming down her face and a look of pure hatred in her eyes.

"He's dead. Stefano is dead." Holy shit. ————————————————————————-Awe poor Lydia. What do you think she's going to do now that he is dead? What's going to happen to Haley and the baby? Will they get revenge? Comment what you think and don't forget to vote!

-Jen

Chapter 21- This Is Not The Answer

Lydia's POVWhen we got to the hospital, I already knew he was dead and that made me numb inside. The doctors said that there was a chance he could still survive but I think they were just giving us false hope.

I feel numb. I can't eat, I can't move, I have this huge pain in my chest and all these different scenarios are going through my head.

What am I going to tell Haley?

One day this baby is going to ask us what happened to it's father and we aren't even going to know how to tell him.

How am I going to get my revenge?

Revenge and hatred were the only things on my mind. I want my fathers head for what he's done. I want him to suffer like everyone else did. I want him to be able to feel fear when he looks at me. I want him to feel the pain that I've been feeling for years. I want him dead. And I am going to kill him.

The minute I saw Haley my heart stopped. "Lydia! W-what happened?" She gives me a hug as tears fall down her face. "It was Carlyle." I said viciously, she shook her head.

"No. I don't understand! He was fine when he left!" Her voice started to sound hoarse from the crying, I told her to sit down because it's not good for the baby.

When the doctor came out, I knew what he was going to tell us. But I was worried for the sake of Haley and the baby, I don't know how much more of this she can take.

"Is he okay? What's going on?" Haley asks the doctor frantically, the doctor shakes his head. "One of the bullets hit a major artery and we tried everything we could. Unfortunately, as we were about to stitch him up, we lost him. I'm so sorry for your loss." I shook my head as tears fell down my face.

"No... no he can't be dead. He was just trying to save me! It should've been me! No. He's okay, he's not dead-"

"Lydia... He's gone." Haley had to try to snap me out of my denial phase, I just couldn't. I know I shouldn't show that I'm breaking for the sake of Haley but I broke down hard.

He was just here.

He was alive.

And now he's dead because of me.

I knew I shouldn't have gone to that stupid dance. If I wouldn't have gone then he could've still been alive.

It's all my fault. Pipers POV"Why are we just sitting here?! She needs us! We should be over there with her!" Brandon protests, Gray shakes his head. "She told us not to."

"Bullshit! Her brother just got killed! She needs us right now-"

"And what could we do for her huh? Gray, Vince and I are the only ones that have been nice to her! Nate, you told Grace to piss off so she told the whole wold Lydia's secret. Brandon, you told Lydia to get out of your life. And Blaire, you have been a bitch to her the past couple weeks and you went and told your psycho bitch of a sister everything! All of a sudden you all care because she's grieving? That's what I call bullshit! If she wouldn't have been fighting with all of you then she wouldn't have had all of this pain inside of her. She probably blames herself for this and all the self hatred is going to result in something huge. So if one of you want to go talk to her then go right ahead, don't expect her to forgive you."

Brandon grabbed his stuff and slammed the front door shut. I knew he was going to talk to her, let's just hope he's ready to see her like that.

Brandon's POVI need to talk to her. I need to apologize. I need to say I'm sorry for her loss. I need to say so many things but there's probably no chance she's even gonna talk to me.

I rang the doorbell and saw Haley with bags and dark circles under her eyes. She looked awful, not that I blame her though considering the situation, but I just feel so bad.

"Lydia isn't here. Try looking for her at the park, that's her safe place." She slammed the door in my face before I could even say anything to her.

I ran to the park and finally found Lydia lying on the grass with her eyes closed. "What are you doing here?" I ask while looking down at her, she cringes at the sound of my voice.

"I'm seeing what it's like to be dead. It seems promising." She replies with a chuckle, I look at her uneasily. That was until I realized what was really going on. "Are you drunk?"

"Are you drunk?" She mimics while sitting up and looking in the other direction. She doesn't even want to look at me. "Lydia, look at me please-"

"Why? So you could tell me how much you hate me and how badly you want me to go away? Well I hate me too so thanks." She opens the flask she was holding and takes another swing of whatever was in it. I shake my head.

"I don't hate you-"

"That's bullshit and you know it Brandon. You wouldn't even give me a chance to explain myself before telling me how much you hated me. I actually loved you and I was going to tell you what really happened in Vegas but you didn't want to hear it. I hate myself! And I know you hate me too." She finally turned around and I melted at the look on her face. She looked so pale, and her makeup was all over her face from crying, I feel so bad.

"I was just angry Lydia. I'm not mad anymore, I don't hate you." She starts laughing and shakes her head. "Yes you do. See that's the secret, everyone hates me! My own damn father hates me. It should've been me that died, not Stefano!"

She went to take another drink but I slapped it out of her hands. "This isn't the answer! Drinking is not the answer to your problems-"

"Well maybe I'm not drinking to solve them! Maybe I'm drinking to end them!" This time a tear slipped down my face. "So that's it huh? You're gonna let that bastard win? What about Haley? What about the baby? That baby is going to grow up without a father and it is all your fathers fault. They need you! Don't take the cowards way out. Fight until you can't fight anymore, you once told me that was what your mother said in the letter she left you before she died. So stop sitting here and trying to kill yourself! Get the fuck up and do something about it! Fight back."

"Don't you get it? He will kill everyone I love! He did it before and he's doing it again. I've found out way too many things this month that I probably shouldn't even know and I feel like I'm going to explode-"

"Good. Now use that anger and sadness to fight back. Do whatever you have to in order to fight back. Fight until you can't fight anymore. Get your ass up and start fighting. If not for me or your friends, then fight for Haley and the baby, fight for your life, and fight for all those you have lost." I know I probably shouldn't be giving her this advice but she needs to hear it. I refuse to watch her slowly kill herself. She needs closure and this might be the only way to do it.

"They are all dead because I let them in. I can't afford to let that happen again. I need to let go of the past in order to win this." Wait, that's not what I meant!

"You're right. I have to fight back and that is exactly what I plan on doing. I have to go, goodbye." She gave me a long passionate kiss before making a run for it.

What the fuck did I just do?

Lydia's POVI knew what I had to do. I'm going to do this. Enough tears, enough crying, it's time to channel my anger.

I ran upstairs and got my duffle bag. I had to start writing letters again. I have to do this. I'm going to say goodbye.

I got in my car and started driving. When I finally reached my destination it was six in the morning, hopefully this will work. Otherwise everything was for nothing.

I rang the doorbell and a few minutes later the door swung open. "I need your help."

———————————————————————————-Sorry for the cliffhanger guys, this chapter was sort of supposed to be a part 2 of the last chapter which is why it was so short. But anyways, what do you thing is happening? Where did Lydia go? What is she planning? Who was at the door? Was it an old friend? Poor Haley, what's going to happen to her and the baby? Comment what you think, and don't forget to vote!

~Jen

Chapter 22- Gone

(GIF of Haley)Haley's POVI heard Lydia come in at about five in the morning so I decided that I was going to let her sleep, she needs it after the night she had.

Truth is Lydia blames herself, which is why last night I let her go to her spot. She has always had a thing for parks, whenever she was upset she would go to one and just sit there for hours. Stefano would eventually go and get her because he worried so much but sometimes I convinced him to let her be.

I don't know how I'm gonna do this on my own. This baby is going to grow up without a father and one day he's going to ask me or Lydia where his dad is and I'll have to tell him everything and the thought of that is killing me.

I figured that I would make her some breakfast to help cheer her up a little. However when I called her down she didn't answer, so I figured I would go up and wake her.

My heart sunk when I saw that she wasn't there. Instead, there was a note on her bed. I started reading it and knew that I had to get all of her friends together and tell them. I went through my phone and scrolled down to see Piper's number, I pressed call and she answered with sympathy.

"Hi Haley, how are you doing?" Even though she couldn't see me, I shook my head and tried to hold back my tears. "Not so good. Um I need you to text everyone and tell them to come to the house, even that bitch Grace. Lydia's missing and there's something I need to show you."

"Oh my god, yeah we will be right over. I'll call them now, see you soon. Stay strong." She hung up the phone and within an hour everyone was in my living room with concerned feelings.

"You've all probably heard by now the news I told Piper, and in that case you have heard correct. I woke up this morning thinking Lydia needed some time to herself, however when I went to go surprise her with her favorite breakfast I saw she wasn't in her room and I panicked. That was until I saw the note she left. I called you all here because I read it and in the note she addresses all of you and I think that in order to make peace with this you need to read it." They all nodded and we read the letter together.

Dear Everyone,   I'm tired of grieving. I'm tired of everything. I have found out so many things that make me just want everything to stop, and if it weren't for my talk with Brandon everything would've stopped for me. When my mother died, she left us a note telling us to fight until we can't fight anymore and that is exactly what I intend to do. I am going to go away for awhile, I don't want you guys to look for me, I don't want anyone to find me unless I come back here.   Haley, I want your baby to have the best life it can ever have. Which is why I can not be in its life while my father is still breathing and hunting me down. The baby already has to grow up fatherless, I couldn't live with myself if something were to happen to you too. I want you to promise me that one day you will tell him/her about me and that I loved them very much. Haley, you have been the best sister I could ever ask for and I want to thank you for that.   Piper, you never failed to make me laugh or even help me with my boy drama. You have been the best girl friend I have ever had and I love you for that. Promise me that while I'm gone you will take care of everyone. Make sure nobody goes off the deep end and especially make sure that nobody comes to find me. If news gets out about where I am, I'm as good as dead. You and Gray are the glue of the group, so please, do me a favor and make sure that you all stay close no matter what. Don't let this change anything.   Gray and Vince, you guys always tried to help Piper meddle in my love life which I thought was the greatest. I was glad to see that people cared about me, and for once I actually felt normal so thank you guys for that. Vince, you take care of Piper for me. She's really gonna need you after all of this. And Gray, I don't want you to make your dad find me. Nobody can find me until this is over.   Nate, what can I say? You were my first best friend, and you never gave up on me. If as you grew up, I was stuck in your head. I want to thank you for getting me out of trouble as a kid and for fake marrying me in order to save Vince and Piper from that evil wedding chapel. I've had some of my most embarrassing moments with you but you never made me feel out of place for them so thank you.   Blaire, even though you were acting like a bitch these past few weeks, we were great friends in the beginning so I want to thank you for always making me laugh, and teasing me about Brandon from day one. If it weren't for you pushing my true feelings about Brandon out, I probably wouldn't have fallen for him so thank you for that as well. Grace, you have been a bitch to me since day one but that's okay because I want to thank you anyways. If it weren't for you spilling my secrets at the ball then I wouldn't be where I am right now and most importantly, I wouldn't be fighting back. I don't know what it is but when I got here I was this scared little girl and then you started being bitchy and that brought the fire out in me. If it wasn't for you then I would still be that little girl who runs away from her problems instead of facing them so a huge thank you goes out to you Grace.   Brandon, I owe you an apology. I snapped at you last night and I was a complete bitch to you when we first met, however you never gave up on me. You turned your life around for me and that actually made me feel something other than useless. You made me feel like me again and I will always love you for that. You always made me feel better when I was upset and you made me realize something last night. You made me realize that instead of cowering in fear, I actually have to get off my ass and do something about it. You have seen me at my worst and yet somehow even then you still managed to bring me out of my slump. I was going to tell you at the ball that you are the one I wanted to be with. I love you with all my heart and nothing will ever change that.   I love all of you (maybe not Grace) in different ways and I want you to know that it's because of my love for all of you that I am doing this right now. Once upon a time there was a scared little girl running from the dragon. The story ends with the girl killing the dragon. I'm writing these letters in case I don't make it back. My father always had a trick up his sleeve, but now I have a few tricks of my own and I'm ready to fight back. Thank you all for having such an impact on my life. ~Lydia

"So that's it? We just go on with our lives? I can't pretend that she was never here. I can't pretend that I never loved her. So what the fuck are we supposed to do? Sit around and wait?" Brandon says angrily. I knew that he was going to have a hard time with this.

"If there's one thing I've learned about her it's that she's a fighter. She'll be back. It may take awhile but she will be back." Grace replies reassuringly, causing everyone to smile. "What?" She snaps, Piper chuckles.

"I think that is the nicest thing you've ever said." Piper teases, Grace rolls her eyes. "I may be a bitch to her but that's only because I'm jealous of her."

Even I was surprised she said that. I mean here we have the queen bee who pretends to hate everyone, yet the truth is she actually likes them. It's priceless.

"Never thought I'd here those words come out of your mouth." Blaire adds on with a smirk, Grace rolls her eyes again as everyone laughs. The happiness soon turned to sorrow when they realized why Lydia really left.

"We need to find her-"

"She told us not to Brandon-"

"I don't give a shit about what she said. I want to have a future with her and that means having her alive. I love her! And I'm not gonna just sit around and wait for something to happen. Gray, you said your dad was a P.I so maybe he can trace her phone and we can look for her." Everyone looked at him with wide smiles on their faces, he grunts.

"Why are you guys so happy?! She's missing!" He protests, I cross my arms and smirk. "You said you could have a future with her." I tease, his face goes blank as he chuckles.

"No I didn't. I said I wanna find her, so are we going to do this or not?" He snaps. Oh the wonderful world of denial! After everything blows over, I am making it my mission to get those two officially together, maybe even eventually engaged.

"We can't Brandon. Whatever this is, she's doing it for a reason-"

"She's gonna get herself killed!" Vince shakes his head in disagreement. "No. Grace is right, she's a fighter. She's angry and she's going to use that anger to fight back."

"If you guys wont find her then I will-"

"No you won't Brandon. Look, we all love her but there is a reason she left and that reason is so she could come back once everything with her father is done-"

"Wait so she's going to kill him? That makes her a psycho!" Grace protests, we all shake our heads but I decided to speak on Lydia's behalf. "She's doing what has to be done. Lydia's father was a monster Grace. You may think you know everything but you don't. Carlyle killed the rest of her family so her and Stefano ran for their lives with the help of their uncle. Technically that was their witness protection. Everywhere they went he hunted and killed everyone who got in his way which included friends, family friends, and even boyfriends. I was lucky that he never found out about me after he killed my brother Wesley. So yes Grace, she will kill him if she has to."

She deserved to know who she has been dealing with all this time. She deserves to know the truth.

"Oh my god... I had no idea-"

"Well what the fuck did you think it meant Grace? A person doesn't just change their name and whole persona just for the fun of it." Brandon snaps, she shakes her head.

"How the hell was I supposed to know?!" She shouts back, Brandon laughs. "Because it's not rocket science! If you actually would've put two and two together then you would've figured it out. But instead you were too bitchy to even ask!"

"I know! And I said I was sorry!"

"You should be sorry! If you didn't do any of this bullshit then maybe her father wouldn't have found out where she was and she wouldn't have run away! It's ALL YOUR FAULT-"

"ENOUGH! Fighting about this is not gonna bring Lydia back! She's gone and your all going to have to learn to deal with it!" It was official. Grayson had snapped. Everyone went silent.

"Grayson is right. You guys are going to have to pretend that you don't care and act like everything is normal, at least for now because you never know when Carlyle is going to make an unexpected visit or if he's still here. We can't slip up. Let's make a pact. No matter what we are doing and where we are, we will not give up on Lydia. She has a plan, and if that plan goes wrong she's going to need us. I suggest that all of you guys take self defense classes just in case. Promise me." They all nod in agreement.

"We promise."

Chapter 23-Did You See Her

Brandon's POVAs the weeks went by, I only missed Lydia more. I started sending her voice memos everyday to keep her up on what was going on and she listened to them for awhile but then weeks turned into months and eventually the messages got left of delivered and I stopped. I know I shouldn't have, but I feel incomplete without her.

She brought out the best in me and she saw a good side in me that I thought was gone. I plan to do the same for her. I just wish that she would come back already. I know it's not safe, but I will do just about anything to see her at this point. It's been 2 months and everyone has been trying to act normal however it's not working.

Grace started being nice to everyone, Blaire went back to her quiet ways, Piper told everyone that she was pregnant so her and Vince moved in together and I guess they are going to raise the baby together. Gray is working really hard to get me and Nate to be close again which is kind of like his distraction for all of this.

As for myself, well I'm a mess. In class I end up spacing out and thinking about Lydia, and then I end up looking at her seat which only gets me into trouble but I don't care. I miss her so much, everyday feels worse and worse and the only thing playing in my mind is that I hope she's not dead. I couldn't handle that, it would kill me. Which is why I am doing my best to stay on the right track so when she does come back I can prove to her that I am responsible enough to actually commit to her and have a real relationship with her.

"Cheer up man. We have our first game in ten minutes." Vince says about basketball as an attempt to make me feel better. I shake my head and sigh. "I can't. No matter how hard I try, I always end up thinking about her. Everywhere I go, it's like she's in my head. I pass the park and I remember the night she left. I pass the cemetery and I remember when she took me to see my mother's grave. And then I pass by her locker and I think of just seeing her face. I just wish I could see her one more time."

"Wow. I never thought you could ever care for someone this much, but you're whipped." He comments with a smile, I nod.

"I know, and I'm not ashamed of it. I love her with everything I've got and I just wish she would come back. At least to see her nephew be born, she deserves to at least see him even if it's only once." Haley found out the gender of the baby about a week ago and I couldn't have been happier for her. Now when that boy grows up she is going to see a little bit of her husband everyday with her, it's beautiful.

"She can't. Whatever it is that she's doing and wherever the hell it is that she went she's going for a reason and that reason is to protect us all-"

"But I can protect her-"

"Not from this Brandon. Yes, you're a boxer but this guy is a trained assassin and you're no match for him. The business he's in is dangerous. Why do you think my dad divorced my mom? She was in the mafia and he wanted no part of it and that's what got him killed. This isn't some video game

Brandon, it's our lives. It's her life. We can't just hit replay when one of us ends up dead because this is reality. I know you love her but you have to respect her decision. And yes, I know it feels like it's been forever but she will be back. Maybe not now, but eventually and I'm sorry but you just have to deal with it."

In that moment I felt awful. I haven't been taking this thing seriously because I've only thought about myself and not anyone else. I've only been focusing on how her leaving effected me, I haven't thought about how this effected Haley, Gray or even Vince for example since he has first hand experience with this stuff.

"You're right. I've been selfish and I'm sorry. Let's focus on the game tonight, we are going to kick some ass." If I am going to be sad about it, I might as well keep it to myself in order not to make everyone depressed and sad. I just have to focus on my school work if I am going to be able to be that guy she wants to spend the rest of her life with.

When the game started, coach had everyone convinced that this game was going to be a good one and he was right. It was the end of half time and we were up by 9 points. As the game continued on, everything got more rough. This one player started to mess with my head which got me angry.

"What's wrong Santiago? Are you afraid?" He said with a chuckle, I smirked. "No Lawrence, why would I be afraid of a chicken legged creep like you?"

"Ha good one. You make me laugh! No I was talking about your girlfriend, she's in witness protection which must mean she's done some pretty awful and rough things. Speaking of rough things, I bet she's a goddess in bed-"

"Shut up."

"Oh what's the matter? Is little Brando getting mad?" The smirk on his face made me want to punch him, but I looked over at Vince who only gave me a glare which I knew was code for "don't do anything stupid or I will castrate you" and I knew that I had to back down.

"No because I understand why you're so bitter. You're just a scared, whiny guy who is so insecure to a point where he has to bully and pick on everyone who gets in his way. But I don't blame you, I would be too if my girlfriend caught me doing it with her brother-" Before I could push his buttons anymore, he pushed me to the ground and I hit my head. For a second, as I went down I could've sworn I saw Lydia in the crowd, but that is probably my concussion talking because that's all I remember before I blacked out.

"Brandon? Brandon wake up!" All I remember is waking up in the nurses office with a really bad headache. I looked at Vince to see that he had a smile on his face.

"Thank god you're awake-"

"Did you see her?" I cut him off in the middle of his sentence. I need to make sure that I am not losing it and going crazy. "See who?"

"Lydia. I saw her before I blacked out, she was there!" He shakes his head. "Dude, you hit your head really hard. And considering that we were talking about her before the game, your sub-conscience was creating an image of something that wasn't there."

"No. She was there, I know what I saw, I'm not crazy!" He gives me a sympathetic look as I protest and carry on. "She wasn't there. It was just us. Lawrence hit you pretty hard, it was a fragment of the imagination."

As if hallucinating seeing Lydia wasn't enough, Piper came in with a worried look on her face. "Guys! It's Lydia's dad... he got Grayson." My eyes went wide and I felt like my heart was going to jump out of my chest, I could see that Vince was scared too.

"What do you mean he got him?" Vince asks apprehensively, she hands us a letter. Damn this guy is like obsessed with writing letters, it's crazy.

To whomever it may concern, I've been watching and looking around and I have yet to see my daughter. And until I see her I will take every one of you like little targets and use you as pin cushions. First on my list is the guitar player. I know my daughter is close with him, but who I am really after for is Brandon and Haley. Can't have any of my family left standing. First is Grayson, then it'll be the others that she loves most in order. Bring her to me and the guitar player won't get seriously hurt. If I don't see her by midnight Friday, it'll be the end for Grayson, and the end for all of you. So for your sake, FIND HER! -Carlyle

"We have to warn Haley. Now that she and the baby are in danger, we need to get her out of here and as far away as possible-"

"No. We need to call uncle Tim. If she's not with him, he will know how to get in touch with her, and we need the both of them right now. They can end this." She whipped out her phone and dialed the number, she made sure to put it on speaker so we could all hear but it went straight to voicemail.

"Tim, it's Haley. Look, I don't know if Lydia is with you or not but I want you to be aware that if she is with you, we need both you and her to come back here. Carlyle is after all of us, he's even after the baby... we got another letter and he kidnapped our friend Grayson. In it he said that if Lydia isn't back by midnight on Friday he will kill him and come after all of us one by one. Please, you have to help us." Before she could say anything else, the voicemail got cut off.

Great. Now we are just a bunch of sitting ducks. "Well what do we do know?" Blaire asks with a tone of worry in her voice, Haley's face went from angry to serious. "We fight."

Chapter 24- Fight Until You Can't Fight Anymore

Lydia's POV (2 months earlier)I got in my car and started driving. When I finally reached my destination it was six in the morning, hopefully this will work. Otherwise everything was for nothing.

I rang the doorbell and a few minutes later the door swung open. "I need your help." I knew that the chances of him taking me in were very low because it would bring my father back into his life after he's tried his hardest to get out of it.

"It's been five years, I've been telling you and your brother to call me if you needed anything and you said no. So now you want my help?" He teases with a chuckle, I roll my eyes. "I know it's early in the morning, and I know the chances of you going full out to help are-"

"Adrianna, I'm your uncle. I'll always help you. What's going on?" He questions while letting me inside, I walk into the living room and sit down. A tear falls down my face.

"It's Stefano... he's dead. Carlyle killed him." His facial expression turned blank. "When?"

"Last night. Carlyle was trying to shoot me but Stefano jumped in the way. He died in the hospital... I am here because I am done running. I want to fight back until I can't fight anymore. I want Carlyle dead, and I know you can help me."

A tear slips down his face as well, but within minutes his sad face turned back to aggravated and normal. He nods. "I can help you. But first I have to show you something that Stefano made a couple years back." My eyes went wide as I followed him into the basement. I looked around and was shocked at what I saw.

"What is this place?" I question curiously, he doesn't even look at me as he replies "my training facility."

"What do you mean training facility?" I ask again, he sighs as he gets whatever he was looking for. He motions for me to sit on the chair. "I was once in the business that your father is in. It was a very dangerous business, still is to this day. Carlyle and I were always in the business, ever since we were teenagers and he fell in love with your mom. Then they got married and he managed to get out of the business and your parents had your brother and sister. Fast forward to you. This is the part that you are not going to like. One night when Carlyle was on a business trip and the kids were at camp, your mother and I had a little fling. About a month or two later she found out that she was pregnant-"

"Wait. Are you saying that Carlyle is not my father? Are you saying that you're my father?" He nods, my mouth hung open in shock. After all that's happened my head feels like it's gonna explode. First Piper being pregnant, then Blaire hating me, then Grace telling everyone my secret, then Brandon hating me, then Stefano's murder, and now this. I don't know how much more of this I can take.

"She was going to tell them, but I was in a really bad place and I was in some trouble with the guys in the business and I thought that it would be best if your mother and Carlyle raised you because at the time he was a good man. But as you grew up, I saw that the colors in his eyes had changed and he was slowly reverting back to his own ways. He found out the truth when he came back into the business and I got out. I told your mother that it wasn't safe anymore and that she needed to take the kids and leave but she wouldn't listen. The night your mother and sister were murdered was the night that she was going to get you out."

"But Carlyle figured it out and by then it was too late. Your mother had a feeling something like that was going to happen so she wrote you that letter telling you that if anything happened to come to me and I would help you. So I helped you and Stefano get away. Shortly after that, I built this training facility because I knew that one day you two would get the courage to stop fighting." More tears started streaming down my face. I couldn't believe it. My father is my uncle and my uncle is my biological father. This is crazy.

"Stefano knew didn't he? Is that why he never wanted me to ask questions? Is that why he was overprotective of what I did?" I started to get angry, but I knew my anger wouldn't be worth it. I have to take this anger and keep it towards my goal in defeating Carlyle.

"This video will answer all of your questions." He put the video tape into the television and pressed play. I almost lost it when I saw Stefano as Lorenzo. When the hell was this taken?

"I don't really know how to start these things but um hi uncle Tim. I know you haven't seen us in awhile and I want to apologize for that but hopefully you will understand why we had to lose all contact with anyone from our past. Anyways, I am making this because Adrianna has been having really bad anxiety and panic attacks to a point where she has night terrors and starts scratching herself and screaming. I recently received a couple of letters from Carlyle. He's found us again. And I am petrified to tell Aide because I'm afraid of what she will do to herself. Luckily her new friends have been there to support her and help her be somewhat calmer but that is beyond the point. I am sending you this because I know Carlyle is planning something and I am willing to do whatever it takes to protect her. I know that you are her father and that is okay because you have been more of a father to us our whole lives then Carlyle ever has. Which is why I know that if something were to happen to me, she will go to you. So I am counting on you to help her. And if she's with you right now, play the next tape."

He knew all along. He knew that Carlyle was watching us from day one of being here and he didn't do anything because of me. I'm the reason he's dead, and I hate myself for it. Tim put the next recording on and it cut to the morning of the winter ball. I know because those were the pajamas he was wearing that morning.

"Hey sis. If you're watching this then that means that you were right and something bad happened. I was going through all of the letters that Carlyle sent us and I finally figured out the hidden message behind it. If you are watching this it means that I am dead right now and if that is the case then I don't want you to blame yourself for it. As your big brother, it is my job to protect you and get you out of trouble through any means necessary. But there are a few things that you need to know." He took a deep breath before holding up a picture of Grayson.

"First off, the reason that you and Grayson have so many things in common is because he is a family member of ours which you will find out later. I found out that Gray doesn't know it either." I was in shock. That's impossible. Gray told me that all of his family died in a car crash when he was 15. There's no way he could be related to us. But if he actually is, then who's kid is he? Stefano held up another picture, this time the picture was of Tim.

"As you may or may not already know, uncle Tim is actually your father. We all thought that it would be safer if you didn't know because it could potentially avoid you turning all assassin on everyone. But considering the fact that you are watching this right now, you need to become one. Tim has all of the essentials that will teach you how to fight back and most importantly, how to survive. It may take a long time but I need you to hold in there. No matter how much anger is pumping through your veins right now do not let it out. Keep it all working up to the moment you put a bullet right through Carlyle's head."

"I want you to understand that your friends are here for you and not to run away and push them away. Fight until you can't fight anymore. Knowing Carlyle, he will try kidnapping and/or killing your friends so they need to know how to fight as well. I know Blaire is basically a martial artist so have her teach them moves and strategies. You have to learn the three most important things in preparing battle. Strategy. Patience. And Control. Those three things will get you to be able to to whatever you want. Tim will be able to help you with these things but you have to trust him. Trust your instincts." He chuckles. What the hell could he be chuckling at? He knows he's going to die!

"When this is over and you defeat Carlyle, I want you to live a long and happy life. I want you to marry Brandon or Nate, or whoever the hell you choose to be with because we never know anymore! I want you to be happy. Stay with your friends and live healthy lives. Have fun, be young and stupid, do all the things I couldn't get to do. But most importantly, take care of Haley and the baby for me. Make sure that my son or daughter have the best life they could ever have, and one day when they ask about me, don't tell them about Carlyle, I don't want them to live with anger like we did. I want that child to know good stories about me, I want them to know that I loved them very much and I died in battle. I want them to live the happy lives that we couldn't. And most importantly, make sure that the baby knows that I love them with everything I've got. I made a separate video for Haley and the baby as well so please show it to them when this is over. I love you Aide.Goodbye."

The screen went dark and I started crying. It was great to see his face again. I really needed advice from my big brother one last time.

"I know you're probably upset-"

"Nope. I'm determined, how soon can we start this self defense thing?" Even though he was hesitant, I begged him and we started right away. It took a really long time for me to be able to get the strength and power to fully fight.

As the weeks went by, I kept getting voice messages from Brandon. He was keeping me up on things and I have to admit it was nice for awhile. That was until a month later when Tim wasn't having it anymore.

"That's it. No more phone." He grabbed it out of my hands and threw it to the ground causing it to shatter on the floor. "What the hell did you do that for?! That was the only way I could keep tabs on everyone!" He shakes his head as I shout at him.

"Nope. You left to protect them. You're not protecting them if Carlyle can track you. Mistake number one. You can't have any connection to them. Now focus!"

Present day Tim got a call from a number that he didn't recognize so he showed me and I almost jumped when it was Haley's number. He declined the call and let it go to voicemail.

"What did you do that for?! She could be going into early labor!" He shakes his head and plays the voicemail. "Tim, it's Haley. Look, I don't know if Lydia is with you or not but I want you to be aware that if she is with you, we need both you and her to come back here. Carlyle is after all of us, he's even after the baby... we got another letter and he kidnapped our friend

Grayson. In it he said that if Lydia isn't back by midnight on Friday he will kill him and come after all of us one by one. Please, you have to help us."

"We have to help them-"

"No." He shakes his head again, I basically growl at him. "What do you mean no? He kidnapped Gray!"

"As your brother said he would. Grayson doesn't know he's your family. If he finds out and most importantly if Carlyle finds out that you know about Grayson, he'll kill him-"

"Then let me call them back and tell them to fight back-"

"No-"

"I DON'T GIVE A FUCK ABOUT WHAT YOU SAY ANYMORE! MY FRIENDS ARE IN TROUBLE AND I AM GOING TO DO WHAT-EVER IT TAKES TO HELP THEM!" I grabbed the phone out of his hands and dialed the number back as he smiled. What the hell is he smiling at.

"Tim?" I almost cried at the sound of Haleys voice. "Haley, it's me-"

"Lydia! Oh my god. I'm so glad you're okay!"

"Yes. I'm okay. Look, I can't talk very long. I need you to pass a message to everyone. First off, you and Piper need to go somewhere safe, I will not have any harm done to your babies. Second, tell Blaire to start teaching everyone to fight, you may need it. And third, I really miss all of you. I have to go now but promise me that you'll tell them."

"I will. We love you Lydia." She replies happily, I chuckle and smile widely. "I love all of you too. I'll be back soon just don't tell anyone. I have to go, bye." I hung up the phone and gave it back to Tim. Ever since I found out he's my father that is all I can call him, obviously I can't call him uncle and

I can't call him dad either because that phrase comes with so many bad memories for me.

"I have to get going-"

"No. There is one more thing you need to learn first and you've got a day to learn it before you have to go back-"

"I've learned everything you've told me-"

"No. The enemy is going to attack at all costs. You'll be weak, you'll be bleeding, but most importantly they are going to try and take your sight. If I know Carlyle, he's all about blinding you at all cost which could mean surprise attacks, coming behind you, or literally throwing dirt in your face. It's up to you to gain the power to fight back with your other senses. So put this on and listen to the sound of my voice." He handed me a bandana to tie around my eyes to act like a blindfold. He's right, I've done every type of training but this is the last resort, and if it means that I can see my friends and family again, I am willing to do anything. No matter how hard or tough it is, I will do it.

Grayson's POVI woke up in what looked like a cave. I tried to move but I couldn't. I was tied to a wall and I had a splitting headache. "Great. The kid is up." A guy in the shadows says sarcastically, I roll my eyes. "You're never gonna get away with this!"

The man who I am assuming is Lydia's dad comes out of the shadows laughing evilly. "Oh but we already have. Isn't that right sweetheart?" He turns his head to a woman that comes out of the shadows. I couldn't believe it. It can't be.

"Yup. I've been getting away with things for years." She says with a smirk, my eyes grow wide. No way.

"		M		o		m		?		"
————————————————————————————-Grayson's mom
is alive! Who do you think she is? How is Gray related to Adrianna and
Stefano? What did you think of Stefano's video? Thoughts on Tim being
Adrianna's real father? Comment below and don't forget to vote! ~Jen

Chapter 25- Something Is Wrong

Haley's POV I know that Lydia told me not to tell anyone but I was debating whether or not to tell them that I heard from her. This is a life or death situation, and Grayson could be dead for all we know, we need her.

I decided to tell them anyways. They needed to know. "Guys, Lydia just called me. She said that we have to start learning self defense, because if Carlyle has Grayson, he can take any of us at any minute. Piper, she also said that you and me should go to our safe house-"

"What? No way! I'm fighting in this." Piper protests, Vince shakes his head. "It's better for the both of you and the babies to stay out of this. I don't want any harm to come to them or the both of you. You guys need to stay safe."

"She's my best friend, I can't just leave her to die! I can't just sit back as you all go into battle!" Piper shouts angrily, I sigh. "Trust me Piper, I want Carlyle's head for what he did to Stefano. But we can't. I am 7 and a half months pregnant and you are 3 months along, now that Carlyle knows about them it's safest for us to hide because he will kill the babies and then us."

"She's right Pipes. You two need to get away, I'll make sure that you get all of your work and your credits to graduate, just please stay safe. I lost mom, I can't lose you too." Brandon pleads. That was enough to get Piper to agree. "Fine. When do we leave?"

"Tonight. So go home and pack your stuff, we leave at midnight." We left the school with our eyes peeled open. Brandon and Vince kept looking around and making sure that nobody was following us back to the house. When we got back, I packed my stuff as Piper went to tell her dad she was leaving.

Pipers POV Convincing my dad is going to be very hard. It was hard enough telling him about the baby which he was not thrilled about either. After a lot of convincing, he said that we could stay in our guest house which was literally in the backyard. But now I actually have to leave and the worst part of it all is that I have to lie to him about it.

My dad hasn't been that productive in my life but that is because he was busy working to make sure that we can have the best lives possible. I plan to do the same for this baby, and if that means going away for awhile then I'll do it. Sorry dad.

I knocked on his office door only to overhear that he was arguing with someone. "But that's not fair! I worked my ass off for this deal and you're going to sit here and tell me that a dead man got it?" Dead man? Who is he talking about?

"So what? Now the deal is just gone? Lorenzo Stone is dead. I did my part, now be a man and step your ass up Carlyle!" I gasped. Holy shit.

He heard me gasp and he turned around after hanging up the phone. "Piper! How long have you been there for?" He asked nervously, I just start hyperventilating. My father killed Lorenzo... that means that Carlyle is not in town! He's been one step ahead of us this whole time. I have to warn Lydia!

"N-n-not long. I have to g-go-"

"Where are you going?" My dad questions while closing the door behind me. Panic sinks in. My heart starts racing. I can't breathe.

"You killed him. How could you do that?" Tears start streaming down my face, he shakes his head. "I did it for us! He was driving the other car the night your mother was killed. He killed your mother!"

"He was an innocent man dad! How could you do that? He had his whole future ahead of him-"

"So did your mother. Yet he had no problem killing her." I shake my head. "No dad. The roads were slippery and icy, it wasn't anyone's fault. And just because Carlyle told you that doesn't mean it's true! He's a conniving liar. You killed an innocent man dad, and I'm going to make sure everyone knows it." I went to leave but he pulled me back by my hair.

"Oh no you don't!" I was thrown to the ground. I felt a stabbing pain in my stomach. Oh no. God please no. "YOU'RE A MONSTER!" I managed to get up and kick him in the crotch. That will keep him busy for a few minutes. I ran out of the house screaming, everyone was ready in the car.

"What's wrong?" Vince looked at me frantically, I shook my head and looked back to make sure he wasn't chasing after me. "Drive. Drive now. Drive anywhere, just drive!" I screamed, he nodded and pressed his foot on the pedal.

I grabbed my stomach and saw that my pants were all bloody. Please no. This can't be happening.

"Piper? Are you alright?" Brandon asks, I nod. If this blood is what I think this means, I can't worry about myself. Everyone needs to get out. "We just need to get out of here. Give me your phones!" Everyone gave me their phones and I threw them out the window.

"What the hell?!" Nate and Grace shout simultaneously, Haley looks at me confused. "What's going on?" Haley questions, I shake my head. "Not here. We need to get as far away as possible-"

"No, we need to get you to a doctor-"

"No! You don't get it-"

"Get what Piper? You're bleeding! Something could be wrong with the baby!" Blaire protests, I slowly nod. "Something is wrong. Somethings definitely wrong I can feel it. But I'm not gonna sacrifice all of you just for myself. We need to get as far away as possible. Carlyle has everyone in on it. He's not the one who killed Lorenzo, it was our dad Brandon. That explains why Lydia never wanted doctors or cops and that's because they are all in on it. Carlyle's got everyone wrapped around his finger. Don't you see? If Carlyle didn't kill Lorenzo then that means he wasn't really here. And what was the last place he was spotted?"

It was as if something clicked in there heads, Haley got out a small phone. I stuck my hand out so that she would give it to me but she shook her head. "Don't worry, this is a disposable phone, it's not traceable." We all nod as she dials a number and puts it on speaker.

"Tim! It's Haley. You and Lydia need to get out of there as soon as possible. Carlyle isn't the one who killed Lorenzo, he just made you think he did so he could be one step ahead! He's been in your town all along, get out now!" There's a chuckle at the other end of the line. That was when I realized that it wasn't Tim or Lydia we were talking to.

"Sorry Haley, this mission has been compromised." Anger started fueling through my body, I grabbed the phone out of her hands and started making demands.

"You son of a bitch. You better not touch a hair on any of their heads or I will end you. You killed my baby and now I'm coming for you." I growled while hanging up the phone. Vince pulls the car over and everyone looks at me in shock.

"Y-you lost the baby?" Vince questions while tearing up, I nod. "The pain started a couple of days ago and I went to get it checked out. The doctor said that if I had anymore stress put on me I could lose the baby, but I knew once I started bleeding. I'm so sorry Vince." He holds my hand and we cry together. "You two switch seats with Grace and I, we will keep an eye out and make sure that we get you to safety." Nate says heroically, we switched seats and headed on our way.

The ride was completely silent. Yes, I am completely torn up about this, but as bad as it sounds, I'm glad that it was me and not Haley. I have my whole life ahead of me, and I can always have a baby with the guy I love. Haley can't. She's seven months pregnant and now a widow because the baby's grandfather killed his father. It couldn't get much worse for her.

"Where are we going?" Blaire questions, Nate smirks. "My birthmother gave me a key and a note for my first birthday. The key unlocks a safe-house that my great grandmother owned. My father always goes up there when him and my step mom are fighting. There should be enough food in there to last you a year. Even if Carlyle tried, he wouldn't be able to find this place."

"Good. But first things first. Blaire, can you track where Tim's phone is?" Blaire nods, I smirk. "Perfect."

"What are we gonna do?" Grace asks, I grab Vince's band hand kiss it before returning to my smirk. "If it's a fight he wants, it's a fight he'll get. I have a plan."

Chapter 26- That's Where You're Wrong

G race's POVAll of this Lydia stuff has been absolutely crazy. And now we find out that Pipers dad actually killed Lydia's brother? I actually feel bad for her. First she loses her mother, then her best friend and now her baby, it's awful.

I feel even worse because I know I am the cause of all of it. If I wouldn't have exposed Lydia at the winter ball then maybe none of this would've happened, everyone could still be alive if I would've just kept my mouth shut. I hate myself for it.

When we arrived it was two in the morning, Vince suggested that Piper get some sleep but Piper refused. She's running on energy, and that energy is pure hatred.

"Piper you need to sit down-"

"There's no time! Everyone could be dead by now! We have to stop him before he kills someone else. Don't you guys get it?! He's targeting us for a reason. We are all connected! And I'm going to do what Lydia couldn't. I'm gonna end this. Nate, you grew up with her so you know where her uncles house is, let's go." Piper stormed out of the safe house and Nate and Brandon followed. Vince was about to go but I stopped him.

"You should stay back with Haley. You're the only one of us that can fight really good, plus if something were to happen to you I think Piper would go over the edge. I'll go, you stay." Before he could even protest, I was already in the car with everyone.

They looked at me curiously, I just snapped at them. "What?"

"Why are you coming with us? You hated Lydia." Blaire asks, I sigh. "I don't hate her anymore. Plus I blame myself for what happened because I exposed her at the dance. She's on the run because of me as well. I want to fix my mistake, and that means fighting for her."

"Do we even know where we are going?" Brandon asks, Blaire shakes her head but Piper nods. "We are going to go to the place where it all began. We are gonna go to Adrianna's house. But first, we have to go to Tim's house and look for clues." Piper says persistently.

It was hours before we actually got there. It was about six in the morning when we arrived at Tim's house. Piper didn't even bother to look around and make sure that there weren't any security traps, she just kicked the door in and stormed in.

Mistake #1.

I gave Brandon that look that said I'll go after her. "Grace, you can hack. I need you to hack into Tim's security cameras to see what happened. Brandon and Blaire, you two are the best fighters. Keep watch."

I followed Piper and Nate into the security room and managed to hack into the system and get footage of the last 24 hours. We watched footage for about an hour, but eventually we saw what really happened.

"I have to get going-"

"No. There is one more thing you need to learn first and you've got a day to learn it before you have to go back-"

"I've learned everything you've told me-"

"No. The enemy is going to attack at all costs. You'll be weak, you'll be bleeding, but most importantly they are going to try and take your sight. If I know Carlyle, he's all about blinding you at all cost which could mean surprise attacks, coming behind you, or literally throwing dirt in your face. It's up to you to gain the power to fight back with your other senses. So put this on and listen to the sound of my voice." He handed her a bandana to tie around her eyes to act like a blindfold. She tied it around her eyes and he hit her.

"What the hell was that for?!" She shouts angrily, he sighs. "I told you, listen to my voice movements. I can sound like I am on one side of you but actually be on the other. Pay close attention." Alarms start going off and they both start coughing as smoke starts filling up the room.

"Tim? The blindfold is stuck! Tim what's going on!" Lydia shouts, Tim looks as if he's about to pass out. "Security has been reached!" They both started coughing hysterically until eventually they passed out from the smoke. A few minutes later a guy and a girl walk in with gas masks and take them off.

We all gasp in shock. "Is that Gray's mom?" Piper questions, Nate shakes his head. "No, that's Lydia's sister Rose." Nate says with his mouth hanging open in shock, I shake my head. "No, that's Grays mom. I've seen plenty of pictures of her, I'm 100 percent sure that's her." Piper says reassuringly.

Nate shakes his head. "That is Rose, I know for a fact."

I shake my head in disbelief. "It can't be."

"But why fake her own death? And most importantly, why is she working with Carlyle?"

Lydia's POV"Sorry Haley, this mission has been compromised." Carlyle hangs up Tims phone and starts laughing. I try breaking out of the chains I'm in but it's no use. "Where's Tim?" I ask angrily, he chuckles.

"Seriously? I smoke bomb my own brothers house with knockout gas, kidnap the both of you, and manage to make contact with your pregnant sister in law and that's the first question you ask? Pathetic."

"No. What's pathetic is you. Now answer her question." Gray demands, Carlyle smirks. "Well look at you! My little grandson making demands! Cute." Did he just say grandson?

"What are you talking about?" Carlyle smirks again. "Oh this is priceless! I can't believe you haven't figured it out yet."

"Figure what out?" I ask curiously again. I want so badly to break out of these stupid chains, but I know that even if I did he would shoot me.

"Rose had a kid when she was 15. Remember when she went to boarding school for two years? Well it was to give birth to the kid, and that kid just so happens to be your friend over here. Grayson's dad raise him and eventually Rose faked her death so that she could stay and help out with you and your brother."

"But that makes no sense. My mother's name is Lucy and she died two years ago. Since Rose died when you were 12, that's impossible-"

"See now that's where you're wrong. Our family is really good at faking deaths. Rose could've easily gotten out of the fire." No way. It's impossible. I shot her.

"You're wrong. I shot her. I watched the life drain out of her body before she bled to death. I saw you light the flame that burned mom and Rose's bodies to the ground. She couldn't have gotten out of there alive." I shake my head in disbelief, someone chuckles in the shadows.

"See, that's where you're wrong." The person comes out of the shadows and I freeze. I recognize that voice... It can't be. "Rose?"

She chuckles easily while holding a bloody knife in her hands. "Hey sis."

Chapter 27- Go To Hell

L ydia's POVI was speechless. I don't understand how this could've happened. "How is this possible? Was this all part of your stupid game to fuck up my life?! Is mom alive too?" I question angrily as Carlyle laughs.

"Nope. That bitch is as dead as your brother is. And as for your sister here, well I gave her a choice. She could either tell me what you all were planning behind my back, or I would kill her along with the rest of you." I look up at Rose and glare.

"And you went along with this?" This time she chuckled and continued to twirl the bloody knife in her hands. "What can I say? I like being alive-"

"Yeah, and apparently you like killing people too. Why did you kill dad and David?" Gray questions, she smirks evilly. "That ones easy. Your father was onto me, he knew my name wasn't Lucy Underwood and he started looking into my past. As for your little brother, well he was just collateral damage-"

"HE WAS FIVE YEARS OLD! HE HAD HIS WHOLE LIFE AHEAD OF HIM! YOU BITCH!" Gray snaps angrily, I look at him in shock. Gray has always been the nice one, to see him going over the edge like this is surprising.

"Snappy and bipolar! You really are part of this family. So here's the deal. One of you is going to die tonight, the other is going to join us. We are gonna give the two of you a choice of who lives and who dies. I'm going to take this knife and leave it for you two to work things out. " Rose says with a chuckle while placing the knife on the ground, Carlyle walks out. "And if we don't?" Gray snaps, Rose looks back with a smirk.

"If you don't, then we will kill all of your friends and their babies one by one and we will keep you alive just for the sake of making you watch them die over and over and over. The tormenting will never stop and it sure as hell will never end. You'll be begging one of us to end your life but we won't. You will be stuck in here for the rest of your life and left with only your dark thoughts. So think about it. Would you rather die or watch everyone you love die at your hands because of you?" Without another word, she slammed the door shut which left us alone in the room with the knife.

I managed to grab the knife with my foot and kick it back to my hands. It took time but I was able to pick the lock on the chains with the lock like Tim had taught me to. I went to untie Gray but he shook his head. "Kill me Lydia."

"Hell no. We are going to fight back-"

"No. Didn't you hear her? They will kill everyone. Do you want all of them to die? Do you want Haley and Piper's babies to die?"

"Nobody has to die-"

"You're wrong-"

"No. I have a plan, but this is gonna hurt."

Tim's POV I heard a loud scream come from the other room. Was that Adrianna?! I need to find a way out but I'm hurt. I need to help them, I refuse to die in here.

I managed to break free from the chains but Rosalinda and Carlyle came back in and I had to act like I was still tied up.

This is ridiculous. How could he bring his family into this? He never used to be like this. When they had Rose he was the happiest man on the planet. Same goes with when they had Stefano a couple years later. Even when Adrianna came along, they were the perfect family.

But perfect can only get you so far. I remember the first time he hit her, that was when he got right where he started, back into the business, and it was all because of his troubled first child.

Rose used to act all perfect, but once she found out about the business she wanted in. When Carlyle wouldn't let her in or give her any information, she came to me, and when I didn't give it to her she found her own way in. She ended up getting pregnant at 15 and that's when Carlyle came back into the business. It went downhill from there.

Adrianna and Stefano believed that she was so innocent and perfect because that's how Carlyle and his wife made it seem. They did it to keep the two of them safe, and most importantly out of the business.

Unfortunately when Carlyle got back into the business, he started to slowly throw his life away. And I guess finding out about Adrianna being my daughter and not his really sent him over the edge.

"Ah the sweet sound of pain. It's amazing isn't it dad?" Rose says with a smirk, Carlyle nods. Maybe she is the crazier one after all. "Where is she?! What did you do to Adrianna?" I shout while acting that I am trying to get out of my chains, Carlyle laughs.

"Oh she's a little preoccupied." He replies with an evil chuckle, my eyes go narrow as my heart starts beating really fast. "What did you do?"

"Oh we didn't do anything. It's what she's going to do that is going to destroy her. But that's what she gets for running away. We gave them a choice. Either one of them could kill the other and join us, or they will both suffer a miserable slow and painful life which will be worse than death. They will be begging us to kill them after they watch everyone they love die but we won't because that will be part of their punishment. But judging by the screams coming from the other room, it looks like they've made their decision. Carlyle, go check if the deed is done. If not, tell her I'll kill Tim." She has a smirk on her face while twirling the knife around in her hands. That's when I realized that she's batshit crazy.

Lydia's POVCarlyle came in the room and smirked when he saw what I had done. "You not only got out of your chains, but you actually killed your own nephew. You really are my daughter." He says with a chuckle, I smirk.

"But I'm not though." His smirk turns into a frown. "You don't know what you're talking about." He snaps. I start laughing evilly as he starts to get angry.

"I mean that's why you're doing this right? You went back in the business and that's how you found out. That's why you killed mom that night. You were just pissed because you found out the truth." He starts breathing heavier, indicating that he's angry. "Stop talking."

"Aw why? Is the big bad wolf angry? I don't blame you. I would be angry too if I found out that my wife had fucked my brother and that resulted youngest daughter is actually being my niece-"

"SHUT UP!" He shouts, I smirk. "You don't have the authority to tell me what to do anymore. All these years! All these years Stefano and I spent running from you and all for nothing. You are a pathetic excuse of a human being and you're going to rot in hell for everything you've done. You call yourself a man? You're nothing but trash. You killed your wife, killed your son, and you killed my spirit. But the thing you aren't going to do is kill me and you wanna know why? Cuz I'm untouchable. All of your attacks on me only made me stronger. I am not that scared little girl I used to be. You in the other hand are a monster. We all get bad and unexpected news in our lives, but you had to go and be a coward!" He starts yelling and then charges at me, I flip him over, grab his gun, and pin him to the ground.

"You won't do it." He says while spitting blood out, this time I smirk again. "You obviously don't know me anymore." I shot him in the leg which caused him to scream. I smiled as I watched the blood poor out of his leg.

"Now get up." He shakes his head. "I can't! Show your father some mercy here!"

"Oh like you showed mom and Stefano mercy? Like you showed Wesley and all my other friends mercy? Or like you're showing all of my friends mercy right now? You're a garbage excuse for a human being and I hate you. You killed everyone I love and I refuse to let anyone else die." I shot him in the leg again. "Now do as I say, and get the fuck up!"

He limped as he got up. I wrapped my arm around his neck and put the gun to his head. "ROSE! GET YOUR ASS OUT HERE OR I SWEAR I WILL KILL HIM RIGHT NOW!"

"Go ahead Adrianna. Kill him. We all know you want to. He caused you all of that pain. So go ahead, pull the trigger." I knew something was up when she wanted me to kill him but I didn't care. "P-please. You don't understand!"

"What do I have to understand Carlyle? You killed everyone I love just for your amusement! And I'm gonna make sure you pay for it." I pushed him out of my arms and continued to hold the gun to his head. "Now get on your knees." He started crying as he got down and looked at the ground.

"You don't understand-"

"SHUT UP! Look at me." He doesn't budge. "I SAID LOOK AT ME!" He looked up while shaking in fear. I smirked as he cried. "I want my face to be the last thing you see, and these words to be the last you ever hear. You took away everyone and everything I love! You killed my family! And for everything you've done you're gonna pay."

He shakes his head and cries harder. "Please don't do this!" I smirk and hold the gun straight to his head. "Go to hell Carlyle." Without hesitation I shot him, Rose just clapped.

"I have never been more proud to call you my sister. Welcome to the business Aide." I went to turn the gun on her but she just laughed. "I wouldn't do that if I were you."

"Oh really? And why is that?" I say snarkily, she smirks and holds out her phone. "Because I have my connections, and with one click of the send button I can get those connections to kill all those that you love most. You already killed my son and our father, now you have to hold up your part of the deal. Join me and nobody dies."

Everything I've been training for has led up to this moment.

"Where's Tim?" I question while still pointing the gun at her. "He's alive. And he'll stay that way as long as you hold up your end of the deal. So what will it be sis?"

"I'm in."———————————————————————————Damn ! That was crazy. Did you expect Adrianna to actually kill Carlyle? Is Grayson dead? What will she do next? Comment what you think and don't forget to vote!

~Jen

Chapter 28- What Have You Done

Brandon's POVAfter watching the footage from the cameras, Piper stormed out with an angered expression on her face while Nate and Grace looked as if they had seen a ghost. "What's wrong? What did you see?" I question, Nate takes me aside and tells me the news.

"We saw Lydia's sister, and she's working with Carlyle. She's alive Brandon." I was shocked, but also part of me was kind of happy because I figured if she was actually alive, then who else is alive?

"Wait, if she's alive then who knows who else is alive. If Carlyle has managed to hide Lydia's sister being alive all these years who knows who else he could be hiding. Others could be alive too."

"Brandon snap out of it. If mom were alive then dad wouldn't have been ordered to kill Lorenzo. He killed him as revenge for moms death because he thinks the other driver was him-"

"But it wasn't. I got a look at the driver before we ran off the road. The driver was a woman, and it looked as if she was smiling. If it wasn't Lorenzo then that means it could've been Rose." I replied apprehensively. Then it clicked.

Holy shit.

"What if everything was Rose? If it wasn't Carlyle in Vegas making every-thing bad happen, and he hasn't actually been in town this whole time then it had to be her. Holy shit we've had the wrong killer this whole time!" I start to panic. Lydia is all alone with that crazy bitch. We need to get her and Gray back in one piece.

"We need to get there now. Nate, do you have any idea where they could be?" Blaire asks Nate, he shakes his head as he thinks about it. Then he looked as if he solved a piece of the puzzle.

"Lydia and I used to play in her basement all of the time. That's it! Ugh I'm so stupid!" We all looked at him confused. "Um, mind filling us in?" Grace says eagerly, Nate smacks himself in the head.

"Her basement was basically like an underground lair. It was like the cat-acombs. Think about it, this whole thing is happening because of events in the past. And what better way to get revenge for the past then the place where it all started?" Piper smiles wide and gives him a bear hug. "That's it! You're a genius! Take us there."

We got back in the car and Nate started driving. "It's about fifteen minutes from here, but if I am right then all that is left is the basement so we have to find a way in first." We all nodded in agreement. I looked out the window until we got there.

The whole ride I found myself questioning my future with Lydia. I love her with everything I've got and I can't help but wonder if she's alive or not and that scares the crap out of me. I can't even close my eyes because every time I do, I see her all bloody and dismantled and just the thought of that alone makes me want to scream.

The main reason I'm doing this is because I want Lydia back in one piece, and most importantly because I want Carlyle dead for what he's done.

"We're here. Now all we have to do is find a way in, be careful though, this house can collapse at any moment." Nate says, we all nod in agreement and get out of the car. We walked slowly around the house until Grace found a way in.

It was a cellar door. Blaire went to touch it but Piper stopped her. "WAIT!" She whisper shouted, we all looked at her curiously as she pointed to a keypad. "Oh crap! How could I forget? Whenever Lydia and I would go down there she would always enter a pin." Nate replies apprehensively, Piper glares at him.

"Well can you remember it?" Piper snaps, Nate nods as he thinks. "She would always talk about this one date. She always talked about her birthday like it was the most glorious day ever."

"When is her birthday?" Grace asks, he smiles and enters the code. 04/16/00. "No way!" Grace said with a smile, we all look at her curiously. "What is it?" I question, she just smiled wider.

"That was the day Grayson was officially born. When we dated he told me that was the actual date but he always celebrated the day before because his mother always left on a business trip for his actual birthday. This is crazy!" I still look at her confused, she rolls her eyes. "What he found out on the footage is that Lydia's sister Rose is actually Grayson's mom. Which makes Lydia Grayson's aunt. The reason Rose left on a business trip every years is so she could come back and celebrate Lydia's birthday. This all makes sense."

Lydia and Grayson are related? What the hell?!

"Why did you guys decide to leave this out when you told me what you saw?" I question nervously, Blaire sighs. "We were afraid of how you would retaliate-"

"Whatever. I just think I deserved to know-"

"Well now you do. So shut up and start walking." Piper snapped as Nathan opened the cellar door. As we were walking, it felt like hours before we actually found something. It was a trail of blood.

"Guys, this is where we need to be careful. Anything could be behind that door." Grace hesitantly cracked open the door where we saw what the trail of blood led to. It was Tim. He had been stabbed.

We ran over to him only to see that he was already out of his chains, he was just so weak that he couldn't move. "Tim! Tim it's Brandon. We need to get you out of here." He shakes his head and grunts.

"No. Get Adrianna." He mumbled. My heart started racing. "Is she still alive?" He nodded. My questions were further answered when we heard yelling in the other room. I rushed over to see but Grace and Nate held me back.

"Are you crazy?! You're gonna get yourself killed!" Grace whisper shouts, I shake my head and peak in the door. We all gasped when we saw Grayson passed out bleeding on the floor.

"You don't have the authority to tell me what to do anymore. All these years! All these years Stefano and I spent running from you and all for nothing. You are a pathetic excuse of a human being and you're going to rot in hell for everything you've done. You call yourself a man? You're nothing but trash. You killed your wife, killed your son, and you killed my spirit. But the thing you aren't going to do is kill me and you wanna know why? Cuz I'm untouchable. All of your attacks on me only made me stronger. I am not that scared little girl I used to be. You in the other hand are a monster.

We all get bad and unexpected news in our lives, but you had to go and be a coward!" Carlyle starts yelling at Lydia and then charges at her, she flips him over, grabs his gun, and pins him to the ground. I smirk. That's my girl.

"You won't do it." He says while spitting blood out, this time Lydia smirks again. "You obviously don't know me anymore." She shot him in the leg which caused him to scream.

"Now get up." He shakes his head. "I can't! Show your father some mercy here!"

"Oh like you showed mom and Stefano mercy? Like you showed Wesley and all my other friends mercy? Or like you're showing all of my friends mercy right now? You're a garbage excuse for a human being and I hate you. You killed everyone I love and I refuse to let anyone else die." She shot him in the leg again. "Now do as I say, and get the fuck up!"

He limped as he got up. She wrapped her arm around his neck and put the gun to his head. "ROSE! GET YOUR ASS OUT HERE OR I SWEAR I WILL KILL HIM RIGHT NOW!"

"Go ahead Adrianna. Kill him. We all know you want to. He caused you all of that pain. So go ahead, pull the trigger."

Don't do it. Please don't do it.

"P-please. You don't understand!" Carlyle pleads while looking at Rose. I thought it was weird that he was looking at her and Rose was just standing there smirking. It's as if this is exactly what she wanted.

"What do I have to understand Carlyle? You killed everyone I love just for your amusement! And I'm gonna make sure you pay for it." She pushed him out of her arms and continued to hold the gun to his head. "Now get on your knees." He started crying as he got down and looked at the ground.

"You don't understand-"

"SHUT UP! Look at me." He doesn't budge. "I SAID LOOK AT ME!" He looked up while shaking in fear. Lydia smirked as he cried. "I want my face to be the last thing you see, and these words to be the last you ever hear. You took away everyone and everything I love! You killed my family! And for everything you've done you're gonna pay."

He shakes his head and cries harder. "Please don't do this!" She smirks and holds the gun straight to his head. "Go to hell Carlyle." Without hesitation she shot him, Rose just clapped.

"I have never been more proud to call you my sister. Welcome to the business Aide." Lydia went to turn the gun on her but she just laughed. "I wouldn't do that if I were you."

"Oh really? And why is that?" Lydia says with a laugh. Rose smirks and holds out her phone. "Because I have my connections, and with one click of the send button I can get those connections to kill all those that you love most. You already killed my son and our father, now you have to hold up your part of the deal. Join me and nobody dies."

"Where's Tim?" Lydia asks while still pointing the gun at her. "He's alive. And he'll stay that way as long as you hold up your end of the deal. So what will it be sis?"

"I'm in." I closed the door and gasped, without hesitation we ran back to the room with Tim in it. "What the fuck just happened?! She killed him without hesitation and she smiled!" Nate whisper shouts, Piper holds her head and starts pacing back and fourth.

"No. That wasn't her back there. She must have a plan-"

"SHE KILLED SOMEONE! And you're saying it was a plan?!" Grace whisper shouts, Piper and I nod. "Think about it. If what I think about

Rose is true, then we need to let Lydia do whatever she's doing. She's manipulative and that is going to get her far in this. As of right now, we need to find a way to get both Tim and Gray out of here. Nate, Grace and Piper, get Tim out of here and take him to the hospital-"

"No way. I'm not going anywhere-"

"You're right. But actually, no one is going anywhere. Alive that is." We jumped at the sound of a woman's voice that is not Lydia's. I turn around and come face to face with Rose. The last thing I remember is telling Piper to get Tim out before she tased me until I passed out.

I woke up feeling very groggy. Most importantly, I was face to face with Lydia who was continuing to tie me up. "Please don't do this. I know this isn't you!"

"Shh shut up. She's going to hear you-"

"I don't care. All I care about is you. I saw what you did to Carlyle, are you okay? Why are you joining her? Is Gray really dead?" She put her hand over her lips as Rose walked back in.

"Alright Rose, the job is done. Where are the others?" Lydia questions, Rose shakes her head and smirks. "You really think I would tell you? After what you pulled today?"

"Are you serious?! I did everything you told me! I killed Gray! I shot Carlyle! I tied up Brandon! I've done everything you've asked me to do. The least you could do is tell me if they are safe." Lydia snaps back, Rose nods. "How's lover boy doing? He doesn't look too good."

"He's fine. So what do we do now?" Lydia questions. I know what she's doing, and by the looks of it I think it's working. "Everything is in place."

"Everything is in place? What's that supposed to mean?" I could tell that Lydia was getting nervous because she does this weird twitching thing with her fingers and starts scratching. "Wouldn't you like to know." Rose teases with a smirk, Lydia's fists start clenching together.

"Yes I would. But most importantly, I would like to know why? Why now? And why leave only Brandon and Gray in here with me?" Rose smirks turns wider. "Well that's a simple question sis. I'm going to make you choose between them-"

"I won't do it." Lydia shakes her head, Rose chuckles. "I thought you'd say that. So I'll give you a choice. You can either stab one of them, or I'll get one of my friends to make sure Haley has a little mishap in her pregnancy." Lydia starts panicking, she looks at me and starts crying.

I nod. "It's okay. Gray is dead, stabbing him any further would be cruel. So stab me, it's okay." She shakes her head. "I can't-"

"Yes you can Lydia. Nothing you do will ever stop me from loving you. Just do it." She slowly walks over to me and starts shaking. I nod and continue to tell her it's okay but she denies. Instead she holds the knife to her wrist and cuts herself. She doesn't even scream or make a noise. She just keeps cutting.

"Lydia no!" She clenches her fist and turns back to Rose. Rose looks shocked but then she smirks. "Not what I had in mind but it'll do. Seeing you in pain gives me almost as much joy as taking those who are close to you away." Rose replied with a smile.

"Why do you hate me so much?" Lydia asks with an angered expression. "Because you were born." Rose takes out her knife and slashed Lydia's cheek. I gasped, but Rose acted as if it was nothing and walked away, making sure to lock the door behind her.

"What happened to fighting back? You're being a coward!" I shout at Lydia, she shakes her head. "No, I'm smart. She has a panic button that can blow this place, plus she has Carlyle's minions parked outside. Once she presses that everyone is as good as dead, including Vince and Haley. I've got a plan-"

"And you had to kill Gray in order to go through with it?!"

"I'm not dead Brandon so please shut the fuck up and listen." Grayson snaps while glaring at me, my heart starts racing. Thank god he's alive! "But how?"

"fake blood. Yes she's being an idiot, but she's saving us all from a fate way worse than death so just go along with this. You'll figure out why she's doing this-" He was cut off by the sound of screaming and fighting coming from the other room.

Lydia ran to the door and started banging on it. It's locked from the outside. "ROSE! DON'T YOU DARE HURT THEM! GET BACK IN HERE I'LL DO WHATEVER YOU WANT!" The screaming stopped. Lydia panicked. "ROSE I SWEAR TO GOD IF YOU HURT ANY ONE OF THEM I WILL FUCKING KILL YOU!"

The door swung right open and Lydia came face to face with Grace swinging keys around her finger. "Do you losers want to get out of here or what?"

"Did you take the button?" Lydia asks, Grace looks confused. "What button?"

Alarms start going off and we heard footsteps coming from the upstairs. Lydia looked worried and she started to cry. "You have no idea what you've done."

"What are you talking about? We saved you-"

"No you didn't. She pressed her panic button which means the others are coming! You thought Carlyle and Rose were bad? The others are ruthless." She ran over to me and Gray and she unchained us.

Lydia's POVI ran into the other room and saw everyone. They looked afraid of me yet happy to see me at the same time but we didn't have any time for reunions. Once I saw that they had knocked out and chained up Rose I panicked even more.

"You guys have no idea what you've just done. You need to get out now!" The alarms go off and the machine starts doing a count down.

10 minutes.

"We aren't leaving without you." Piper argues, I shake my head. "Do you see that timer? She rigged this place to blow and if we don't get out of here we are all gonna die!"

They looked at me hesitantly but I told them to grab Tim and go. I told Nate the way out and they made their way out. I stayed.

"What are you doing? Let's get out of here!" Brandon snaps while pulling me, I shake my head. "I need to stay."

"Are you crazy?! You'll die!"

"I need to finish this. I need to make sure she's really dead. Go, I'll meet up with you guys at Tim's." I give him a kiss but he shakes his head. "I'm not leaving without you. I lost you once, I won't go through that again."

7 minutes.

Rose was waking up, I turned her gun on her and made sure she didn't have her knife. "Well well what do we have here? Are you actually helpless for once?" I say snarkily, she shakes her head.

"I knew you'd betray me for them-"

"Of course I would! Do you think I'm stupid? I know everything!" I shout, she chuckles. "Oh honey, you don't know a thing."

"Oh really? I know that all this time I believed it was Carlyle, but he was just a pawn in your little scam. I know that after he killed Wesley, he realized that what he's doing was wrong. And I know that you were behind this all along. You faked your own death. You burned down the house. And you made Carlyle hunt us down. You knew he was scary so you got everyone he could to spy on me and Stefano and you ordered him to be killed And most importantly, I know that it was you who switched out my meds which caused my consistent panic attacks in Vegas. But all I want to know is why?"

"You and Stefano were always the ones mom and dad compared me to. I was the rebel child who got pregnant at 15 and they hated me for it. I've been planning my revenge since you were born! And once I got involved in the gang, I found out about Tim being your real father and of course, I told dad. He was ready to go off the edge but I stopped him. I told him the plan and everything was ready to take place." She stood up. What the hell? How did she get out of her chains?

"But then you stopped him so the plan changed. I wore the bullet proof vest and put in the blood packets so that wherever you shot me, I wouldn't get hurt." She says with an evil laugh, I roll my eyes.

"But then we got away-"

"Yes! You got away with the help of your father which is why we had to take him here along with you. I didn't think you were smart enough to figure out that it was me all along but apparently you are. So now I'm gonna have to kill you both." She points the gun at Brandon and fires but I shoot at her and jump in front of him.

4 minutes.

She hit me right in the chest. I knew that soon enough I'd be unconscious given the place where she shot me so I had to do this fast. I step over her and shoot her again, this time in the leg. "That's for Wesley."

I shot her in the chest. "That's for Stefano." And finally, I shot her in the neck which caused her to choke. "And that's for mom."

I watched as she choked on her own blood. I smirked as she took her last breath but Brandon pulled me away and we started running. I was starting to feel weak in the legs. I was losing too much blood.

"Brandon... If I don't make it out-"

"You will." He says reassuringly, I shake my head as I fall to the ground. He picks me up and continues to run. We're almost at the exit.

1 minute.

"I love you" Seeing the fire coming behind us was the last thing I remember before I passed out.

BOOM

Chapter 29- I Can Save Her

Lydia's POVI woke up on the ground. The old house was on fire again and everyone was crying. There were also a bunch of ambulances around and cops on the scene. This is bad. This is really bad.

I saw Tim being carried into the ambulance so I ran over to him. "TIM!" He was awake but it was almost as if he didn't see me. So I ran over to Piper and everyone in hopes to ask what was going to happen to us but I got no answer.

"Guys, this isn't funny! I'm okay! Is Brandon okay?" I question, no answer. I go over to two cops and overhear them talking about what happened. "It's really a shame, they were so young, they shouldn't have to go through this trauma." One of the cops says, the other nods in agreement.

"How are the victims?" The second cop asks the first, he shakes his head. "The man is going to be okay. The boy had some head trauma but nothing too serious."

"And the girl?" The First cop shakes his head as they take away another body. I looked at that body and started to panic when I saw that it was me. Oh god, am I dead?

"No you're not." A voice says with a chuckle, I look over and see a tall figure standing next to me. "Well not yet." He says again while walking away, I run after him.

"Wait!" All of a sudden, I was in an old fashioned restaurant and the figure was sitting across from me. It took me some time to realize who it was, but when I did I was jumping for joy.

"I can't believe I didn't recognize you. You got hotter, too bad you didn't hit puberty before my dad killed you. But please, explain to me if I am dead." I question Wesley, he shakes his head as the waitress gives us our burgers.

"You're in what I call the place of return. You can either stay and your sins will decide whether you become a guardian like I am or, if you're one of the lucky ones then you can decide if you want to go back-"

"Okay. Well how do I go about doing that?" He smiles and laughs. Gosh I missed him so much. "Typical Adrianna. It's not that simple. You have to deal with your demons in order to be able to choose. Unless you choose to stay, but most people go through it either way and decide." I nod.

"Well how do I face it?" He shrugs. "It comes to you. It's like a dark wave, you feel weak and then just drop. It's kind of like an out of body experience but at the end it will show you what happened to you and you will have a choice. But in the meantime you just have to wait-"

"That's ridiculous! I'm not waiting!" I went to get up but it was as if something was pulling me back and I couldn't breathe. "I told you. That's not how it works. Unless you want to die without a choice I suggest you sit down and wait." So there I was. In the middle of nowhere, talking to my first love and waiting for death to show me how to come back and live again.

Brandon's POVWhen I woke up, I felt as if someone put a jackhammer in my head and started banging on it. My vision was blurry and I was really confused. But there was only one thing on my mind. Lydia.

"You're awake! Oh thank god!" Piper grabbed me and hugged me, I winced in pain. "Sorry. Does that hurt?" She asks, I nod and look around.

"Lydia. Where's Lydia?" I question as my vision starts coming back, she gives me a sympathetic look and tries to change the subject. "Do you remember what happened?"

"Don't change the subject Pipes, where is she?" I snap, a tear slips down her face. Oh no. Please don't say she's dead.

"She was hurt pretty bad. She lost a lot of blood and the blast from the explosion really destroyed her. She needs a blood transfusion but since her blood type is so rare, none of us are a match, not even Tim." She grabs my hand and squeezes it before continuing. "It's really bad Brandon, the doctors said she might not make it."

I feel tears start to well up in my eyes but I wipe them away and try to get up, Piper stops me. "What are you doing?"

"Tell them to give her my blood. I need to see her." She pushes me back down. "You can't get up, you'll open your stitches and hurt your leg even more. I'll go get the doctor and he will explain the process to you." She walked out and a few minutes later the doctor came in.

"Hey Brandon, how are you feeling?" I glare at him. "How would you feel if your girlfriend is lying on her death bed and there is only a one percent chance you can save her?" I reply sarcastically, he sighs.

"Okay. Well your sister tells me that you want to give Lydia your blood. In order to do that we have to ask you your blood type and a couple of follow up questions." The doctor replies with a smile, I nod as he clicks his pen and gets ready to write on his clipboard.

"I am O negative." The doctor nods and writes it down. "Any STD's?" I shake my head. "Any diseases or sickness that runs in your family?" I shake my head again. "Are you up to date with your shots?" I nod, the doctor smiles.

"That's great. You are a perfect candidate. Are you sure you want to do this?" He asks, I nod again. "I've never been more sure of anything in my life. How quick can we get this thing started?"

"I'll have one of my nurses come in and get to work. They will be taking 2 pints of blood so make sure you lay down and keep drinking juice and staying hydrated afterwards. You'll feel very weak but give it a day and you should be up and running again." The doctor said with a smile before walking out.

The nurses came in a few minutes later and took my blood. "You're very generous for doing this Brandon." One of the nurses says, I smile.

"I love her, and I'm willing to do whatever it takes." I replied with a smile, the nurse nods. "Alright, all done. You did good. This could save her. Now remember, drink your juice and stay hydrated. The doctors want to keep you overnight to run some tests but you will be free to go in the morning." The nurse continued to smile walked out of my room, I looked at Piper with a wide smile on my face.

"Did you hear that Pipes? I can save her!" She gave me another sympathetic look. "Brandon, there's still no guarantee that you will save her. Even if the transfusion works, she could still be asleep for a long time. She's gonna be in a coma." My smile soon faded and sadness overcame me again.

"So no matter what I do, she's not gonna wake up." A tear falls down my face, she shakes her head and grabs my hand. "No, that's not it at all. You definitely increased her chances of surviving by doing this. Just the damages caused by both her getting shot, stabbed and the explosion were too much for her. Her body couldn't take it. The doctor told Tim that the explosion knocked her out and unfortunately she wasn't as lucky as you." At that point, Tears start streaming down my fault.

"Its all my fault. I did this." She shakes her head. "No. It wasn't your fault. Rose was a crazy evil bitch who was willing to stop at nothing. It wasn't your fault." I shake my head in denial.

"I could've protected her! Rose was going to shoot me back in the basement, but as she fired the gun Lydia jumped in front of me and it hit her instead. It's all my fault!" I start crying hysterically as Piper tries to convince me it's not my fault.

It's my fault. I killed her. ————————————————————————————————Hey guys! Sorry this chapter is pretty short but I had to get both Lydia and Brandon's point of views in one. What do you think is going to happen next? Will Brandon save Lydia? Will Lydia be able to save herself? Comment below and don't forget to vote! Thanks,-Jen

Chapter 30- I'll Never Forget You

Lydia's POV"How's Haley? She must have felt awful after Stefano's death." Wesley asks, I look at him confused. "How did you know about that?"

"I was his guardian, just like I am yours. He unfortunately was one of those who ignored the process and was stuck here for good-"

"Wait. Are you saying he's here? As in right now?" He shakes his head, I sigh. "He was able to move on. Your mother was my guardian, she told me that I should stay and watch over you and Stefano. She was a great woman."

"Why are you telling me this? Are you trying to get me to stay here with you, my mother and Stefano? Because I can't! I promised I would protect them and I can't leave them now!" He shakes his head and starts to get defensive.

"Aide stop getting so defensive! I'm trying to help you forgive yourself! The whole reason you are here right now is so you can come to terms with your past and forgive yourself. You blamed yourself for your moms death. You blamed yourself for what you thought was Roses death. You blamed yourself for my death, and now you're blaming yourself for putting your friends in this situation. But you need to stop!" I start getting angry. How dare he?!

"You don't think I've tried? You don't think that every day that goes by I try to convince myself that none of it was my fault? I went to therapy for that shit! I almost killed myself because I felt so guilty for your death! So don't you dare tell me that I haven't tried to stop blaming myself!" I shout at him, he chuckles.

"You think you have it all figured out? Nothing is easy Adrianna! Some things you just have to cope with and you're not going to be able to leave here until you cope with it." He grabs my hand and all of a sudden we were in the hospital. Brandon and Piper were crying.

"It's all my fault Pipes. I could've protected her." Brandon says in between tears, I shake my head. He can't blame himself! It's my fault.

"No. You can't blame yourself!" A tear falls down my face as I shouted at him, Wesley shakes his head and grabs my hand. "They can't hear you. I know you love them, but maybe it's time to let go." Wesley says, I glare at him and pull my hand away from his.

"I'm not giving up without a fight." I went to look back to Piper and Brandon but instead I found myself in the safe house with Vince and Haley. She was crying hysterically.

"She can't die. I can't do this on my own!" She cries, Vince shakes his head. "She's a fighter. You know that more than anyone, she's going to be okay. She's going to keep on fighting."

"The doctors said there's a 50 percent chance that she will wake up. Odds are never in our favor Vince and I'm petrified." She starts holding her stomach and realizes she's bleeding, I scream.

"NOOOO!" Before I could reach her, we were back in the old house. "You can't help them Aide." I turn to Wesley and start punching him.

"Why are you doing this to me?! Is this some sort of punishment for everything I've done? Or is it some scheme to get back at me for letting you die?" He doesn't respond, I chuckle. "Wow. Well I guess I've got my answer. The fact that you think I would let you go sickens me-"

"You did let me go! You moved on!" He shouts while clenching his fists together. He has some nerve to be getting mad. "I loved you with every-thing I had! I tried reviving you and so did the doctors! I even gave you my blood but the doctors told me it was no use Wes because you were already sick! You never told me that you were dying. I loved you with everything I had and after your death I tried killing myself multiple times and that only made things worse. I had severe depression and anxiety and I learned to deal with my PTSD! You think that was easy for me? You think letting you go was easy?! Letting you go was the hardest thing I ever had to do, so don't you dare punish me for something you lied about Wesley!"

"I didn't want you to have to go through the pain of losing me to cancer-"

"So instead you let my father kill you, and you were perfectly fine with letting me take the blame for it? Gee and here I thought you were an honest and trustworthy person. Thanks for letting me destroy myself." My anger was getting the best of me as tears started welling up in his eyes and I hated it.

"I'm sorry-"

"Sometimes sorry's aren't good enough Wes. Now take me back to Haley, I need to see what's going on." He shakes his head. "I can't." I glare at him.

"Why not? You did it before, why can't you do it again?" I snap, he sighs. "There is a time limit on how often you can visit people. You used your time." My eyes went wide.

"What do you mean I used my time? You mean temporarily right? I can see them again tomorrow?" He shakes his head. "I'm afraid there will be no tomorrow."

"What do you mean?" I question anxiously, he sighs. "When you're here, things are different. You get to see whoever you want for a limited time and then poof. You never get to see them again. That is until you are able to make your decision. If you decide to stay or don't get a choice then you will end up like me until someone you love is in the same situation you're in right now." I shake my head.

"This isn't fair! Haley could be losing the baby right now! Brandon and Piper are crying, and I didn't even get to see Tim and the others. This isn't fair!" He pulls me into his arms as I cry my eyes out. Images of everything that's happened pops into my head and I feel even worse. "I know. Which is why you have to hold on and fight this. It may take awhile but I am going to help you do whatever it takes to stay alive." He starts rubbing my back as I continue to cry into his shoulder.

"Everything is going to work out sweetheart." Chills went down my spine as I recognized the voice. I started crying even more once I actually turned around and saw her. "Mom?" She smiles and holds out her arms, I grab onto her tight.

"I don't understand. Wes said you moved on after helping him. How is this possible?" I ask, her smile turns wider as she chuckles. I missed her so much. "My good deeds got me into heaven. They showed me that one day you would be here with Wesley and in this exact situation so I asked what I could do to see you again. They said that in order for me to be able to see you that I have to help someone you love. Then Wesley came along and I helped him get through it. My favor was granted to me and ever since then I've been hanging around here."

"I missed you so much!" I just hold her tight. I can't forget this moment, it's too important. "I missed you too sweetheart. But we have to try and get you back as soon as possible." I shake my head.

"But I don't want to leave you." She wipes a tar from my face. "Awe sweetheart, as much as I would love for you to stay, you can't. You've got your whole life ahead of you. You've got a guy that loves you, you've got friends that love you, and most importantly you have Haley and the baby that love you. That baby needs you and Haley needs you too. You have to go back for them."

"But I don't deserve to live after what I've done." I reply, both mom and Wes shake their heads. "Are you kidding me Aide? You saved everyone's lives. You're a hero!" Wesley encourages, I shake my head.

"No. I ran away from my problems and that ended up in getting everyone killed. I'm the reason the both of you are dead. And I killed two people! I don't deserve it-"

"Stop. Stop it right now. You did the right thing. Don't you dare feel guilty for killing Satan and his spawn. They were risks to society and tried to kill everyone. They killed Stefano, they killed Brandon and Piper's mom, they killed Grayson's dad and little brother, they put you in a coma, they tried killing Gray and Tim, and they killed me and Wesley. You did what was right and you got rid of those monsters so don't you dare feel bad." My mother scolds, I sigh and put my face in my hands.

"I can't help it. These last few months I've felt like my head was going to explode. I found out so much about my life that it became so much to handle. I guess when I slit my wrists and took the bullet for Brandon, part of me wanted to die. I felt like if I was out of their lives then they would live a more perfect life. Now I don't know."

"That's not true. You protected and saved them. You should become a detective when you graduate because you can solve crime cases and lock up criminals and make sure that they don't get out." Wesley says with a smile, I shrug. "I don't know. I just want to get away for awhile-"

"Then take the year off and go to college late. Explore the world, I'm sure everyone will understand. Plus you've already graduated online so it's not like you have to worry about summer school." Mom replies.

"Do you really think that if I go back, everything will be okay?" I ask, they both nod. "You have nothing to worry about anymore. Since Rose and Carlyle were the head of the business, Tim will take over and can change the business to whatever he wants and you can live the life that you have always dreamed of. Everything will be good.You have to go in a few minutes so I'll give you this necklace. It's a picture of me and you in the hospital when you were born. Promise that you'll always carry this with you." She hands me a necklace, I look at her confused as I start seeing the black fog that Wesley was talking about.

"Will this be with me when I get back?" She nods and gives me a hug. "I will do everything in my power to make sure that it does." She replies with a smile.

I give her a bear hug as the fog comes closer. "I'm gonna miss you so much."

"I'll always be with you. We all will. I love you Adrianna." She gave me another hug before she disappeared. Then it was just me and Wesley alone as the walls starting crumbling down.

"I have to admit, I'm really going to miss you Aide. But I want you to promise me that no matter what you will be happy and live a good life. Travel the world, go to college, get married, be crazy! Do everything I never got to do." He says with tears in his eyes, I nod and give him a kiss.

"I needed to do that one last time. I'll never forget about you Wes." I replied with a smile, he smiles wide and nods as the darkness starts spreading around me. "I love you Aide. We all do, never forget that. Now before you go, can do me one more favor?"

I nod. "Sure, What is it?" His smile turned to a smirk. "Go get the guy" He replies with a wink, I chuckle.

"I will. Thank you for everything. I'll never forget you." I felt my eyes becoming heavier and my knees becoming weaker. The last thing I remember was seeing his smiling face before I was back in my old home. I freaked out even more when I saw my five year old self giggling and laughing with my family.

This is it. This is how my life is going to start again. First I have to face my demons. Let's do this.

Chapter 31- Adrianna Daniels

Lydia's POV This is it. This is how I'm going to get my life back. This is going to be very painful.

5 Year old Adrianna "Happy birthday Aide! You're five years old!" Rose says with a smile while hugging me, I smile. "Do you like my dress?" I ask while doing a twirl, Rose smiles and nods.

"I love it! You look beautiful. I have to go to work but I promise I'll be back for your birthday party." She replies, I pout. "You promise?"

"I promise." I'm so excited!

Hours went by and people were starting to arrive in our backyard. Mommy rented a bouncy house for all of the kids and daddy got me the best present ever!

"Here you go princess, I hope you like it." I smile wide as I see how big it is. I unwrapped the paper and saw the big box. "ITS A BOX!" I shout excitedly, everyone laughs.

"Yes, but look at what's inside the box." Mommy says, I open the box and squeal out of excitement when I see what's inside. "A BARBIE DREAM HOUSE!!!"

"Do you like it?" Daddy asks, I nod fast and smile harder. "I love it! Thank you!" I give him and mommy a hug.

Steffy gives me a small box. "This is from me and Rose, I hope you like it." I rip open the wrapping paper and smile when I see a Hannah Montana doll with extra clothes to dress her up with, plus she sings! "Thank you Steffy!" I give him a giant hug before looking around curiously.

"Where is Rose?" I ask, Steffy looks at mommy with a concerned look, mommy just smiles. "She should be here soon. Why don't you go play in the bounce house with Stefano." Steffy grabbed my hand and took me over to the bouncy house.

As I kid I never really understood what disappointment meant. But as the years went by and I got older, I found out.

6 Year old AdriannaIt was the day of my kindergarten graduation. It was a happy day. My class sang our school song, and a couple other childhood songs and it was really fun.

I even got flowers from mommy and daddy, and Steffy and Rose got me a bike and a diary.

It was one of the best days ever.

7 Year old Adrianna diary entryDear Diary,   I never see daddy anymore. He is always at work and mommy is always mad at him. When I do see him, he acts funny and says very mean things to mommy and Stefano. Things are not the same anymore. I'm scared.

8 year old AdriannaIt was the day of my school play. I was so excited because I was the lead and the play was Aladdin. It was my favorite movie as a little kid, almost my whole family showed up to the play. Tim, mom, Stefano, and Nate and his family came.

I'm really upset because my microphone string fell through my costume and it looked like I was wearing a saggy diaper. It was horrible, everyone laughed at me backstage and I was humiliated.

What made it even worse was the reason I was even distracted and the string fell in the first place was because my father burst through the doors drunk out of his mind screaming "THATS MY GIRL! TELL HIM OFF!"

The ride home was horrible. Nobody spoke to each other and Stefano knew that I was angry and upset so he tried comforting me.

"It's okay Aide. Dad is just not feeling good-"

"That's a lie and you know it Stef. Dad is drunk. I may only be eight but he's been doing this for a year now and it's getting out of hand. I shouldn't have to deal with this!" I stormed out of my room and sat on the staircase but I could only hear my parents arguing.

"How could you do this to her Carlyle?! She's humiliated!" Mom shouted, dad laughed. "I'm just showing support for my daughter! Is that so bad?"

"No. What's bad is you coming home either drunk or high out of your mind and it's bullshit. The only reason I deal with you is for the sake of the children! They are the only things that are keeping this marriage alive. You're nothing but dirt and the bottom of my shoes. You're a bastard-" Dad cut mom off by slapping her across the face. I gasped in shock and ran into my room.

I cried the rest of that night.

11 Year Old AdriannaThis was the day that things were supposed to change. She was supposed to leave him. Instead she dealt with it by getting drunk too.

Why does she keep going back?!

"Get up." I demand. She grunts and throws her pillow over her head, I grunt in anger. "I said get up!" I tried pulling her but she pushed me to the ground instead. By the time I stood up, I was ready to snap at her, and so I did.

"Look at yourself! You hate dad because he spends his days doing god knows what and comes home drunk off his shit! You are supposed to be the one that's protecting us. If we stay here, we are going to die and I won't make it past 13. WAKE UP!" I scream, she starts crying, I roll my eyes as I hear the front door slam shut.

"You're late. Dinner is in the fridge, go heat it up." I say to my father with anger on my voice, he chuckles. "Forget dinner! Go get me another beer." He slurs, I roll my eyes.

"No, you're already drunk enough." He glared at me. The look in his eye scared me. Don't show fear. Don't show fear. "What did you just say?" He growls, I shake my head fast.

"N-n-nothing." I continued walking down the stairs and went to the fridge. When I saw there were no beers, I freaked out a little, but then I saw an empty bottle and decided to make my own concoction of alcohol.

I mixed vodka with rum and put it into the bottle. After I mixed it together, I gave it to the monster and he took a sip. Unfortunately for me, he realized it wasn't beer.

"What is this shit?! This isn't beer!" He throws the bottle at me, it cuts me and tears threaten to leave my eyes but I refuse to let him see me cry. "Adrianna... I'm sorry-"

"Save it."

I had to get seven stitches that night, and the shards of glass just missed my artery so I got lucky.

12 Year Old AdriannaThis was the day that my life changed forever. This was the day my mother was murdered. This was the day that my life would forever be changed.

I remember hearing mom and dad fighting so Stefano took me outside while Rose dealt with them and made sure Carlyle stayed in line. Some job she did, bitch.

"Come on Aide, let's go throw a ball around, it'll be fun." Stefano grabbed his football and took me into the backyard. We could hear mom and dad arguing but he kept talking to me so I could block it out.

"So what's the deal with Nate? I had you guys have a little thing going on." He teases, I roll my eyes. "None of your business." I reply with a chuckle, he pretends to be hurt.

"As your big brother, it is my business. But I see how it is, be that way!" He continued with a laugh. That was until we heard screaming and the sound of glass breaking.

I went to run in but Stefano grabbed my arm. "Aide no-"

"She could be hurt. I have to." I ran inside and saw my dad pulling at his hair with blood on his hands as he freaked out. "Dad? We heard screaming. What's going on?" He doesn't look at me, instead he just starts scratching himself to a point where he started bleeding.

"Where's mom?" I ask, he doesn't answer. I felt something drop on my face so I went to wipe it off. Once I realized it was blood, I looked up. It was coming from the attic. I have to find her.

I went to run up the stairs to the attic but dad stopped me. "You can't go up there." I glare at him. "There's blood dripping from the ceiling. My bet is that it's mom. I have to save her!" I continued to run up the stairs but instead, he threw me down.

"I said no! It's too dangerous!" He whisper shouts, I glare at him. "You killed her didn't you? Oh my god... you killed my mother!"

"No. It wasn't me! You don't get it! She's up there. And she wants revenge." He whisper shouts again, I look at him curiously. "She's not as innocent as she seems."

"I don't believe you. Mom! Mom are you okay?!" I got up, ran up the stairs, and pushed the attic door open. I saw Rose standing over her body covered in blood. I ran over to mom with tears in my eyes.

"Mom? Mom wake up! Please wake up!" I plead, Rose shakes her head. "She's dead Aide."

I look up at her only to see that she has a smile on her face. I thought it was weird but I didn't really think anything of it. "Did he do this?" I question angrily, she slowly nods as he comes up the stairs.

"Adrianna, I want you to do as I say and pick up the gun. Take it and shoot your sister." He demands, referring to the gun that's at the bottom of my mothers blood pool. I look at Rose and then dad and shake my head.

"I can't." He rolls his eyes and slaps his head. "You are so naive. Don't you understand that I didn't do it? It was her! Pick up the gun Aide." Dad shouts, I shake my head as tears stream down my face.

"I won't do it!" I shout back while shaking my head, he chuckles and pulls Stefano close. He holds a knife to his throat. "Fine. We will do this the hard way. Either you pick up that gun and kill her right now, or I will slit his throat on the spot. You choose." Stefano has always been there for me. But Rose is my sibling as well. I can't do this.

"DO YOU WANT ME TO KILL HIM RIGHT HERE?!" Dad screams, I shake my head fast, he smirks. "Then pick up the gun. And shoot her!"

I can't let him die.

I slowly picked up the gun and took the safety off. Mom had taught me to use a gun just in case I had to defend myself, now is the time.

Rose shakes her head. "Aide... Aide please don't do this!" Rose pleads, I shake my head. "I have no choice! I'm so sorry Rose." I close my eyes and pull the trigger. It hit her right in the heart and she went down without suffering.

"Good girl. Now stick with your brother and go outside. We are going to get far away from here. But first, we have to get rid of the past.

Me and Stefano ran downstairs, outside, and just kept running until we reached Tim's house. Tim hooked us up with hair dye, color contacts, and new ID's and he called his friend who took us to Canada.

I can't believe I didn't remember it being Rose who killed my mother. Now I understand why every time I thought about Carlyle I would pull my hair and start scratching... I was remembering repressed memories. He was actually trying to protect us. I just killed him for nothing. Holy shit.

Chapter 32- Kate Georgsson

----

13 Year old Kate (Adrianna) Today is my 13th birthday. Things have been great this past year. Stefano and I have been able to laugh again and know what it's like to not be afraid for once. It was nice.

"Are you ready to party tonight?" My best friend Phoebe asks, I nod excitedly. "Totally! It is going to be so much fun!"

"That's a fact. We are going to have fun music, games, and decorations. Trust me when I say you're gonna love it." My other best friend Tyler replies while singing his arm around the both of us, we all laugh as the bell rings.

"Okay, well I have to get to class otherwise Mrs. Liona will have my head. Let's meet back here after school and then we can ride our bikes to the park." They both not in agreement. "Sounds great. Happy birthday Kate."

A couple hours later school was out and it was time for my party. I was so excited. Phoebe and Tyler had worked it out with their parents and we are having a party in the park.

"You look great!" Phoebe says with a smile, I smile back. "Thanks. Let's get this party started!" Luckily we reserved a small area in the park so that we wouldn't be bothering people with our music.

Tyler cranked up the music and everyone was laughing and dancing. We even played all sorts of games.

The night was going great until Stefano showed up and pulled me away from the party. "What the hell Stef?!" I shouted angrily, he motions for me to be quiet.

"That's not my name here Kate. But these won't be our names for much longer..." He replied apprehensively. There's something he's not telling me, I can tell.

"What's wrong? Why did you pull me away?" I question while calming down, he sighs and hands me a letter. I look at it and start reading. When I realized who it's from, my heart felt like it was going to jump out of my chest.

Dear Children,   After everything we have been through, honestly think you can hide from me? Sorry to break up your happiness but I have my sources and they have already found you. Now, I know you're going to try and run but it's no use because I have made sure that your passports and credit cards have been declined and destroyed. You can try to run but I'll always find you. See you soon.-Carlyle

I started to panic. "He's found us." Stefano nods, I start to hyperventilate. "We are going to get through this okay?"

I couldn't even look at him. My vision was starting to turn blurry and he was starting to worry about me. "Aide, what's happening? Are you okay?"

I don't answer. I just start scratching and my hands start shaking. "Aide, you need to breathe!"

"Is she okay?" Tyler and Phoebe ask while walking over to us. Stefano puts me in his arm and sighs. "Unfortunately no, I'm so sorry guys but our grandmother is terminally ill. My mother just called me, we have to leave immediately."

"Oh my gosh, I'm so sorry. How long are you guys going to be gone for?" Phoebe questions, Stefano shrugs. "I don't know, it could be a long time. Mom signed us up for schools down in Texas. We have to get going right away."

Phoebe walks up to me and hugs me, I cry onto her shoulder. "We really are going to miss you Kate. Promise you won't forget us?" Tyler says, I nod and give him a hug as well.

"I'm going to miss you guys so much. I promise I'll try to write you guys letters once a week. Hopefully we will see each other again soon. I really have to go. Goodbye." I turned and left them with tears in my eyes.

Worst birthday ever.

I never saw them again. We drove home as fast as we could that night. We packed our stuff, got in the car and called Tim from a pay phone three cities down. He hooked us up with new names and stuff and we were able to rent an apartment in Massachusetts. I hate the fact that Stefano lies to them about going to Texas but now I realize that it was needed.

If only I could see them one last time to explain everything. I wish.

Chapter 33- Ashley Davis and Morgan Sage

There is not much to tell about my next two lives as Ashley Davis and Morgan Sage. Both were really short and just worsened my mental health.

14 Year old Ashley Davis It's been a year since Carlyle found us. We were able to settle down again and Stefano found a cool job at an art museum.

I refuse to make any friends because I know that the minute I settle down, we are going to have to run again. It's not fair. Why can't I ever be happy? I wouldn't wish this kind of life on my worse enemy.

At school, I make sure that everyone stays clear me. Stefano doesn't like it because I cause chaos in order for people to stay away but it's my method of coping.

I haven't been able to stop thinking about when he's going to come for us. He killed mom and now he's destroying me mentally. Stefano doesn't understand. Everyday goes by and he acts as if everything is okay and like we didn't just run away from a murderer who is our father.

"What's wrong Aide? Why are you doing this to yourself?" Stefano asks as I have my meltdown. I just laugh in his face and start scratching again.

"What's wrong is that I can't stop thinking about what happened and you're just acting as if we didn't see anything." I snap, he sighs. "Aide, you can't think about it-"

"How can I not think about something that has been tearing me up for years?! Carlyle killed mom and then he killed Rose! I could've stopped it! I could've stopped him-"

"There's nothing you could've done Aide." He says sympathetically, I get angrier. "Bullshit! I could've seen the signs, I could've done something. I could've told somebody what he did to us! I could've helped them. I could've saved them." I start panicking and scratching as I think of that night. The events just keep playing in my head over and over.

"Aide... calm down." Stefano tries to touch my hand but I pull away and freak out more. "Don't go up there. I said no!" I shout, recalling memories of that night.

"Aide you're scaring me-"

"Kill her or I'll kill him!" I shout again, holding a knife to my wrists, Stefano shakes his head. "Stop it! This isn't you!"

"I can't. Don't you see? This is never going to end unless I make it end. I need to! I need this!"

The last thing I remember from that day was blacking out after I cut myself and waking up in the hospital. He found us through my medical records.

14 Year old Morgan SageI didn't even go to school as Morgan Sage because of what happened before I was hospitalized. Stefano set me up with a

therapist and I was homeschooled all of the three months we were actually in New York.

"I don't want to see a therapist! I'm not crazy!" I shout angrily, Stefano shakes his head. "Of course you're not. But you can't keep hurting yourself! I almost lost you back there and you don't even seem to care!" She shouts back, I roll my eyes.

"Maybe I would be better off dead. Did you ever think of that? I could've stopped it. It should've been me and not her. I should've taken that gun and put it to my head. It should've been me! Not her!" Tears start falling down my face as he shakes his head, grabs my hands and shows me my now bandages wrists.

"Look at these! This needs to stop. Your bad thoughts are why I'm taking you to Dr. Green. She can at least try to help-"

"NOBODY CAN HELP ME!" I shouted so loud that my voice became hoarse. "You're going to Dr. Green weather you like it or not. You need to talk about your issues, so get your ass into the car and shut the fuck up. I am here to help you get better and I intend to do so." I was shocked, he's usually think nice flowers and rainbows kind of guy. I guess I never realized how moms death effected him as well.

"Hello Morgan, I'm Dr. Green. Today we are going to do what I usually do with my patients to start the session. We are going to do this with ink drawings. I am going to show you some drawings, and you are going to tell me what you see. Next visit I am going to analyze your responses and explain on how we are going to help you get better. Sound good?"

"I don't want to be here. But if all I have to do is what you just said then fine. Let's start." She took out a bunch of square paintings and asked me what I thought they were.

"Blood" She shouldered me the next. "A scared person." Next one. "Crow." Next one. "Knives." And the final one. "Murder."

As I left her office she looked sad. She seems smart so she probably already interpreted my emotions based off of everything. I would be scared too. ————"Morgan, I've analyzed your interpretations of the paintings and I have to say I'm quite impressed. Usually kids your age see bunny rabbits and rainbows, but you've turned it to a new level. I can really tell that you've gone through something horrible. So let's start at the beginning-"

"You do realize I'm not actually gonna admit anything to you right? The reason I'm here in the first place is because I couldn't keep my mouth shut and I tend to keep my mouth shut from now on."

It was a really long session. She tried to get everything out of me but I just wouldn't budge. That was until my very last visit with her. —————-"So tell me Morgan, how are things?" Dr. Green asked, I rolled my eyes and chuckled. "Just peachy miss! How are things with you?"

"These sessions aren't about me-"

"I know. These sessions are for you to get paid to tell me how crazy I am. Well I'm not crazy, I just had a moment and you would too if you were in my situation." I snapped, she sighed and told me to take a seat.

"You're not crazy Morgan. Tell me what's been going on." She says calmly, I shake my head. "I can't tell you because if I tell you then you'll be dead in a couple of days."

"What do you mean Morgan?" She asks apprehensively, I laugh and plop on the chair across from her. "People die when I tell them things. I get to know people and let them in and the boom their dead. I'm not crazy, I'm just spitting facts. You want me to open up but I can't because I don't want you to die."

Her eyes went wide. I could tell she was nervous. "Morgan, you're scaring me..."

"You should be scared. I'm running from my past and it's about to catch up to me. No amount of therapy is ever going to make me forget what I've done."

"What have you done?" She asks, I sigh while looking at my nails. "I've hurt, I've lost and most painfully I've killed. My spirit is dead and no amount of therapy is ever going to fix that." I walked out of her office without another word and got into Stefano's car. We drove to our next state to start our new lives.

Chapter 34- Alison Carters

This is where my story gets even more twisted. I was comfortable here, but my father had to ruin it.

14 Year old Alison CartersOkay this is just getting really ridiculous now. I give up on making friends, I give up on any hope that one day I am gonna be happy again or even start a family. I give up on everything.

As I sit here in Drama class listening to the tragic tale of Macbeth, I can't help but laugh at the fact that my life is even more twisted then the mind of Macbeth ever was.

I was cut out of my train of thought by some boy talking to me. He's been talking for awhile now, I've just been ignoring him. Ugh why did I have to talk to him. "I'm sorry what?"

"Mrs. Fletcher said we have to partner up. We are doing Romeo and Juliet and everyone is partnered up already which leaves me with you. So come on, let's practice." He said sarcastically, I roll my eyes and start reading lines.

Weeks later...We ended up getting an A on the project. Apparently we did so good that Mrs. Fletcher paired us up for the rest of the year.

"Hey Wes, my sister is having a party tonight, wanna come?" Nina Sanders. Gosh I hate that bitch. She thinks she owns everyone just because her dad is the senator. And of course she wanted Wesley. Everyone wanted him. How could you not? He's got the cutest dimples and those green eyes could melt anyone's soul.

He looked at me and smirked before wrapping his arm around me. "Sorry Nina, I have a date with Ali." Her eyes went wide, he gave me a look that told me to play along so I smirked.

"You two are dating?" We both nod, she rolls her eyes. "Well, if you change your mind you know where to find me." She winks at him and then glares at me as she walked off.

"Thank you so much, you saved my ass from an uncomfortable groping session." He says with a chuckle while hugging me. "Yeah, she's really into you isn't she?" I replied with a chuckle.

"Yeah, but I've got my eye on someone else." He replies with a wide smile, I smile back and try to get it out of him. "Ooooo who is it? Is it Tina? Laura? Madison? Paige?" He shakes his head, I start hitting him.

"Tell me you jerk!" I tease, he laughs and continues to shake his head. "Sorry Ali, but I can't tell you yet. Not till I know she likes me back. You'll know soon." With that sentence, he walked away which left me speechless.

I want to know so badly who it is and part of me is hoping that I'm the one he likes. I know I shouldn't but I think I'm falling for him.

15 Year old Alison Carters"Happy birthday Ali!" Wesley says with a bright smile while giving me a hug and twirling me around. "Thanks Wes. I have a good feeling that today is going to be a great day."

"I think it will. Especially since I got us these!" He hands me a ticket and I freak out when I see who the tickets are to see. My favorite band 5 Seconds of Summer. Front row. Holy shit.

"No way! Oh my god I love you!" I guess it was a spur of the moment thing but I jumped into his arms and kissed him of the cheek. His face was turning red, I couldn't help but laugh.

"I know how much you love Michael Clifford so I figured I would make this day special for you. You said it yourself that you haven't had a good birthday in years. I am here to change that. So Alison Carters, will you be my date to see your favorite band in concert?" He asked with a smile, I nodded really fast and hugged him again.

It was one of the best nights of my life. It was the night that Wesley and I officially became an item. Unfortunately for us though, his sister (Haley) was dating my brother. We should've stopped our relationship there... maybe things would've been different a year later.

16 Year old Alison Carters"No no no! This is bad. This is really really bad!" I freak out, Wesley tried comforting me but it didn't work. I started scratching again. "What's going on Alison?" I shake my head and turn away from him and scratch harder, starting to open up my scars.

"Stop! You're gonna hurt yourself! Just tell me what's going on Ali! Please, open up to me!" He turns me around, I shake my head again. "I love you so much Wesley... but I can't see you hurt. It'll kill me."

"I'm not going anywhere. Please just talk to me. Whatever it is Ali-"

"Please stop calling me that. That is not my name! My name is Adrianna!" I snap. Shit. He looks at me with a concerned look. "What?" My heart melted, he looked so hurt.

"I've said to much-"

"No Adrianna! You haven't said anything and that's the problem. These past two years have been amazing but I knew something was up with you since day one. I love you okay? And nothing is ever going to change that but you have to open up to me or you're going to end up killing yourself! I'm not stupid. I see your scars, and you're just continuing to scratch. Please open up to me, I can help." He holds my hands and makes me look into his eyes. I start crying as someone bangs on my door.

Stefano comes barging in. "Aide, we have to go now. Wesley are you with us or not?" Stefano says apprehensively, Wesley nods and runs with us.

He didn't even know what he was getting himself into and that's how much he loved me. I explained everything to him in the car but just as he was about to speak, we were hit head on with a car.

I woke up in my old basement. I thought the place had burned down but I guess not. "Ah she's awake!" Carlyle says enthusiastically while holding a knife to my throat.

"Let her go!" Wes shouts, I shake my head. "No Wes, it's okay." Carlyle looks between the both of us and just smirks.

"Actually no, everything is not okay. Your little girlfriend here owes me her life-"

"Don't you dare hurt her!" Wes shouts with tears in his eyes, Carlyle turns to look at him as I shake my head. Don't do it. Please don't do it.

"Or what? You're just a love sick puppy. What could you possibly do?" Carlyle teases, Wesley looks at him with daggers. "I love her-"

"Love is pain and will only result in death. You are weak if you even believe in love." Carlyle spats, Wesley laughs. "I may be weak but at least I'm not a heartless monster. You are incapable of love. You hurt you children and wife just so that they can fear you and that is what I call being a coward-"

"Oh please! What do you know? You're just a 16 Year old weakling whose falling for a little whore. I hope you enjoy the show. Because right after I blow your girlfriend's brains out I'm coming for you next." Don't do it Wes. Please don't.

You don't have to do this!" Wesley shouts, dad chuckles. "You don't know what I have to do. You know too much. And people who know to much snitch, you know what snitches get? Stitches!" Dad screams, tears are streaming down my face as Wesley turns around. Before he could say anything to me, my father shot him' making his blood splash over me in the process.

"NOOO! WHAT DID YOU DO?! WHAT THE FUCK DID YOU DO?!" I screamed while running over to Wesley, dad laughs. "That boy is dead as a door nail. You think you can leave me and go without me knowing? You and your brother think you're so slick but you're not Adrianna! Oh wait, I forgot you go by Morgan now. Or was is Alison? I can't quite remember."

"You're a bastard!"

"Yeah, but so is your brother. And you're nothing but his little bitch. What, are the two of you into incest now or something?" He comments with a sly grin, I glare at him. "You're sick!" I shout while grabbing his knife and holding it to my wrists.

"Sick? No. Psychotic? Maybe. So why don't you put the knife down before you hurt yourself-"

"YOU'RE MAKING ME DO THIS! You fucked up my brain! You messed with my head! I JUST WANT THIS TO BE OVER! I WANNA DIE!"

"Don't do this Adrianna-"

"Or what? You can't kill me if I'm already dead! I loved Wes and YOU KILLED HIM!"

"He knew too much! My sweet, sweet girl." He goes to stroke my hair, but I stabbed his hand in the process. "YOU LITTLE BITCH!"

"I'd rather be a bitch than be your daughter. You're a psychotic piece of shit! You killed them! You killed them all! I'm gonna make sure you pay for it." I scream, he laughs.

"And what are you gonna do? Shoot me?"

"YOU KILLED THEM! Now it's your turn to die!" I charged at him and stabbed him until he was the one that was down on the ground. Then I ran back over to Wesley.

"Wesley! Wesley please wake up!" I shake him. He doesn't budge. I start screaming and crying over his body as Stefano and Haley come barging in the room. Haley started hysterically crying as well while Stefano only asked me what happened.

"He killed him. He killed them all!" I went to grab his hand again but Stefano pulled me and Haley away. "I can't leave him!" I scream with tears streaming down my face, Stefano sighs.

"I know you don't want to, but you're going to have to. If we stay here Carlyle will suck his men after us. We have to go!" He picked me up, threw me over his shoulders and started running. I screamed and screamed for him to leg me down but he never did.

We left Carlyle to die but unfortunately we weren't that lucky because he found us in California.

Wesley's death literally destroyed me, probably even more than my mother's death did. I wanted to die so badly after but Stefano and Haley kept me on strict watch. I never even got to say goodbye. In a way I'm glad that I was able to see him and mom again because they are what is motivating me to go back. If it wasn't for them, I would be staying here and dying. But I have to live. And this is the only way for now. I can't wait to move on from my past.

Chapter 35- Lydia Stone

After Wesley's death, Haley and Stefano thought it would be best to keep their eyes on me for a year so they homeschooled me. Which is why when I actually started school, I was so nervous.

17 Year old Lydia Stone

"Stef I'm nervous." I say to my older brother, he rolls his eyes. "Damn it Aide, how many times did I tell you we have to use our new names. It's Lorenzo now Lydia."

"Fine. I'm very nervous Enzo, I feel like something bad is going to happen and you know I'm never wrong." It feels like I have a rock in the pit of my stomach that's trying to push out. I'm scared.

"You can't be nervous, you just have to think positive-"

"How can I think positive when he's out there looking for us?" I snap angrily, he sighs and grabs my hand. "I promised myself that I would not let anything bad happen to you and I am going to keep that promise until the day I die. He's not going to find us this time, just keep your contacts in and keep your head held up high. We are going to go to school. We are going to make friends. And we are going to have a good life. From now on we have to forget about him and start focusing on our lives alright sis?"

I slowly nod. He's always found us, what says this time it's going to be any different?

"Okay good. Now get going, you're going to be late for your first day of senior year!" Before I could protest, he shoved my car keys in my hand and pushed me out the door. Stupid Stefano.————-The cafeteria was packed inside so I decided to go to the quad where others have lunch, at first I was eating while reading my book alone until I was approached by the guy in the SnapBack from earlier. "10 Things I Hate About You, excellent choice but have you seen the movie?"

"Yes I have. Didn't think a guy like you would though." I replied sarcastically, he smirks. "What can I say? I guess I'm just a hopeless romantic. So do you have a phone?"

"Maybe I do maybe I don't. What's it to you?" I flipped to the next page in my book, not even looking up at him. "Maybe I can call you sometime."

"Yeah sure my number is 555-N-O-T- gonna happen." I looked up at him only to see him with a smirk plastered on his face. What is this guys' problem?

"You're tough, I like that." He winks, I rolled my eyes. "Yo Brandon! Let's go!" One of his friends called, he flipped them off and looked back at me with an innocent smile.

"Duty calls, see you around Lydia." I forgot to mention he is in my math, gym and drama classes so now he knows my name. Wonderful. ————-You see that brunette?" Piper asks, pointing to a guy wearing a leather jacket, I nod. "That's Mrs Thomas' stepson Nathan, although he takes his birth mothers last name which is Davis. He runs the school along with my brother and their goon squad." Piper adds on with an eye roll. She clearly doesn't like them.

"The one that is playing the guitar is Grayson, he is the only good one in the group meaning he doesn't undress girls with his eyes like the rest do." Piper's friend says with a smile.

"The one with the jawline sculpted by god is Vince, him and Nathan are the ones you really have to watch out for. And lastly the one in the SnapBack that you were just talking to is my brother Brandon. Oh and this is my friend Blaire, she's pretty cool and her fashion sense is on poi nt."——————Damn, I really felt like kicking ass today." Piper grunts causing me to chuckle. "Why?"

"Grace is up my ass today." She replies while face palming herself, I give her a questioning look. "Who's Grace?"

"Let us embrace you into the wonderful world that is my evil sister. She's blonde, she's perky, and most of all she's a stone cold bitch." Blaire says with a chuckle, I look at her as if she had three heads. "She can't possibly be that bad-"

"Hey hobbit. Who's the fresh meat? The boys are going to eat her up! Honey I don't know why you would hang out with my ugly sister and her dumb friends instead of living the cool life with me. Here's my number if you change your mind. Kisses!" First she took my phone and put her number in it, then she blew a kiss and walked away.

"Yeah never mind she's a bitch." I reply dryly as we watch her walk away, the girls just laugh. "I told you. She started referring to me as hobbit because she feels as if I resemble smeagol from Lord of The Rings." Blaire says with anger clear on her face, I shake my head.——————-Nathan caught up with me. "Hey Lydia! Do you want a ride?" I decided to say yes because I don't feel like dealing with people's bullshit on the bus today.

"Sure." The minute me got into the car, it was silent. That was until he decided to break the silence and turn the radio on. "Can I ask you something?" He questions, I sigh while looking out the window.

"That depends on what you're going to ask." I reply with a chuckle, he smiles. "Why do you hide behind this tough wall of hate and bitchiness?"

"I don't know, why do you and your friends fuck everything without a penis?" I reply sarcastically, he smirks. "Touché"

"Alright well since you asked me I have to ask you now. What really is midnight madness? I keep getting bits and pieces of information but I don't know exact details." He starts laughing. What the hell is he laughing at?

"Well let me fill you in. Midnight madness is basically an excuse for everyone to get drunk, for girls to dress slutty and for everyone party hard. People get high, have sex, dance, and sing. After all of the craziness, Me, Blaire, Piper and Gray help Vince clean up and we usually get so drunk that we start spilling secrets but that's a story for another time. Oh and the iconic midnight kiss. To be honest I have no idea how that even came to light, it just became a thing. Any more questions?"

"Actually yes. This one is completely random but are you into Blaire? Because if you are I think you two would make a cute couple. I've seen the way you guys look at each other, it's got love written all over it."

"Nah, it's not like that-"

"Oh come on! You guys would be so adorable!"

"Lydia I don't think you understand." He replies with a chuckle, I look at him confused. "What do you mean?"

"She doesn't like me because she doesn't like boys. She's into girls." That was enough to make us go silent. "Oh." I said awkwardly, he just started laughing hysterically.

"It's not funny Nate I didn't know!" I punched his shoulder which only made him smirk. "You're cute when you're angry." He says randomly, I smirk.

"Only when I'm angry? Sorry dude, I'm cute all the time!" I reply while doing a hair flip. Its a joke. Don't get triggered.————-"So are we going to talk about what just happened back there?" Nathan questions awkwardly, breaking the silence. I chuckle. "What? The kiss, it was nothing-"

"No, I mean the fact that you freaked out when we talked about the pictures being leaked. Is there something going on that you're not saying? Do I need to call child protective-"

"No! It's nothing like that. Just please delete the pictures. Delete them all. I can't be traced." That sounded so sketchy. Way to go Adrianna!

"I can't delete what others posted. What's so dangerous about one little picture? Are you afraid that your brother is going to ground you?" He questions, I shake my head. "Yeah, something like that."

If only you knew...

"If you're afraid about your brother, I can fight. I'll protect you-"

"That won't be necessary. I'll be fine in my own-"

"No. I insist-"

"I can't be in a relationship with you. I shouldn't even be friends with any of you. You need to stay away from me, I can take care of myself and-"

"That's ridiculous! Why would I stay way from you?" Jesus Nate just cooperate! "Because you don't want someone like me in your life. Where I go, danger follows. I don't expect you to understand."

"Then make me-"

"I can't Nate! You don't get it! I can't be with you nor can I be friends with someone like you! Thanks for the ride but I no longer need your assistance. Do me a favor a delete those photos." That was it, I snapped. I got out of the car and the front door of my house swung open. I could see the disappointment on Stefano's face.

I'm sorry.

I was yanked into the house by my brother and thrown onto the coach. "Are you insane?! What the hell is wrong with you! Did my speech mean nothing to you?!" He shouts, a tear falls down my face, but then anger consumes me.

"I deserve to live life to the fullest Stef! You got to live the high school dream and what did I get?! School after school! Name after name! Hair color after color! It's endless-"

"Your mistakes may have just cost you your life! Say goodbye to your friends, make an excuse, I really don't give a shit. You crossed a major line Aide! You not only disobeyed me, but you drugged me and then got yourself so drunk that it's all over social media! We stayed out of the news for a reason! No pictures. No phones. No technology. Nothing that can trace back to us Aide!" He screams, I'll admit I saw a bit of our father in him and that made me petrified.

"I need freedom!"

"Freedom my ass! You know what Carlyle will do once he finds us. If we don't run, if we don't hide! It'll be the end for everyone! I understand you're a teenager now, I understand you want to have fun, but this is your life now Aide! Our father is a monster and we are on the run! You want to be normal?! We will never be normal after what we saw! We will never be normal after what he made us do! HE'S A MONSTER AND I DON'T WANT TO DIE AT THE HANDS OF THAT BASTARD! So keep your nose out of everyone's business and stay away, otherwise I'll make you." The tone in his voice was indescribable. He was stern, he was angry, but most of all, he was scary. And that's all I needed to hear in order to get my act together.

"I hate you! Sometimes I feel as if you are just like him. You're trapping me-"

"I'm protecting you-"

"From what?! You can't protect me from the world Stef! I could die any day at the hands of our father! Might as well live it to the fullest." I screamed at him and then the world stopped. He hit me. He's never hit me before.

"I HATE YOU!"—————-"Hey hobbit. Hey slut. Hey demon. Nice costumes." Grace says sneakily, smirking at the names she gave me, Blaire and Piper. I chuckle and take an intimidating step towards her.

"Hey Grace. Your costume is pretty nice too, what are you again? I forgot. Was it a hooker or a prostitute? Oh no wait I forgot this year you decided to go as the dumb blond! Hm, it suits you."

"Oh SHIt! Go babe!" Brandon chants, making a circle of people surround us. Grace and I find ourselves caught up in a stare down. She tried to look intimidating so she took a step forward just as I did. I'm not backing down. "I'd watch what I say if I were you-"

"Or what? You have nothing on me." I reply with a growl, she smirks evilly. "I can ruin you."

"I'm already ruined. Sorry, but your bitchiness can't bother me. I know that you are just sad and insecure and that is why you pick on everyone else. I really don't know how Grayson puts up with you, if I were him I would just throw you down the garbage shoot and take out the trash."

The crowd erupts in a spur of 'Oooohs'

I just chuckle as her cheeks go red. "You're gonna regret that bitch-"

"Yes I am a bitch and I'm proud. I don't regret anything and I never will. Your reign here as queen is over, move over there's a new bitch in town." I walked away without a care in the world and went over to the karaoke section.

"Grace, this ones for you." I stood up and made sure people could see me, specifically so Grace could see me and I started singing. "Said lil bitch you can't fuck with me if you wanted to!"———-

I drove to school with a smile on my face, I was ready to tell him everything. This was my chance. I held my head up high even as I got glares and glances by a bunch of people. I didn't care who was staring at me, I was going to go up to Nate and tell him.

I skipped over to his locker with a smile. "Hey Nate." I said flirtatiously, he didn't flinch. "Hey." He said shortly, I looked at him as if he had just said something wrong which in my opinion he did. He never talks dryly with me, I'm the only one he really opens up to.

"What's up?"

"The sky." He closed his locker and was slammed against the locker by some girl. I didn't think anything of it until the girl started kissing him. Then I got a good look at the girl who was looking right at me only to realize that it was Grace.

Anger started building up in my body. I hate her. I was so angry that tears started forming in my eyes. I would not let her win, I will not let them see me cry. I just ran in the opposite direction. I sat in home room, slammed my books on the floor and buried my head in my arms. I'm tired of getting spit on. Can't I just have one thing that is good in my life?!

"Lydia, are you okay?" Brandon questions, I glare at him with tears rolling down my face. "Do I look okay to you?" I snap angrily, he sighs.

"No you don't, that's why I'm asking you. Look I may act like a douchebag but I have feelings too, you can talk to me. What's wrong?" He goes to grab my hand but I pull away and sniffle.

"As if I would ever tell you. All you want is a ticket into my pants-"

"That's not true-"

"Oh really? Ever since I got here you have been talking about having sex with me to all of your stupid friends. You all have your stupid book and call yourselves the overachievers because you take pride in taking people's virginity. I'm not a virgin so forget about that and I'm not some ticket that you can use whenever you want either. I'm a person, and people have feelings." I let all my anger out on him but I didn't feel one inch of guilt.

"This is about Nate isn't it?" He questions, I roll my eyes and wipe away my tears. "You know what, just forget about it."

"No. What he did was not cool. He led you on and pretended to be Grayson's friend just so he could get to Grace. He's in the wrong-"

"Don't talk to me about being in the wrong. You've done bad things too Brandon. So don't try and pull the crap on me."

"Are you actually defending him? He first spread rumors about you, then led you on, broke up Gray and Grace, and then started going out with

Grace. And yes, I admit I have done some bad things but thats not really me, I'm just hiding behind the death of my mom okay? But I'm done being like that. I want to be good. And you're going to help me." He replies with a smile, I roll my eyes and glare at him.

"And why would I do that?" I snap, he chuckles. "Because, if Nate sees you hanging out with me more and more then maybe he will start to get jealous. I know that what ever is happening to him is all because of Grace, she's a master manipulator and she's not gonna stop until she gets what she wants and that was Nate. You'll help me be good and I'll help you get Nate back. Think about it." He got up out of his seat and walked to his first period class as the bell rang.

I decided to follow him to his locker, once he closed his locker and saw me standing there he jumped. "Alright Santiago, I'll give it a shot. Lesson one of being good, get to class on time."

"Jesus Lydia! You scared the crap out of me!" He shouts, I chuckle and smirk. "Good. At least I know I have your attention now. See you later."

"Wait, you can't just do that!" He calls out, clearly shocked, I laugh. "I just did." I shout back while walking to class. ---------"So what's the deal with you and Brandon?" Piper questions with a tone of worry in her voice, I shake my head. "Nothing. We are helping each other that's all. I'm teaching him how to be a good person and in return he's helping me make Nate jealous."

"Wow. You really are evil." She replies with a big smirk, I chuckle. "I'm not evil. I just know what I want."————-Why are you telling us this?" She questions, I sigh. "My brother got a letter from our father. He found us again, I wanted you guys to know for two reasons. One, because I might have to leave again and I want to keep you guys out of danger, and two because Grace knows everything somehow and I'm pretty sure that is what she has on me."

Piper immediately grabbed her stuff and got up. "I have to go. I'm sorry." She ran out as fast as she could leaving me to start crying again, while Brandon comforted me. "This is why I didn't want to tell you guys. I'm so sorry!"

"No, there is no reason the be sorry." He starts rubbing my back as I cry in him arms. I knew this was a bad idea, I shouldn't have brought them into this. "I was afraid to tell you because I was afraid that what Piper just did would happen. I shouldn't have dragged you into this. I should've just stayed away-"

"Hey, I'm right here. I'm not going anywhere." He tries to reassure me, I shake my head. "Brandon he's dangerous, I don't want what happened to my ex to happen to you. Or even Piper, Blaire or Vince." Nice save Aide, nice save.

"Let's just say I know how to fight-"

"B, you know what I mean. He's got weapons and power and he's all sorts of ruthless. I don't want you being in the middle of that. I did it once and look how that turned out." He grabs my hands and makes me look at him, he sighed before saying "let me ask you something. What are you really afraid of?"

"I'm afraid he's going to kill me and everyone I care about. I'm afraid that he's going to hurt everyone I care about just to get to me. I'm afraid that he will kill my brothers baby once he finds out. I'm afraid of many things Brandon, the list goes on and on. I can't let anything happen to any of you, all of your lives are in my hands and-"

"It's okay-"

"No it's not okay! If he finds us then it's game over. He will get into my head and make me do very bad things which will end in chaos and my main goal is protecting my little niece or Negev and I don't know if I can't do that and it's really freaking me out and-"

"Lydia."

"And hopefully everything will be fine because I'm really starting to like you and all your friends and if he finds me he-"

"Lydia!"

"He will find a way to hurt me mentally and then we are all screwed. I'm so sorry this is all my fault."

He kissed me.

He kissed me?!

What. The. Fuck————It look about an hour for us to finally find this so called chapel, Brandon was MIA and Nate and I had to pretend that we were looking to get married just because they aren't allowed to give out their guests names and since the guy at the desk said that the guests staying there are invited to the wedding so we decided to fake being engaged.

"Okay fine, well I guess we were actually asking because our friends got married here and we wanted to share the joy with our recent engagement and all. You can invite everyone, when can we book an appointment? My honey bear and I wanna get hitched as soon as possible!" I fake slur, Nate catches on to my plan and winks.

"Yeah man! I had to put a ring on it otherwise she wouldn't let me smash. Virgins, am I right?" He replied while acting drunk as well. This time Grayson stepped forward, he was going to pretend to be the sober one that talks the drunks out of things. "Sir, I am the only sober one here but you have to understand how kids do dumb things when they are drunk. So what do you say we have a fake wedding but make it look real for them?" Gray added on with a chuckle, the guy wasn't having it.

"We don't do fake marriages-"

"Fake?! OUR LOVE IS REAL!" I pretend slur, the guy smiles. "That'll be $450."

"Deal. Do you take fifty dollar bills?" My eyes bugged out, I pulled Gray aside. "Gray, that's too much money. I can't ask you to do that, it's all the money you have for this trip-"

"Piper is like a sister to me. And since her brother is being a dickhead at the moment, I'll step up. You guys can get a divorce very easily, I won't tell Brandon that you guys are married as long as we can get Piper and Vince the hell out of here. The school bus leaves in 4 hours, we have to act fast."

"Sir, how fast can my sugar bear and I get married?" I question going back into drunk mode, the guy smiles. "We happen to have an opening in an hour, dresses, room, rings, and tuxes are included in the price so you can go pick them out now if you'd like. I'll come knock on the bridal sweet door when it's time, here is your room key. Have fun!"—————-"Lydia wait!" It was Brandon, he was running after me, I shook my head. "You have to go back Brandon-"

"No. Not without you." He shakes his head and grabs my hands, I sigh. "I have to do this Brandon, you don't understand-"

"Then make me understand! He's dangerous Lydia and he could kill you! If something happened to you I don't know what I would do. You saw light in me when nobody else did and you brought it back out in me. I know you say you don't want to be anything and that's okay but I can't stand seeing you walk into a trap. It's suicide!" I cupped his face with my hand, hoping that this will make him understand.

"I couldn't live with myself if something bad happened to any of them, especially you. You make me feel something that I haven't felt in a very long time. But you have to understand that my father is dangerous, and he will kill whoever gets in between him and my brother and I. I'm going to be as careful as I can, don't worry he's not going to hurt me. He wants me and my brother alive for now, you can't follow me or he will kill you. So please, if not for yourself then do this for me. Stay here and make sure that nobody leaves, go into everyone's room and lock all windows and doors to make sure no one can get out. Nobody is going to die on my watch today."

"You really are a hero Lydia Stone." He replies with a big smile, unfortunately a tear also fell down his face which I wiped away with my thumb. "Don't be sad. I am going to be okay. I promise. I'll be back before you know it." I decided that now was the time to show him how I feel without actually saying it, I kissed him so passionately it felt like the world around us had stopped. Time stood still and it was just the two of us.

Sadly I had to pull away because I had to leave. "I'll be back soon. Stay safe okay?" I reply while giving him a hug and smiling. He always smells so good, I don't know what cologne he uses but it is very comforting. And if this is the last thing I ever get to smell then at least it'll be something good.

As I was walking to the staircase, - because elevators are the route of all evil- he said something that gave me hope. I knew I had to come back for him.

"Hey Lydia?" I turned back with a smile. "Yeah?"

"I love you."

"I love you too Brandon." I wish I could've stayed, but I needed to do this. This ends today.

My house was only a couple of blocks away, so I ran as if my life depended on it. I made sure to check the perimeter, when I saw my father wasn't there

I was confused. But I decided that I was going to visit my family's grave and keep my guard up just in case.

I decided to take a seat next to the grave of my mother and start talking. "Hey mom, it's Adrianna. I know it's been awhile since we've talked but that is only because Stefano and I are carrying out your wish. We got out as soon as he started the fire, Stefano knew it was something that you would tell us to do so we ran. It's been five years and he's found us yet again. He's created chaos and I don't know what I'm going to do to stop it. I'm sorry I failed you."

All of a sudden I heard a slow clap and laughing, I looked up to see the devil himself. "A family reunion, how precious! I knew I would find you back here."

"What do you want Carlyle?" I snap, he smirks. "Please stop with the formalities, call me dad Adrianna-"

"It's Lydia now and I will never call you my father."

"That's not what you said when I killed that boyfriend of yours." Anger fueled through my body at the mention of Wesley. "You didn't ask my question. What do you want?"

"Well, part of me wants to kill you but the other part of me wants you and Stefano to come back so we could be a family again-"

"You know, I really would it's just you are a narcissistic psychopath and I don't want to sleep with one eye open every night because of the constant reminder of what you made me do-"

"Oh you loved it! I saw the look in your eyes when you drove the knife through your sisters heart. Why do you think I chose you and not Stefano? I chose you because you're special Adrianna. You had the same look in your eye that I did when I first killed someone. Come back home, I can teach you my ways."

"Never. Tell me what you did to my class." I demand, he chuckles and pulls out a knife. "Oh that was nothing! First I just had to cut the oil tank so that the bus would stop, then I made sure to put a little something extra in your classes breakfast. Eggs and a bit of drugs, whoops! The plan was to make you hallucinate so that you'd come back with me but you weren't even there for breakfast so here we are."

"If you brought me here just to threaten me into coming back, it's not going to work. I will never work with you. You're a monster!" I shout angrily, he slashes my arm with the knife.

"Don't you dare talk to me like that-"

"And why not Carlyle? You're not my father anymore. My father was a kind and generous man until he got into the drug and alcohol business. You are not my father, you're nothing but DNA and I hate you for it!" He slashed me again, I winced in pain. "Go ahead dad, what are you going to do? Kill me, Your precious little girl? You've already killed my spirit, I died the day you murdered my mother so go ahead. Kill me. I know you won't do it because you're a coward!"————-I made my way over to Brandon and his new stoner friends. "What the hell do you think you're doing?" He started laughing, his stoner friends walked away from us as he replied "I'm having fun. Try it!" He blew the smoke in my face, I waved it away and grabbed the joint out of his hand and stomped it to the ground. He only got angry at me but I didn't care.

"Hey that was expensive-"

"I don't really give a shit Brandon. What are you doing huh? You're wasting your life, that's what you're doing! And for what? Because you're sad?"

"You don't know what it's like-"

"MY MOTHER WAS MURDERED BY MY FATHER! And you say I don't know what it's like? Bullshit. I know what it's like to blame yourself, I know what it's like to feel numb and I know what it feels like to lose a mother."

"I don't know what to think anymore! I'm tired of everyone questioning me today! I'm tired of all this drama and most importantly, I'm tired of you. I'm out of here!" Tears were forming in my eyes but I refused to let them fall. I just followed him to the parking lot and sat in his car.

"Get out." He growls, I shake my head as anger flows through me. Stay calm Lydia. Stay calm."No. You don't get to do that. You don't get to say you love me and then take it back when you're sad, that's not how things work! Talk to me B. I've confided in you for all my issues, now it's your turn. Come on, this isn't you-"

"You don't know who I am-"

"Yes I do. You used to be this ball of sunshine and then your mother's death turned you into a player, I knew that. But you were able to come back to your good self and I know you are still that person. Brandon just talk to me." His face starts to turn red, indicating that he is about to cry.

"It was all my fault." He buries his head in his hands and starts to cry, I rub his back. "No, whatever happened was not your fault. I know how you feel right now. You blame yourself and you feel numb. You feel as if you can't breathe and like someone is literally shattering your heart into pieces. It's good to let it out, it's okay to cry."

"No it's not. It was my fault, I'm the reason she's dead. Everyone blamed me, my father blamed me, Piper blamed me, even my grandmother blamed me, I even fucking blame me because it was my fault."

"Tell me what happened, you can talk to me." I grabbed his hand and intertwined our fingers, I saw a small smile appear on his face, but that smile was soon turned into a frown when he remembered what happened.

"We were on vacation at a ski resort and I went to a party with this girl I met at the resort. I got really drunk and I had sex for the first time with that girl and my mom caught us. She started yelling at me and I yelled back and said things I shouldn't have and she hit me. So I ran downstairs and got in the car, I wanted to blow off steam but she got in the car with me. I never planned on it, but I knew she hated when I drove fast so I was driving real fast. We were arguing and I turned to face her for one second and then I heard a truck honking. It was coming at us so fast, it was out of control. Mom grabbed the wheel and the car swerved away from the direction of the truck but the car spun around on the slippery road and hit us. We went off the cliff and into the frozen lake and I got knocked out. When I woke up in the hospital, they told me what happened and that she didn't make it. I killed my mother and last thing I said to her was that I hated her... I never even got to apologize."

He starts hysterically crying, I hug him as an attempt to get him to feel better, obviously it didn't work. "It wasn't your fault Brandon. The roads were icy and the guy driving the truck was in the wrong lane. That wasn't your fault. And while it was unfortunate that things went down the way they did, everyone fights with their parents. She grabbed the wheel because she wanted to protect you. She knew you didn't mean it, believe me."

"I never got to say I'm sorry! It's all my fault...she probably hates me. And now I'll never see her again." I made him look at me before I cupped his face with my hands and wiped away his tears. "Listen to me. If there's one thing I've learned about mother's, it's that they will always forgive you no matter what. There is nothing more special then a bond between a mother and her child. Where is she buried?"

"Evergreen. Why?" He gives me a questioning look, I smile and grab his hand again. "Because I want to meet the woman who birthed such a wonderful human being that had a huge impact on my life."

For once, I actually saw his lips twitch, turning into a little smile. It made me so happy. "But first, we have to make a little pit stop so let's switch spots because you can't cry and drive, and I know how you feel about your car but-"

"You can drive it. If there's one person I trust, it's you." I was surprised he let me drive his car, he treats his car like his child. He doesn't even let Piper touch it, I feel special.

We switched seats and I drove to the nearest flower shop and picked up pink roses, I knew they were her favorite flower because Piper said they were her favorite as well. The drive to the cemetery was quiet, but once we were approaching his mother's grave I was holding his hand.

The tombstone said "Here lies Kathleen Danielle Santiago, loving daughter, mother, and wife." I could tell he was nervous, his hands were shaking, but I only smiled at him and whispered "You can do this." He just gave me a look of fear so I reassured him by sitting down next to her grave.

"We are going to be here awhile. It's okay to sit down, this way it'll feel as if the two of you are face to face. Don't be nervous, it's okay." He placed the flowers on the grave and sat next to me.

"H-hi mom. I brought your favorite flowers, I hope you like them… but most of all I h-hope that you're not mad at me. I have made so many mistakes in my life and saying what I said to you before the crash was one of them. I don't hate you, I never hated you mom. I love you with all my heart and I'm so so sorry. This past year I have carried so much guilt with me and that made me do so many things that I am not proud of. But I guess the truth is that I did those bad things because I blamed myself. I always thought maybe if I hadn't gone to that stupid party or even met that girl, you would still be alive. Now I understand that god has a plan for everyone, and you are in a better place." A tear falls down his face, I place my hand on top of his as a way to tell him it's okay.

"These past few months have been an emotional rollercoaster. But I think you would be proud of me when I tell you that there is one person that was able to bring me out of my spiral downwards, and that is this girl right here. Mom, this is Lydia. She has made such a huge impact on our lives. She brought me back to my old self, and she even got Piper to start smiling and laughing instead of thinking bitterly like she used to. I love her mom, and I hope that you are able to watch over us growing old together. I want you to know that I really miss you, and I guess when my time comes which hopefully isn't for a long time, that we will find each other some day." He kissed his fingers and then touched the grave, I smiled. I'm so proud of him, I knew what I had to do next.—————Once I found Brandon, I saw he was fueled with anger. "B, I know your mad-"

"Mad? Ha funny. Mad would be an understatement Lydia, I'm furious! How could you? I t told you things that I could never tell anyone else, I trusted you, I opened up to you, I fucking changed for you! And for what?! For you to spit it all in my face?!" I shake my head as tears fall down my face.

"No! It's not like that! I'm in love with you-"

"Don't you dare say that word. You don't have a right to say that word. You don't love me and you never did! If you loved me then you would've have gotten married to one of my best friends behind my back!"

"But you don't understand"

"Oh I understand clearly Lydia. What, was this all some joke? Let's try to get him to trust me, maybe I can get him to fall for me! Right? I loved you more than I have ever loved anyone before, I let you into my home and I protected you multiple times all for nothing."

I shake my head as tears continue to stream down my face. "Brandon-"

"Don't text me. Don't call me. Don't even talk to me. I don't EVER want to see your face again! I hope your father finds you and takes you back to the hell hole you came from." With that said, he stormed off into the crowd of people that were watching our fight, I broke down. I was so upset and so angry that I screamed and punched a hole into the wall.

I was going to keep going but my phone started ringing. It was Stefano.

"What?" I snapped while answering. "Lydia listen carefully. You have to get out of there." The panic in his voice scared me, my heart started to race.

"Stefano, what's wrong? Why do you sound worried?"

"I'm coming up the block now, just listen. Get out now. The moon shit that he's been saying in his letters, I figured it out. That means today. He's here Lydia, you need to leave that party now!"

"Oh my god. I'm on my way out, I'll see you in the car." Piper found me right as I hung up the phone and she saw the look on my face. It was pure fear. "Lydia? Lydia talk to me, what's wrong?"

"Everything. I-I have to go." She grabbed my arm and chuckled. "What? That's ridiculous-"

"Piper. I need you to let me go before I punch you. I need to leave now or everyone in here is going to die."

"What are you talking about?" She asks apprehensively, I shake my head and try not to hyperventilate. "He's here. My brother just called me, he said that the moon meets the stars crap that my father has been saying in his letters means today. I need to get out of here right now."

"I'll go with you-"

"No, stay in here where it's safe. Get Grayson, Vince, Blaire, Nate and Brandon and lock yourselves in the bathroom. I'll call you when it's safe to come out but please, no matter what you hear, do not open that door. Promise me." She nods fast. There was a look of shock on her face, I feel so bad for springing this on her. "Okay. I'll do it. Stay safe." She gives me a bear hug, I return it.

We parted ways and I started walking out, I was about to call Stefano but I heard the sound of a speeding car and I panicked. I froze when I saw my father driving with a gun pointed at me.I dropped my phone, closed my eyes and waited for the pain.

"LYDIA!" I opened my eyes when the shots stopped firing and the car was nowhere to be found but I didn't feel any pain. I opened my eyes to see Stefano on the ground screaming in pain.

"NO! HELP! SOMEBODY PLEASE HELP!" I couldn't even use my phone because it broke when I dropped it. Please someone help.

A bunch of people from the party came out, I was staring at Stefano's eyes. His face started turning pale, his lips started turning blue. "You have to stay with me. You can't die! You promised nothing bad would happen!"

"M-mom told me t-t-to do whatever I h-had to do in order to p-protect-t you." He said with a smile. That was before he started coughing up blood. "She didn't tell you to take a bullet for me. Come on Stef, you have to stay with me. If you're not going to stay for me then stay for Haley and the baby. They need you! I need you! Please." His eyes started closing and his breathing got heavier.

"No! Stef! Stefano wake up! You can't die. You promised nothing bad would happen! You said everything would be okay! This is not okay! I need you! Please don't leave me!"

He grabbed my hand and smiled. "W-we will m-meet again. P-promise m-m-me y-you'll find h-him and k-kill him." I nodded fast and squeezed his hand.

"I promise. I promise you I will do whatever it takes for as long as it takes. But you're going to be okay, the ambulance is on its way! Everything will be fine." He shakes his head. "T-tell Haley I L-L-Love h-her."

He coughed one last time and he stopped breathing. I screamed so loud that I'm pretty sure the whole town could hear me. No amount of crying is going to bring him back. I want revenge. I want blood.——————-Adrianna, I'm your uncle. I'll always help you. What's going on?" He questions while letting me inside, I walk into the living room and sit down. A tear falls down my face.

"It's Stefano... he's dead. Carlyle killed him." His facial expression turned blank. "When?"

"Last night. Carlyle was trying to shoot me but Stefano jumped in the way. He died in the hospital... I am here because I am done running. I want to fight back until I can't fight anymore. I want Carlyle dead, and I know you can help me."

A tear slips down his face as well, but within minutes his sad face turned back to aggravated and normal. He nods. "I can help you. But first I have to show you something that Stefano made a couple years back." My eyes went wide as I followed him into the basement. I looked around and was shocked at what I saw.

"What is this place?" I question curiously, he doesn't even look at me as he replies "my training facility."

"What do you mean training facility?" I ask again, he sighs as he gets whatever he was looking for. He motions for me to sit on the chair. "I was once in the business that your father is in. It was a very dangerous business, still is to this day. Carlyle and I were always in the business, ever since we were teenagers and he fell in love with your mom. Then they got married and he managed to get out of the business and your parents had your brother and sister. Fast forward to you. This is the part that you are not going to like. One night when Carlyle was on a business trip and the kids were at camp, your mother and I had a little fling. About a month or two later she found out that she was pregnant-"

"Wait. Are you saying that Carlyle is not my father? Are you saying that you're my father?" He nods, my mouth hung open in shock. After all that's happened my head feels like it's gonna explode. First Piper being pregnant, then Blaire hating me, then Grace telling everyone my secret, then Brandon hating me, then Stefano's murder, and now this. I don't know how much more of this I can take.

"She was going to tell them, but I was in a really bad place and I was in some trouble with the guys in the business and I thought that it would be best if your mother and Carlyle raised you because at the time he was a good man. But as you grew up, I saw that the colors in his eyes had changed and he was slowly reverting back to his own ways. He found out the truth when he came back into the business and I got out. I told your mother that it wasn't safe anymore and that she needed to take the kids and leave but she wouldn't listen. The night your mother and sister were murdered was the night that she was going to get you out."

"But Carlyle figured it out and by then it was too late. Your mother had a feeling something like that was going to happen so she wrote you that letter telling you that if anything happened to come to me and I would help you. So I helped you and Stefano get away. Shortly after that, I built this training facility because I knew that one day you two would get the courage to stop fighting." More tears started streaming down my face. I couldn't believe it. My father is my uncle and my uncle is my biological father. This is crazy.

"Stefano knew didn't he? Is that why he never wanted me to ask questions? Is that why he was overprotective of what I did?" I started to get angry, but I knew my anger wouldn't be worth it. I have to take this anger and keep it towards my goal in defeating Carlyle.————Carlyle came in the room and smirked when he saw what I had done. "You not only got out of your chains, but you actually killed your own nephew. You really are my daughter." He says with a chuckle, I smirk.

"But I'm not though." His smirk turns into a frown. "You don't know what you're talking about." He snaps. I start laughing evilly as he starts to get angry.

"I mean that's why you're doing this right? You went back in the business and that's how you found out. That's why you killed mom that night. You were just pissed because you found out the truth." He starts breathing heavier, indicating that he's angry. "Stop talking."

"Aw why? Is the big bad wolf angry? I don't blame you. I would be angry too if I found out that my wife had fucked my brother and that resulted youngest daughter is actually being my niece-"

"SHUT UP!" He shouts, I smirk. "You don't have the authority to tell me what to do anymore. All these years! All these years Stefano and I spent running from you and all for nothing. You are a pathetic excuse of a human being and you're going to rot in hell for everything you've done. You call yourself a man? You're nothing but trash. You killed your wife, killed your son, and you killed my spirit. But the thing you aren't going to do is kill me and you wanna know why? Cuz I'm untouchable. All of your attacks on me only made me stronger. I am not that scared little girl I used to be. You in the other hand are a monster. We all get bad and unexpected news in our lives, but you had to go and be a coward!" He starts yelling and then charges at me, I flip him over, grab his gun, and pin him to the ground.

"You won't do it." He says while spitting blood out, this time I smirk again. "You obviously don't know me anymore." I shot him in the leg which caused him to scream. I smiled as I watched the blood poor out of his leg.

"Now get up." He shakes his head. "I can't! Show your father some mercy here!"

"Oh like you showed mom and Stefano mercy? Like you showed Wesley and all my other friends mercy? Or like you're showing all of my friends mercy right now? You're a garbage excuse for a human being and I hate you. You killed everyone I love and I refuse to let anyone else die." I shot him in the leg again. "Now do as I say, and get the fuck up!"

He limped as he got up. I wrapped my arm around his neck and put the gun to his head. "ROSE! GET YOUR ASS OUT HERE OR I SWEAR I WILL KILL HIM RIGHT NOW!"

"Go ahead Adrianna. Kill him. We all know you want to. He caused you all of that pain. So go ahead, pull the trigger." I knew something was up when she wanted me to kill him but I didn't care. "P-please. You don't understand!"

"What do I have to understand Carlyle? You killed everyone I love just for your amusement! And I'm gonna make sure you pay for it." I pushed him out of my arms and continued to hold the gun to his head. "Now get on your knees." He started crying as he got down and looked at the ground.

"You don't understand-"

"SHUT UP! Look at me." He doesn't budge. "I SAID LOOK AT ME!" He looked up while shaking in fear. I smirked as he cried. "I want my face to be the last thing you see, and these words to be the last you ever hear. You took away everyone and everything I love! You killed my family! And for everything you've done you're gonna pay."

He shakes his head and cries harder. "Please don't do this!" I smirk and hold the gun straight to his head. "Go to hell Carlyle." Without hesitation I shot him, Rose just clapped.

"I have never been more proud to call you my sister. Welcome to the business Aide." I went to turn the gun on her but she just laughed. "I wouldn't do that if I were you."

"Oh really? And why is that?" I say snarkily, she smirks and holds out her phone. "Because I have my connections, and with one click of the send button I can get those connections to kill all those that you love most. You already killed my son and our father, now you have to hold up your part of the deal. Join me and nobody dies."

Everything I've been training for has led up to this moment.

"Where's Tim?" I question while still pointing the gun at her. "He's alive. And he'll stay that way as long as you hold up your end of the deal. So what will it be sis?"

"I'm in."————-Rose was waking up, I turned her gun on her and made sure she didn't have her knife. "Well well what do we have here? Are you actually helpless for once?" I say snarkily, she shakes her head.

"I knew you'd betray me for them-"

"Of course I would! Do you think I'm stupid? I know everything!" I shout, she chuckles. "Oh honey, you don't know a thing."

"Oh really? I know that all this time I believed it was Carlyle, but he was just a pawn in your little scam. I know that after he killed Wesley, he realized that what he's doing was wrong. And I know that you were behind this all along. You faked your own death. You burned down the house. And you made Carlyle hunt us down. You knew he was scary so you got everyone he could to spy on me and Stefano and you ordered him to be killed And most importantly, I know that it was you who switched out my meds which caused my consistent panic attacks in Vegas. But all I want to know is why?"

"You and Stefano were always the ones mom and dad compared me to. I was the rebel child who got pregnant at 15 and they hated me for it. I've been planning my revenge since you were born! And once I got involved in the gang, I found out about Tim being your real father and of course, I told dad. He was ready to go off the edge but I stopped him. I told him the plan and everything was ready to take place." She stood up. What the hell? How did she get out of her chains?

"But then you stopped him so the plan changed. I wore the bullet proof vest and put in the blood packets so that wherever you shot me, I wouldn't get hurt." She says with an evil laugh, I roll my eyes.

"But then we got away-"

"Yes! You got away with the help of your father which is why we had to take him here along with you. I didn't think you were smart enough to figure out that it was me all along but apparently you are. So now I'm gonna have to kill you both." She points the gun at Brandon and fires but I shoot at her and jump in front of him.

4 minutes.

She hit me right in the chest. I knew that soon enough I'd be unconscious given the place where she shot me so I had to do this fast. I step over her and shoot her again, this time in the leg. "That's for Wesley."

I shot her in the chest. "That's for Stefano." And finally, I shot her in the neck which caused her to choke. "And that's for mom."

I watched as she choked on her own blood. I smirked as she took her last breath but Brandon pulled me away and we started running. I was starting to feel weak in the legs. I was losing too much blood.

"Brandon... If I don't make it out-"

"You will." He says reassuringly, I shake my head as I fall to the ground. He picks me up and continues to run. We're almost at the exit.

1 minute.

"I love you" Seeing the fire coming behind us was the last thing I remember before I passed out.

BOOM————-All of a sudden I was back into my hospital room and Brandon was holding my hand and sitting next to me. He was crying.

"The doctors said you might not wake up again. Tonight is the cut off for your life support. It's been three months. Tonight was supposed to be the best prom night ever, but I couldn't have picture going without you. I can't picture a life without you in it and I refuse to. I love you so much Lydia and nothing is ever going to change that. I'm tearing myself up here. I would do anything to see your beautiful smile, or hear your cute laugh, or even hear you tell me I'm an idiot. Now I understand how you felt with Wesley and it's awful. So please wake up. I'll do anything. I'll take you all around the world, I'll marry you, I'll do whatever it takes, I don't care if I'm 18, I love you. We have been through hell and back and I want you to know that if you wake up you don't have to be afraid anymore. Rose and Carlyle are gone. You're free to be whoever and do whatever you want but I want to have a future with you. And I know this sounds selfish but I don't care. I love you Lydia Stone and I will shout it from the rooftops if I have to. Just please wake up." He leaned his head back into my hands, I smile.

Suddenly I start to regain feeling in my body again. I no longer feel cold, there is a sudden warmth.

Everything is dark again.

I can move my fingers.

I'm waking up!

I intertwine our fingers and smile. He looks up at me and cries out of joy while giving me a hug. "It's a miracle!" He says excitedly while giving me a kiss, I chuckle. "I love you Brandon Santiago."

"I love you with everything I've got Lydia Stone."

Chapter 36- Perfect Life?

B randon's POVWords cannot describe how happy I am that she is okay. My prayers have been answered and I finally have her back. From this day forward, I promise that I will never let her go no matter what happens.

"I'm gonna FaceTime Piper." I tell Lydia, she smiles and nods. I called her and she answered with a sympathetic look on her face. "Hey. Are you okay?"

"I'm better than okay. Someone wants to talk to you." I give Lydia the phone and Piper starts screaming and crying. "It's a miracle! Oh my god! I have to go find Blaire and the others!" She started running until she found them.

They all were smiling and happy that she was alive. "I can't believe it! I don't care if this is prom night, I'm coming to see you." Grayson says enthusiastically, Piper turns the phone back to her and smiles. "We will be there soon."

Lydia's POVI felt bad that they were missing their prom because of me but I was glad to see them. Apparently I was out for a really long time, but I'm glad that I'm back.

"So what happened? Did you see a light?" Vince asks, I shake my head. "No. I saw something even better. I saw my mom. It was a very weird experience but apparently I had to go through my whole life and forgive my past in order to get back. I realized that it wasn't Carlyle all along, it was Rose. She killed my mother and Carlyle just got roped into it."

"Well you don't have to worry about them now. They are both dead for sure this time, and Tim took over the business and is making sure that nobody will ever bother you or your family ever again. All who worked for Carlyle can finally live happy lives. Everything's going to be great Lydia." Blaire says while grabbing my hand, I look at all of them and smile. My smile turns to a frown when I remember what I saw about Haley.

"Wait, Where's Haley? Is she okay?" I ask apprehensively, Grace smiles and nods. "She's great. Actually, we called her and she's right outside. Come on in Haley."

Haley walked in slowly with a baby in her arms. I almost started crying out of joy. "Oh my gosh Haley, he's beautiful! What's his name?" I ask with a smile, Tears well up in her eyes as she said "Wesley Tyler Stone. Wesley for my brother, and Tyler for the middle name because that was Stefano's name when we first met. Now he will have both his uncle and his father with him everywhere he goes."

"Can I hold him?" She nods and puts him in my arms, I smile and hold his tiny little hands. "Hi Wesley. I'm your aunt Lydia. I'm sorry I wasn't around these past two or three months but I am here now and your mommy and I are going to make sure you live the best life you can. Sound good?" We all laugh as he smiles. I can tell things are going to be good. From now on I'm going to live the best life I can.

Tim comes back into the room with a wide smile on his face. "What did the doctors say?" I ask, his smile only turns wider. "They said they are going to keep you one more night for observations and then if everything goes okay you should be ready to go home tomorrow. How does that sound?"

"That sounds amazing. Honestly, living my life without being afraid is going to be a weird concept for me but I'm ready. I have nothing to be scared about anymore. I'm ready to live."

"So where to first? Paris? Australia? London?" Gray asks, I shake my head. "I just want to be here with all of you. You are all going off to college soon and I don't want you guys to miss it."

"They are all going to colleges which are around here. I have decided to take the year off and explore the world. College can wait, but we are only going to be 18 once. So what do you say? Explore the world with me?" Brandon asks with a smile while holding out his hand, I nod and intertwine our fingers. I really love this boy.

"Awww! How cute. The fact that you're holding Wesley makes it even cuter because you guys look like a little family." Haley teases with a laugh, we all chuckle. "No babies for a long time for me."

"That's okay. I can wait." Brandon says with a wink, I feel heat rising to my face as Blaire and Piper start gushing at his cuteness. "We should have a road trip this summer! We can go anywhere we want. Oh this is going to be great!" Grace says enthusiastically, I look at her feeling uncertain. "In the beginning of the year, you hated me. What changed?" I ask, she sighs.

"I was being a bitch and I finally realized it. You were the only one that actually had the balls to stand up to me and I admired that about you. When I found out the truth, I wanted to help save you. I'm sorry for everything." I hand Wesley back to Haley and hold out my arms to hug Grace. "If there's one thing I've learned from this whole experience, it's not to hold grudges. So I agree, let's go on this road trip, it'll be our last trip as high school kids."

"How about we have a little adventure tonight?" Brandon questions, we all look at him curiously, telling him to go on. "We should sneak you out of here and into the prom!"

"As much as I would love that, I can't. I'm going to be under observation. But I will be there tomorrow for your graduation." Piper gives me a sad look before saying "wait, you aren't graduating with us?"

"I didn't know how long it would be till this whole thing was over so I took online courses and graduated online. Technically I'll still be graduating with you guys because I'll be in the crowd cheering for you guys." Vince shakes his head.

"No." He says angrily, Piper tries calming him down but he wouldn't. "Vince it's really fine-"

"No it's not Lydia. After everything you have been through, the least you deserve is an actual graduation service. As student body president, I am going to do everything in my power to get you to graduate with us." He stormed out without another word, I sigh.

"He's right. You deserve at least one normal high school experience before we are out in the real world." Grace replies, I shake my head and smile.

"I've had plenty of experience this year. I've experienced going to parties and dances. I've experience best friend and boy drama. I've even experienced the typical cliche fight with the mean girl. Sure graduating with you guys, or even going to prom would be awesome, I can't and that's just the way it is. At least I have gotten to experience some high school moments. Even through everything, we all managed to stay friends and I want you to know that I love you guys so much and I hope that we can all stay friends until we are gray and old."

"If we can get through an explosion and murder then I'm pretty sure that we can get through anything. But the question is, are you guys ready?"

They all nod, Brandon grabs my hands and replies "I'm all in. Here's to the future."

The next day"Okay Lydia. You are free to go." The doctor says with a smile, I nod and thank him. Tim and I basically ran from the hospital to the car just so that we could get home and I could get dressed and we could make the ceremony on time.

I'll admit it, I kind of tuned out until I saw that it was Vince's turn to speak as valedictorian. "Good morning everyone. I'm proud to say that these past four years have been the best years of my life. I've loved, I've lost and basically just had the best high school experience as possible. As many of you know, my friends and I used to run this group called the overachievers, and I would like to apologize to anyone who was hurt in the process of that group forming. This year started off pretty rocky, but there was one key factor that changed this year for the better. That key factor was a girl who had a pretty tough life growing up. She managed to change all of us for the better and she literally saved us from our own inner demons. Unfortunately, she had been hospitalized these past couple of months and she hadn't been able to attend school. I asked her father to send the school her online records of school that she was doing while she was away and the school approved it. I can gladly say that this girl turned me and my friends' lives around, and if there's one person who deserves to graduate the most, it's her. So will Lydia Stone please come to the stage."

What the hell is happening?

I got up out of my seat and people started clapping for me as I approached him on stage. All of a sudden Brandon and Piper came over to me with a cap and gown and they helped me put it on.

"Lydia Stone, you are now officially a high school graduate, congratulations!" Vince says with a smile while handing me a diploma. Tears of joy start welling up in the back of my eyes. "How did you do this?" I ask happily, Vince shrugs.

"Well, first I sent out a mass text telling everyone the situation and we all chipped in for prices for your cap and gown. Then Tim gave Nate your online records and Nate gave them to his stepmom and explained everything and since she's principal, what she says goes and she approved the idea. I hope you're not mad at me." Vince replies with a chuckle, I laugh. "Are you kidding? I love you so much! Thank you!" I gave him a bear hug as everyone clapped and chanted my name. I smiled and sat with the rest of my class.

Mrs. Samuels took to the stand and said "It's been my pleasure to have you all as my students. I wish you the best of luck in the future. Congratulations, you all are now graduates of 2018!" Everyone started chanting and hugging each other, Brandon ran over to me and kissed me. I felt sparks fly through my body. It was one of those kisses where you can actually feel the magic.

"Alright lovebirds, break it up. It's picture time." Nate says with a chuckle while wrapping his arms around us. We all do a normal group pose, and then we started doing silly ones. It was a really fun day. It feels amazing not having to be afraid and genuinely having a great time with friends. I hope the rest of my life is like this.

2 weeks later...We all decided that this summer we are going to take a road trip and explore as much of the world that we can before Labor Day. I was a little apprehensive about leaving Haley and the baby but she kept convincing me to go.

"Are you sure you don't want me to stay?" I ask while packing the last of what I'm bringing in my suit case, she shakes her head. "We will be fine. Besides, it's not like we are going to be alone, Tim agreed to help out. And don't worry, he is not mixing business with family. Go have fun, we will still be here when you get back."

I convinced Tim that we needed him around. I wanted to get to know my father, and this baby needs a male figure that isn't an 18 year old in his life. Plus he completely changed the business. Carlyle was leader out of fear, whereas Tim is the leader that actually is giving everyone an out. He is making it less dangerous for everyone and I really appreciate that.

Pipers honks her car horn. "Come on Lydia!" She shouts loudly, I chuckle and give Haley a hug. "Call me if you need anything or need me home, wherever I am I'll take a plane or a bus or-"

"I'll be fine Lydia, go!" She pushed me out of my room and led me downstairs. I kissed Wesley and said goodbye. Then I hugged Tim. "Take care of them please."

"I will. Have fun kiddo." He kisses me on the cheek and opened the door for me. I walked over to the RV that Piper and Vince rented and greeted everyone.

As we were on the bus, I took out the 10 Things I Hate About You book and started reading again. Brandon had a SnapBack on again and he just couldn't help himself. "10 Things I Hate About You, excellent choice but have you seen the movie?"

"Yes I have. Didn't think a guy like you would though." I replied sarcastically, he smirks. "What can I say? I guess I'm just a hopeless romantic. So do you have a phone?"

"Maybe I do maybe I don't. What's it to you?" I flipped to the next page in my book, not even looking up at him. "Maybe I can call you sometime."

"Yeah sure my number is 555-N-O-T- gonna happen." We both start laughing hysterically as he sits next to me. "If only first day of school you could see us now."

"I think first day of school me would be happy because of everything I've accomplished. As for present me, well I'm pretty happy." I hold his hand and lean on his shoulder, he kisses my forehead.

"I can tell that the future is going to be good for us. What do you say we have that perfect life we were talking about of that bus back in Vegas?" He questions with a smile, my face turns red as I think of that day.

"Oh god, that day was so awful! But our conversation did calm me down a lot. I think we should give our perfect lives a shot. So what do you say? Perfect life?" I reply with a smile, he winks at me and kisses my forehead again.

"My perfect life is with you. Whenever I am with you everything feels perfect. I want that white picket fence dream that I told you about with you. So, will you make me the happiest guy in the world and have the perfect life with me?" He asks, I smile so wide. "Are you asking me what I think you're asking?" He nods, my heart starts racing.

We may only be 18 but if there is one thing I've learned my whole life, it's that life is way too short and anything can happen at any minute to make your world stop. I am at my happiest point when I am with Brandon. I love him with everything I've got.

"Yes, I will." He smiles and kisses me, Piper comes running back to where we are sitting with a huge smile on her face. "Did I just hear what I think I heard?" She asks excitedly, we tell her to shush.

"Are you guys engaged?!" She whisper shouts excitedly, we both nod. She starts dancing in her seat. "Whoop! I did that! Best matchmaker ever right here!"

We just start laughing as she continues to do her dance. "Alright guys, we have reached our first destination. You ready?" Vince pulls into the parking lot of the hotel, we all look at each other and nod.

Here's to the future!————————————————————————-

Epilogue

1 0 Years Later (Lydia's POV) Today is the day that we tell Wesley about his father. Today is the day that we finally are going to watch the video that Stefano left for Haley and Wesley that he titled "For The Future".

Haley invited everyone over to the house so we could watch it together. Things have been pretty hard for Brandon and Piper after they found out the truth about their father working for Carlyle whereas I made peace with it. I don't want to have any bad ties with my past, I have forgiven it all.

"You ready to go?" Brandon asks, I nod as I take my makeup off. I work at the same law firm that Stefano worked in, surprisingly I even got his old office. After his death, they refused to give it to anyone because it was disrespectful. However, they thought it would be special if they gave it to me. So everyday, I get all dressed up and make Stefano proud.

"I'm ready to cry, but that's okay. I need to see his face again." Brandon gives me a kiss and then hugs me. "Haley sent me a picture of the movie thing Wesley set up. It's adorable." He showed me the picture and I couldn't help but laugh.

Wesley is an artistic kid, just like his mom. He loves drawing and he's been drawing the seating outline for this for about a month now. The plan is that we are going to watch a movie that Blaire is in and then we are going to show him the special video from Stefano. Haley told Wesley about what happened to Stefano, but she just said that some bad men hurt him which is why he isn't with us anymore. He always asked about Stefano so Tim, Haley and I had no problem telling him how brave his father was.

"I'm so glad that the gang is going to be back together again!" I say enthusiastically, he nods in agreement. "Yeah, it should be really fun."

Our end of high school road trip was really fun, but after college was when our lives really took off. Blaire started acting in her school plays and talent scouts eventually got her information. She now is an actress in some big time shows and movies.

Grace is currently flying in from Australia where she had a modeling gig. She sent out some photos to some agencies and eventually she signed a contract and is now modeling for Victoria Secret.

Grayson took up his passion for music. While he's not famous yet, he's getting there. He posts videos on YouTube and performs with his band in pubs on weekends. Sometimes I like to perform with his band during my free time and it feels just like it used to.

Piper and Vince are happily married and they are expecting a baby pretty soon. The two of them moved out of town after college and Piper is now 7 months pregnant, she couldn't be happier. I'm so happy for them, after everything they really deserve this.

Nathan is a child services social worker. He wants to help kids that are in the same situation I was in years ago that come from troubled homes. He believes in giving them another chance to live a happier and healthier life.

Brandon now works as a detective for the FBI and solves criminal cases. Brandon said he wants to lock away those who are like Carlyle and in order to do that, he must crack the case of who did it and why. From there, I deal with actually locking them away and throwing away the key.

As for Brandon and I, well we are still the way we were when we left for the road trip. Don't get me wrong, we are madly in love, but both of us haven't had any time to actually get married because we have been so busy. But we are living together and we are happy with the way things are, so whenever we actually decide to get married we will be 100 percent ready.

As we got in our car and drove to Haley's, I couldn't help but think of some of the good memories I had here. But with good memories also come bad. I've had my share of panic and anxiety attacks but I'm okay. I'm right where I want to be. ———We arrived at Haley's after everyone else had. Wesley answered the door and immediately pulled us into the backyard where he had set up everything. He had bean bag chairs, popcorn, and a projector screen set up for everything. What made it even better was that everyone was here.

"Lydia!" Piper shouts while running over to give me a bear hug, I hug her back. "Ugh I missed you so much!"

"I missed you too. You two have to come into town more often. I'm so nervous, can you believe today is the day?" Piper shakes her head and sighs. "I know, you and Haley have waited 10 years for this. Now you're finally going to see his face again. Anyways, how have you been? How are things with your lover?" She teases, I chuckle and hold my stomach.

"Things are going pretty good. What about you and Vince?" Her eyes pop out as she realized what I was trying to say, she smiled so wide and squealed. Everyone looked at her, she glared at them "what? I haven't seen her in a year. Let me be happy"

Everyone turned back and continued what they were doing as she turned back to me. "Are you pregnant?!" She whisper shouts excitedly, I smile and nod, she squeals again, I tell her to be quiet.

"Shh. I haven't told Brandon yet. You are the first one to know, I plan on telling him later." She gives me another hug. "Aw congratulations! How many weeks are you?"

"8. I went to the doctor yesterday because I wasn't sure, he confirmed it." She smiles and laughs. "Oh my god I'm so happy for you!"

"What are we talking about?" Grace and Blaire ask with a smirk, I chuckle. "Nothing, I'm just so happy to see you guys again-"

"Stop lying Lydia, we can see right through you. Now what is it? Do I sense a wedding?" Blaire questions with a giant smile, I shake my head. "No. We both have been way to busy with everything to even try to get married."

"Oh yeah, you guys have been very busy." Piper says with a wink, Grace's mouth hangs open. "No way. Shut up!" Shit she figured it out. Thanks a lot Piper!

"What am I missing?" Blaire asks with a pout, Grace squeals. "I'm so happy for you!" Grace gives me a hug, Blaire still is trying to figure out what is is.

It was like a lightbulb went off in her head when she realized it. "Oh my god! Congratulations!" Now she gave me a hug, I just smiled and laughed.

"Thanks guys. But look, I haven't told Brandon yet. I've been waiting for the perfect time but it never has seemed right. I think I'm going to tell him tonight." Before they could say anything else, Haley interrupted. "Okay everyone, time to watch the movie."

After the movie, Wesley was so happy and excited, we pulled the best birthday present ever on him. "That was the best movie ever! Aunt Blaire, you did such a great job!" He hugs her, we all smile.

"Well Wesley, we have one more surprise for you that I think you're going to love." I say with a smile, his mouth hangs open as he jumps up and down in excitement. "What is it! What is it! What is it!"

I lead him over to where he was sitting before in front of the projector screen as Haley is about to tell him. "You have always asked me about your dad and I have always told you that he was a wonderful man. You are beginning to look more like him every day that you grow older. Before your daddy passed away, he left us a video message. I've been waiting for the time to be right and now it finally is. Are you ready to see what your father was like?" Wesley nods really fast, we all pay attention to the screen as she hits the play button.

I almost cried when I saw Stefano's face. He looked so happy. "Hey Haley. If you're watching this right now then that means everything went okay with the pregnancy and our beautiful baby boy was born. Yes, I know it's a boy because I went to Dr. Coldon and she told me. First off, I want to say that I love the both of you with everything I've got and that will never change."

"Second, I want to talk to my son. I'm so sorry that I can't be there to watch you grow up and have kids. None of this was supposed to happen, but the world works in mysterious ways which is why I am sitting in front of a camera right now taking to you. I want you to live the best life you could possibly live. I just know that you are going to be a leader one day. You're going to make a lot of friends, you are going to have fun, and you are going to grow old and have children, and even grandchildren. Know that whenever you have a problem, if you need help with something, that your mother will always be there for you. You can even go to aunt Lydia or uncle Grayson or Grace, Blaire, Brandon, Piper, Vince and Nathan, they will all help you get through whatever it is that you need help in. I love you so much son. And I want you to know that I'll always be with you."

A tear falls down my face as he blows a kiss to the camera. "Haley. You are the love of my life and I just know that you are going to be a great mom to our child. I don't want you to be sad, I want you to live the rest of your life to it's fullest. I remember when I first met you at the coffee shop. You were in the worst mood yet I kept hitting on you. It took a couple of weeks but once I got a job at the coffee shop with you, I finally got you to go out with me. And once Carlyle found us and killed Wes, you were so angry yet understanding as to why we were trying to protect you guys. You just packed up everything and left with us and I'm so glad you did. If you didn't, then we wouldn't have our little boy right now. Take care of him for me. I love you both. Oh and most importantly, keep Lydia out of trouble. Make sure she has beautiful babies with Brandon and lives the best life possible. I don't want any of you to be sad. And knowing you girls, one of you is crying right now. So wipe those tears and put on a smile because you've got the whole world to see. Don't give up. I love you all. Goodbye." The screen went dark and I went up to Wesley who was smiling.

"So Wesley, how do you feel?" I ask while wiping away a tear. He smiles wider. "I just met daddy!" He starts clapping and giggling, I smile back.

"You're not sad?" I ask, he shakes his head. "This is the best birthday ever! I'm not sad, he's always watching. He wants us to be happy and that's what I will be. He also wants you and uncle Brandon to give me cousins so hurry it up!" We all laugh, Piper gives me a firm look that tells me to tell Brandon now.

"Actually Wesley, you won't have to wait much longer. In fact, you'll only have to wait 7 more months." I look at Brandon who looks confused. "What?" A smile starts rising to his face.

"You're gonna be a dad Brandon." He smiled so wide I thought his face was going to explode. It was adorable. "We're having a baby? We're having a baby! I'm gonna be a father!" He runs over to me and twirls me around, all of the guys smile.

"Congratulations guys! We need to celebrate!" Haley says excitedly, Wesley starts jumping up and down. "We are celebrating right now! Let's party!" Wesley says with a wide smile.

"But it's your birthday! We don't wanna ruin your party-"

"Are you kidding? This is the best birthday I could ever ask for. I got to see my dad for the first time, and we are all fulfilling his wishes. This is the best birthday ever, nothing will ever be able to top this. I love you all so much, thank you for making this the best birthday ever." He gives me a bear hug which caused me to tear up.

This kid has a pure heart of gold. He's definitely Stefano and Haley's son.

I couldn't have asked for a better family. I'm glad that I went through all the bad stuff, because without it, I wouldn't be where I am today. Stefano never would've met Haley and had Wesley, I would never have moved so much. And most importantly, I wouldn't have met all of these great people.

Sometimes you have to go through bad things in order to live a better life. I'm thankful that everything happened to me because I wouldn't be the woman that I am today without my crazy messed up life. I got everything I could have ever asked for and I couldn't be happier.

The End————————————————————